GEOFF GENTRY IS DEAD . . .
AND WHEN A MILLIONAIRE IS MURDERED, ALMOST EVERYONE HAS A MOTIVE.

BETH LACY—an elderly widow and Geoff's close friend. She was paying to have one mystery solved, but there were others she wasn't talking about.

ALAN GENTRY—the grandson. Why do good families always turn out such rotten kids?

BARBARA GENTRY—the granddaughter. She was a Barbie doll wired with dynamite who *always* got what she wanted.

BUTCH BANUCHI—the "businessman" from Chicago. Business for him meant danger for everyone else.

MELVIN DAVIS—the sheriff. How much can you expect from a lawman on the take?

AN INTERESTING GROUP . . .
BUT KILLERS ARE ALWAYS FASCINATING.

LEGACY OF THE LAKE

MICHAEL SMITH

AVON
PUBLISHERS OF BARD, CAMELOT AND DISCUS BOOKS

LEGACY OF THE LAKE is an original publication of Avon Books. This work has never before appeared in book form.

AVON BOOKS
A division of
The Hearst Corporation
959 Eighth Avenue
New York, New York 10019

First Avon Printing, August, 1980

AVON TRADEMARK REG. U.S. PAT. OFF. AND IN
OTHER COUNTRIES, MARCA REGISTRADA,
HECHO EN U.S.A.

Printed in the U.S.A.

TO PAT, TIM AND JULIE

LEGACY OF THE LAKE

ONE

The water snake danced in and out of his consciousness until he awoke suddenly and discovered that it was real. It gave him such a fright that he jerked involuntarily on the fishing line, and that caused his fear to turn into annoyance. The scales of the snake were light brown, with a pattern of darker brown bands on its back. It knifed through the water effortlessly, apparently headed for a clump of grasses and reeds on the other side of the spot where Jack Olsen had beached the boat hours earlier. He had unloaded the ice chest, thrown in a fishing line, lain back and closed his eyes.

Jack watched the snake disappear below the surface of the water, and a chill passed along the back of his neck. What if it went after the bait and he had to pull it in? He decided to reel in his line, telling himself that it was for the purpose of checking the bait. The worm was still there, but it was dead, pale and water-soaked. He snorted contemptuously, remembering the bait shop salesman's assurances that the crappie were running.

He looked at the old man in the fishing boat bobbing not far off shore, and suppressed a temptation to yell out and ask about his luck. The man was flicking his line near the branches of an uprooted tree that had fallen into the water. Jack could see the lures pinned into the band of the man's hat—a sign Jack associated with *knowing* how to catch sport fish. He remembered the string of black speckled rainbow trout he had seen at a marina one day, and the fisherman's proud story of the fight they had put up. Maybe Kate would demonstrate the intricacies of fly casting, the next time they were out in the boat.

The summer sun had burned the bridge of his nose during the day, and the reddening skin contrasted with the freckles that generously splotched his face. He was thankful for the late afternoon shade provided by the oak-hickory forest that crowded its way to the water's edge. Still, it was hot. Jack used his palm to blot the sweat on his forehead and dried his hand in his hair.

While he was thinking about moving to a new spot, a sleek motorboat shot into view, sending up a spray of water as it turned sharply into the cove. Waterskiers, he mumbled. If they churned up the water in a series of oval passes, he'd have to move for sure. Jack watched the boat skim across the surface of the lake deeper into the cove until the driver pulled back on the throttle and the hull settled into the water.

Jack waited for the two occupants of the boat to throw out a tow line and skis. Instead, the boat turned slowly, reared suddenly out of the water and headed toward the open channel. Jack admired the sleek lines of the craft. It seemed connected to the lake only at the point of the white water outrush of the inboard motor. He noticed one of the men had moved forward and was bracing an oar against the bow rail so that it was at a right angle to the length of the boat. At this point, Jack stood, dropping his rod and reel.

"Hey!" he shouted, more to himself than anyone else.

The speedboat headed directly toward the fishing boat. Damn kids, he thought. They'll swerve at the last minute, hoping to swamp the old man. But Jack watched in horror as the sleek craft rammed the low-lying fishing boat at midsection. Because its bow was naturally elevated, the speedboat easily overrode the fishing boat. There was a sharp grinding sound of metal on metal. It happened quickly; the fisherman flew from the boat, as if he had been struck.

Jack focused on the speeding boat for several seconds, snapping mental pictures to be examined later. Briefly, he considered jumping into his own boat and giving chase, but then he thought of the old man.

Jack shook off his moccasins, extracted his billfold from a back pocket and dropped it on the sand before diving into the water. It was about two hundred feet to the boat, but Jack's heart was pumping in earnest as he tried to cover the distance as fast as possible. It was an old metal fishing boat, painted the standard green. The impact of the collision had buckled the boat near the center and it was taking on water rapidly. The outboard motor was not in sight, and Jack assumed it had come loose and sunk. Neither could he immediately see the old man, until he swam to the other side of the boat.

The fisherman's life jacket had worked properly by rolling him onto his back, but the front portion of the boat had drifted over him and the old man's face was submerged. Jack yanked him from under the boat. His hopes that the fisherman was alive ended when he cupped the back of the old man's neck and felt the head move forward in a rubbery motion. The eyes were vacuous, and a nasty bluish-black welt covered the expanse of his lower forehead.

Jack looked around the cove. No homes, resorts or marinas. It was the reason why he often fished near the east end of the Shawnee Bend peninsula—for the solitude —although it didn't serve the old man's purpose at the time. He grabbed the shoulder of the dead man's life jacket and began scissor-kicking toward the shore, guiding and paddling with his right hand. He dragged the body onto the sandy beach, where he sat down to catch his breath. He looked at his watch. It was four-thirty.

He hit the beach west of the concrete boat launch at a fairly fast speed, shutting off the motor at the last minute. The boat plowed straight ahead through the sand and mud and then slipped sideways to stop a few feet beyond the shoreline. The impact broke the lock that held the outboard motor in running position and snapped a blade off the prop. Jack surveyed the damage idly, calculating that the repairs would probably cost a hundred dollars or more.

He strolled purposefully toward the marina, walking out

onto the floating dock toward the building that served as boat rental office, headquarters for fishing supplies and coffee shop. He knew he could have made a less dramatic appearance by idling the boat into one of the dock's vacant slips. But he was conscious of the body in the boat and wanted somehow to protect the old man from the trifling stares of anyone who might walk by.

He ordered a beer, his first in nearly six weeks. Then he told the wide-eyed girl that a fisherman had been struck and killed and that she ought to call the sheriff.

Back by the boat, he sipped the beer and lit up a cigarette. He turned to look again at the fisherman, who was sprawled lifelessly in the back of the boat, one arm having slipped between the portable fuel tanks. Jack tried to remember how many times he had seen that fixed stare, indicating that the lights were out inside.

Jack watched the man leave the building and walk along the swaying dock. He had expected him. It was the same man who had sold him the red worms shortly before noon and guaranteed the crappie.

"The girl says you pulled a dead man from the lake," he said, sucking on a toothpick. "That right?"

"Take a look for yourself," Jack said, motioning toward the boat. The man looked, and the toothpick dropped from his gaping mouth. Then, he turned and scampered back toward the marina.

A Missouri water patrolman in a green uniform arrived next. He tied his patrol boat to the dock near the fuel pumps and looked Jack's way as the bait salesman provided an animated explanation.

When he reached Jack, the patrolman looked suspiciously at him and then glanced inside the boat. "Jesus Christ. Is he dead?"

"Yes."

"What happened?"

"Couple of guys in a boat ran him down."

"Goddam." The patrolman climbed gingerly into Jack's boat and poked at the body. "Don't look like he got cut up by the prop. Did he drown?"

Jack frowned and pointed toward the main channel. "Don't you think you ought to take a description of the boat and see if it's still on the lake?"

Embarrassed, the patrolman stumbled out of the boat, alternately walking and jogging back toward the marina.

Jack followed him and gave him a concise description of the killer boat, which the patrolman relayed over his boat radio. "It's a very distinctive boat. Quite expensive, I'd say. A modified vee bottom with a long rake. Rides high out of the water but the front end dips, like the Concorde."

"The what?"

"The airplane. You know." Jack used his hands to illustrate the turned-down beak. "It was an inboard. Lots of horses, I'd guess, by the speed it was traveling. Also, the console is in the middle."

"What about the color?"

Jack strained to remember. "There are two panels along the top of the hull on each side. They're about a foot wide at the stern and taper to a point at the bow. Each panel is black except for a gray-colored lightning strip. It looks like a Z, except it's stretched out. The rest of the boat is red. It looked new."

"Okay, I gotcha," the patrolman said, preparing to shove off.

"Wait a minute," Jack protested. "Don't you want to know about the guys in the boat?"

The patrolman looked like a berated schoolboy.

Jack corrected himself. "One of them could have been a woman. The one driving had long hair and was wearing a hat, a white T-shirt and yellow trunks. The other one had on blue trunks and was definitely a man. A big man."

"You didn't see how tall they were, did you?"

Jack thought the patrolman was being a little sarcastic. He hesitated before answering. "Like I said, the one that moved to the front of the boat looked big, although he was stooped. The other one was sitting down."

"I'm going out for a look around," the patrolman said, suddenly galvanized into action. "You stay here until the sheriff arrives."

Jack didn't expect the patrolman to do any good, since he doubted the two in the boat had stayed around very long. He went back to his boat, lit another cigarette, and waited.

There was no mistaking them when they arrived: a car sliding to a stop on the gravel road, two sheriff's deputies

13

leaping out and slamming the doors hard enough to make the vehicle rock on its wheels. A van-type ambulance came shortly thereafter. Camden county sheriff Melvin Davis arrived while the ambulance attendants were removing the body from the boat. The sheriff, unlike his two deputies, parked his car leisurely, stood gazing out over the lake for a few minutes and then walked down to the beach. He was a stout man, with a beer drinker's stomach.

Jack noticed a crowd forming on the dock around the bait salesman, and he congratulated himself on his decision not to tie the boat up at the marina. He ran painstakingly through the details of the accident again for the benefit of the sheriff, who stood with his lower jaw thrust out, rubbing his hands and looking out over the lake.

"You got a good memory, fellow," Davis said, removing his hat to scratch his bald pate. "Most people don't have such good recollection, especially at a time like this. You tell all this to the water patrolman?"

"Yes. He said he was going out to look around."

"Know who that is? . . . was, I mean," the sheriff asked, as the ambulance drove off.

"No," Jack replied.

"Geoffrey Gentry, the second. Important man around here. Retired millionaire. Owned a lot of property on the lake. People listened when he talked."

They both turned to watch the water patrolman bring his boat to shore.

"Hi there, Ted," Davis said in a neighborly manner. "Find anything?"

"Didn't find the boat, but the rest of the patrol are on the lookout. If this fellow's description is any good, we'll find them."

Jack noticed that the patrolman had regained his composure, and was compensating for his previous lapses by being overly professional.

"The dead man's boat was still in the cove, around the fifteen-mile marker," the patrol said, giving the distance of the cove from Bagnell Dam. "Found this too, Mel," he added, holding up an oar.

"I just remembered something," Jack interjected.

"What's that, fellow?" Davis asked, chomping on his gum.

"The man in the boat who was up front had an oar

14

propped against the bow rail, sticking out the side of the boat." Jack snapped his fingers, thinking he finally understood the significance of what had happened. "I think they were trying to hit the fisherman with the oar!"

Davis looked keenly at Jack. "You see that happen?"

Jack frowned. "I'm not sure. Everything happened too fast."

"Well, we'll just let the coroner tell us what killed Gentry then, if you don't mind." The sheriff again jutted out his jaw and looked across the lake. "Did you get a good look at either one of the people in the boat, other than to notice the color of their swimming trunks?"

"No, except that the man, or the one I know was a man, was barechested," Jack replied.

"Didja see any tits on the one with the T-shirt," the sheriff snickered, poking the water patrolman.

"No, it was too far away for that."

"What about the color of their hair?" the sheriff asked, again serious.

"The big man up front with the oar had medium-length hair. Light brown, or blond if it was wet. The one driving had longer hair. Brown. It stuck out from under his—her —hat; one of those hats with beer emblems on it."

The sheriff grunted, picked up several rocks and tossed them into the lake. "What's your name, fellow?"

"Jack Olsen."

"You just down here on a fishing trip, Olsen?"

"No, I've been staying here for over a month."

"Whereabouts you staying?"

"Off the Y-Road, north of Camdenton."

"Which resort?"

Jack kicked at the ground. "I'm staying with a friend."

"You understand," the sheriff prompted. "We have to know where, in case we need to talk to you again."

"I'm staying with Kate Carter," Jack said, a muscle twitching in the side of his face.

A broad grin spread across Sheriff Davis's face. "Oh, yeah, I heard. No wonder you got such a good memory for details, huh?"

Jack began to walk toward the marina, to telephone for a ride, when a thought turned him back. "I'm sure the prop on that speedboat was damaged. If you find one that meets the description, you might check that."

"Hey, Ted, did that thought ever occur to you," the sheriff said mockingly. The water patrolman only sneered, shaking his head from side to side.

"You just rest your mind, Mr. Olsen," the sheriff said. "We may not be big city cops, but we know how to do our job."

Jack dialed the number, fighting the urge to drink another beer.

TWO

The day was like a gift; one of those summer mornings recalled from Jack's boyhood when he could smell the heat rising from the earth, mixed with the fragrance of pine trees, flowers and mowed hay. The day had promise, which distinguished it. When he was in the city, those days seemed lost forever.

Jack drove the battered red pickup truck south on Highway 54 toward the Lake of the Ozarks. Early in the morning, he had driven to Eldon, Missouri, and was waiting outside the boat dealer's shop when the man came to open up. Sure, they could fix the boat. It would take anywhere from two days to two weeks.

Jack took the business route across Bagnell Dam, looking out over part of the nearly one hundred square miles of water and undulating shoreline. The highway was crowded with vacationers coming from St. Louis, Chicago and elsewhere. The parade of cars crossed the dam and encountered "the Strip," a mile-long stretch of highway cluttered with tourist attractions.

He followed the highway past the turnoff to the Horseshoe Bend peninsula, on over the Grand Glaize bridge, where he could look west over the water and see the tip

17

of Shawnee Bend. Farther on, his feelings of comfort with the day were jarred sharply by the large roadside sign pointing the way to Tan-Tar-A, located on the south shore of the Turkey Bend peninsula. Jack set his jaws tightly and ground his teeth at the memory of his experiences at the large resort hotel.

He continued along the highway until Camdenton, the county seat, located near the southern tip of the lake. There he turned onto State Highway 5 and began driving up the west shore. As the pickup dawdled over the Niangua River branch bridge, Jack thought of spending the day tramping in the forest.

But he had to go and see Elizabeth Lacy, a widow who lived on the north shore of Shawnee Bend. She had called Kate and asked if Jack would come by and visit with her Wednesday morning about ten. When he had questioned Kate, she would only say that the widow and Gentry, the dead fisherman, had been close friends. Jack tried to fathom the nuances of that statement, but Kate could be very stonefaced and noncommittal when she wanted. He did know the two women had talked on the phone at some length.

Jack supposed the widow wanted him to recount the last hours of Gentry's life two days ago. How many times had he been in that situation before: the survivors pressing him for details, the slightest clue that would indicate—what? That the victim's last thought was of his friends and family? That he or she died peacefully? That the victim's life was somehow redeemed in that final gasp? He never understood totally the motives, but appreciated that this cross-examination was a natural accompaniment of death.

Jack drove through Hurricane Deck toward Sunrise Beach, towns whose names suggested action and excitement, but which were actually sleepy hamlets with a combined population of less than three hundred people. At Sunrise Beach, he turned east onto the peninsula, picking up a county road designated as Double-T. It was the route he had taken to go fishing the day Gentry died. It was a quiet and dignified area of rolling forests, hidden resorts and attractive homes.

The widow Lacy's home, a unique A-frame facing the

18

lake, was no exception. Its prow-shaped front opened onto a concrete porch that extended about two feet into the water. As a result, a boat could be moored at the front door.

Jack was looking out at the view when a woman called his name. He turned to face a slim, elderly woman wearing a bright print dress and an infectious smile. He grinned back in spite of himself.

"Mrs. Lacy?"

"Yes, yes, and you're Jack," she said, taking his arm and guiding him into the house. The sliding glass doors were flanked by stone on each side; partitioned glass windows extended from the top of the doors to the roofline. As a result, Jack stepped into a combination living room and dining room that was as bright as the outdoors.

"This is a beautiful home," he said, taking in the room at a glance.

"Yes, it is, isn't it," Mrs. Lacy agreed. "My late husband, Eldon, built this house himself. He was a carpenter, and I think it shows. Would you like some coffee, Jack?"

Her voice was low-pitched and came from her throat. He liked the way she said his name so naturally. "Yes, that would be fine."

"Maybe some coffee cake, too?"

"Sure."

Fitted into a corner along the wall opposite a massive fireplace was a four-tiered curio stand, made entirely of glass except for the stainless steel framework. Jack sat on the end of the sofa nearest the stand. It was handsome itself, but could in no way detract from the beauty of the delicate hand-painted porcelain objects placed on its shelves. There were figurines of eighteenth-century nobility, country boys and girls and an exquisite Dresden coach. There were also trinket boxes, a dinner bell, a floral basket, a pitcher-shaped vase and many birds—canaries, cardinals, blue jays and robins.

"That's what I do in my spare time," the widow said, returning with a tray and coffee set of expensive pewter. "And Lord knows, I've got plenty of time on my hands these days." Her pale green eyes sparkled as she laughed easily at the joke on herself.

"Do you collect these?" Jack asked.

"In a way," she replied. "I buy them unpainted and then do the work myself."

Jack was awed by the concentration that was obviously required to paint tiny eyes and fingernails, and to capture the shades of red on a cardinal's wing.

They sat on the edge of the sofa to be nearer the coffee table, while the widow served.

"So you're Kate's young man."

Jack shrugged, feeling slightly ill at ease. "Yes, well, we, that is, I'm staying there temporarily."

"I heard you had curly hair," she said, reaching over to touch his head lightly. "Blond with a sort of reddish tinge, isn't it?"

He nodded politely. She had touched him easily. He could tell it was part of the way she communicated with others, something natural.

"I've talked to Sheriff Davis about Geoff's death," she said, suddenly solemn as she smoothed back her shoulder-length gray hair. "I don't want you to think that I invited you here to engage in any maudlin conversation about how Geoff died, or to find out whether my name was the last word he spoke. You should know, however, that we were constant companions, and lovers, for several years now. Really since 1974, a year after Geoff's wife died."

Lovers, he thought, and decided he could imagine it on the widow's part. She was vivacious and alive.

"What is it you want with me, Mrs. Lacy?"

"Beth, please," she said, touching his hand.

Intimacy wasn't so easy for Jack in such circumstances, but he agreed, "Beth, then. I'm afraid I don't know anything more than I've already told the sheriff, and I'm sure he will undertake a thorough investigation."

"Mel Davis?" The tone of her question hinted at several qualifications. "We first came down here in 1966 when Davis was in his early thirties. He worked for the county road crew awhile, then was a mechanic, and even tried running a café until he and his wife were divorced. Then he became a deputy sheriff and two years later somehow got himself elected sheriff. And even re-elected."

"But you don't think highly of him?"

"As a politician, he may have found his niche in life.

20

He's shrewd in a shifty sort of way. Knows how to manipulate people. As a policeman, I've got my doubts."

Jack stared at her noncommittally. So she didn't want sympathy, she wanted revenge. That was the other side of the coin.

"Last year, one of our friends came home one afternoon and surprised a burglar, who shot him dead. That happened just up the road. Sheriff Davis never made it to first base in solving that crime, and that was a year ago."

He wondered if she had any idea how many times that happened. What if it had been some guy on his way to Los Angeles, who had just stopped off to pick up a few items for a hock shop in Kansas City? He wouldn't leave a clue. He would slip out just as he slipped in.

"Besides, the water patrol has jurisdiction over this . . . 'accident,' " she said, stressing the last word. "But they really aren't an investigative agency. They'll turn it over to the state police, who'll want to retain control of the case, but they'll ask Sheriff Davis to do most of the work. But he won't do anything, since he's not in charge. Do you see what I'm getting at? It can fall through the cracks."

Jack's image of the widow changed slowly as she spoke. There was warmth and mirth about her, but she was tough and perceptive too.

"How do you think I can help?" he asked.

"You were a Chicago policeman, right? You've worked with professionals. I figure you know how to go about an investigation."

"Are there any secrets among the people who live down here?" Jack asked, trying to sound casual but unable to conceal a measure of frustration. He was the type of man who preferred his private life to remain private.

The sparkle and devilishness were back in her eyes. "This is worse than your usual small town, Jack. Not only have some of the families been here for generations but there's all us 'outsiders' to further define them." She laughed that deep, throaty laugh, throwing her head back. "And believe me, you're still an outsider even after twelve years."

Jack set the coffee cup back on the tray and looked at his hands. "Maybe you already know this, but I left Chicago to get away from police work. I'm down here on . . . ah . . . an extended vacation."

"Now don't go worrying that Kate would tell anything *personal* about you." She paused and Jack sensed that she was thinking carefully about how to proceed.

"Mind you, I never said there was a premeditated crime committed," she said. "Sheriff Davis may be right, in fact. Just a couple of drunken boaters. It's happened before. Still, accident or not, I loved Geoff. Old people like us don't have much to look forward to. We can only take joy in each other. That's what Geoff and I did, and it made these past years much brighter than I had expected, especially after Eldon died. I just want someone to make certain that those responsible for Geoff's death are brought to justice."

Jack again contemplated his folded hands. "I was a street cop, never a detective. Besides, you don't know me."

"That's true," she replied, "but then I don't know any private investigators. If I have a firm from Kansas City or St. Louis send out a man, I'll still be taking potluck."

She rose, walked toward the fireplace and turned to face him. "But I do know Kate and I trust her judgment." She paused for effect, and then spoke rapidly, in a businesslike voice. "I'll pay you one hundred dollars per day, plus expenses."

A look of incredulity spread across Jack's face. Did she have any idea what a Chicago cop made? Did she have that kind of money?

"One-fifty," she said defiantly, answering his silence.

"Wait a minute! I mean, a hundred was more than plenty."

"You'll do it, then?" she asked, returning to sit beside him.

"I didn't say that. I don't know. I'll have to think about it."

"Jack, all you have to do is look around a few hours a day. I don't expect you to give up your daily fishing trips. Just make sure the investigation doesn't stall; that nothing is overlooked. That's not so bad, is it? And it's a way for you to make some money."

Again, he looked closely at her in an attempt to fathom any underlying meaning. Did she know he was nearly busted? That he was feeling guilty about sponging off Kate?

"Okay, I'll look around," he said, making his decision.

"But if I don't find any reason to stay on the case, I'll tell you straight out, okay?"

"Fair enough, Jack."

He picked up the coffee pot and poured himself another cup, signaling that the conversation was not over.

"I've a few questions," he said.

"Yes?"

"Gentry. Where did he live?"

"When you turned into my driveway, you could have continued along the road. Geoff's house would have been the second on the left. There's only one house between us. It's owned by a couple from Kansas City. They're rarely here, except in August."

"How old was Gentry?"

"Seventy-eight."

"He must have been fairly vigorous, for his age," Jack said, remembering the bulk of the fisherman's body, the muscles in his neck.

"Yes—he was ten years older than I am, but I couldn't keep up with him."

"Did he usually fish off Shawnee Bend?" Jack asked, calculating that Gentry was killed about five miles east of his home.

"Most of the time, yes. I used to worry about him in that terrible old fishing boat. He could have afforded the best. But he was like that—sentimental about old things."

Jack hesitated as the widow momentarily lost herself in remembrances. "Did he have any enemies that you know of? I doubt that's the case, but I need to know."

"Enemies? I suppose. Geoff was a rich and powerful man. He was outspoken about many things, especially commercial development on the lake. He probably stepped on a few toes along the way."

"But no one special comes to mind?"

He detected a slight hesitancy on her part, as if she were making a decision. "Recently, there were quite a few telephone conversations I overheard. Couldn't help but hear them. All I could determine was that Geoff was adamant about whatever was being discussed. Sometimes it sounded as if there were heated exchanges."

"Who are Mr. Gentry's natural heirs?" Jack asked.

"There are two grandchildren." She paused, deep in thought. "There are no other living heirs."

23

Beth Lacy rose and walked to a desk beside the fireplace. Returning, she handed Jack a card. "You should see this man, Roy Cousins. He's a lawyer. Geoff may have changed his will. It may or may not be important."

THREE

Crossing the Osage River channel south of Hurricane Deck, Jack watched a half dozen people churn up the lake water with the new jet ski contraptions. When his prop was fixed maybe it would be a good idea to do his weekday fishing at the nearby Pomme de Terre lake. It was less likely to be crowded there. On the weekends, he'd stay home. There was no escape from the tourists anywhere, then.

He drove by Gentry's house after leaving the widow and saw Sheriff Davis's car parked in front. He considered going in and talking to the sheriff, but he couldn't think of any good reason for doing so at the time.

But he did plan to stop and visit the lawyer, Roy Cousins, whose office was in Camdenton. Jack was curious to find out more about the widow's puzzling comments regarding Gentry's will.

Cousins had a second floor office in one of the older buildings in the shopping area on the east side of Route 54. The lawyer's office was small and dusty. Cousins sat behind an ancient roll-top desk, which was piled high with books and papers.

They introduced themselves, and Jack was offered the

use of an old captain's chair. His first impression was that the office suited the man.

"So Beth Lacy sent you over, did she," Cousins said, scratching with one hand the long white hair that hung to his collar and reaching with the other for a much-used pipe.

"Yes. She wants me to make sure there are no hitches in the investigation of Gentry's death."

"She never did trust Mel Davis," he grinned, drawing fire deep into the bowl of the pipe. The old man's gray suit was crumpled and shiny from too much dry cleaning.

"She thinks there may be too many fingers in the pie. Scared something will fall between the cracks."

"Uh-huh. May be right about that."

The old man seemed overly cautious to Jack. Or had he mistaken the natural tremors of old age for nervousness?

"I don't think there's much to this case," Jack said, trying to put the old man at ease by minimizing the issue.

"Maybe not."

"I hear boating accidents aren't that infrequent on the lake."

"That's right," the lawyer said from behind a haze of blue smoke. "But you tell me, son, whether you thought it was an accident. You were there, I hear, and that's an advantage no one else has."

Jack hesitated. The old man had put him on the spot, and Jack wasn't prepared for that question. He considered the incident with the oar, but thought better of mentioning it specifically. On the other hand, he sensed the need to be honest with the old lawyer.

"There seemed a sort of deliberateness about it to me. My first reaction was that they were trying to swamp him. Maybe that was it, and the boat just got away from them."

"Even so, that could be manslaughter, especially since they left the scene."

Jack agreed by nodding his head. "Mrs. Lacy said Gentry argued recently on the telephone with someone, or perhaps several persons. Also, she indicated he may have changed his will. Is there any reason to believe either of these things were related to his death?"

Cousins poked around in the pipe bowl with a pipe tool before replying. "Let me tell you a little about Geoff Gentry. It may not help your investigation any, but you

26

might just be interested in learning more about the man.

"He first started coming down here from St. Louis in the late fifties. Used to stay at an old fishing lodge that folded up years ago. I met Geoff through Louis Dupré, who sold real estate around here until he died a few years back. Louie and several of us used to have coffee every morning at the drug store, and Geoff joined us now and then. He and I became good friends. You'll hear how clannish we are down here. Don't take to outsiders and all that. But Geoff was a good man who everyone liked. Most everyone."

Cousins took time out to thump the pipe against the heel of his hand. "That might sound kind of strange, since Geoff was president of a large manufacturing company. Oftentimes, men like that don't cotton to small town folks. But Geoff treated us like kin from the first day he sat down to drink coffee with us, and most of us treated him the same way. Of course, he wasn't really a big city boy. He was born and raised in Chester, Illinois. I suppose that's why he felt comfortable with us.

"He eventually bought some property from Louie. First place he bought was a house in Lake Ozark. Later on, though, Geoff bought the house on Shawnee Bend, and he and Elsie retired to that place in sixty-two. She was a delightful person, too. Her and my Maude would have gotten on great but Maude died the winter before."

Cousins suddenly thumbed through some papers on his desk, and then abandoned the search with a frown. "Geoff bought up a lot of property around the lake throughout the years. Bought several parcels on Turkey Bend. Wasn't much out there, then. That was a few years before they built Tan-Tar-A, which was really the start of the tourist boom down here. Geoff always said land was one of the best investments. 'There's only so much of it, Roy,' he used to say. And he was right, of course. Geoff's landholdings alone are worth a small fortune today."

"Would it be out of line for me to ask how much Gentry's estate is worth?" Jack interrupted.

"Well, yes and no, young man. The will hasn't been read yet, nor filed for probate. The executor of the estate hasn't officially been announced and naturally hasn't begun to catalog the estate. So I really can't tell you specifically what Geoff Gentry's material possessions are worth, and

27

some might say that it woudn't be appropriate for me to tell you before the rightful heirs."

The old man was again tamping tobacco into the pipe. Jack maintained a respectful silence. The lawyer's refusal wasn't absolute; he had qualified it.

"On the other hand, I don't suppose it would be inappropriate for me to tell you in general terms about Geoff's estate," Cousins continued. "He was president of a manufacturing firm located in St. Louis. Geoff started working for the company when it was little more than a small foundry making manhole covers. But Geoff had an aptitude for mechanics, and he was awarded a patent for an improved grain auger. That's when he acquired part ownership of the company. Under his leadership, they diversified and eventually became one of the nation's largest manufacturers of components for elevators."

Jack sensed that the old man had a feeling of pride in Gentry's accomplishments and realized that a deep friendship had existed between the two men.

Cousins wagged a cautionary finger at Jack. "But Geoff didn't rest on his laurels in the manufacturing world. He *invested* wisely, acquiring an admirable portfolio of blue-chip stocks. There were other buildings and landholdings besides those here on the lake, and then there were bonds, savings accounts, even royalties from a book on how to patent new equipment designs."

Cousins held both hands forward, palms up, in a questioning pose. "I don't know. I'd guess it's all worth several million."

"Who inherits?"

The old man rose from his chair, a smile on his face. He was tall, but had a slight stoop. Jack noticed a cane leaning against the far side of the desk.

"Now that, son, is a horse of a different color. A lot of people might make an educated guess about the value of Geoff's estate, but I'm the only one who knows the contents of his will. And that's because I was his attorney."

Cousins grasped his cane, and Jack sensed that the conversation was drawing to a close.

"You drew up Gentry's will, then?"

"I *revised* his will in recent years. Geoff had a will before he came to live in this area, of course. A man of his achievements knows a lot of lawyers, has dealings with

28

them. Geoff never trusted lawyers much, though." Cousins chuckled at the widespread distrust of those in his profession. "But, as I said, we became friends. So Geoff looked to me to make changes in his will, such as when his wife died. Said he trusted me more than those city lawyers. I'm not so sure that was smart of him."

The old lawyer picked up a lightweight straw hat, placed it on his head and began walking toward the door. "C'mon, son, I'll walk you to your car. I'm going over to the local cafe for an extended lunch. Several of us old duffers sit over there for a couple of hours, drinking bourbon from a flask and telling lies."

Jack hurried to open the door. "I suppose it's logical to assume that Gentry's grandchildren will inherit his estate?" Jack ventured.

Cousins continued talking, as if he hadn't heard Jack. "You know, they say that having to climb stairs is good for the heart, but I just consider it a pain in the ass. I wish to God they'd put an elevator in this building."

As they walked the flight of stairs side by side, Jack considered taking the old man's arm but worried that Cousins might be offended.

They stepped out of the coolness of the building into a blazing June sun.

"Now that starts the juices flowing, don't it, boy."

"It certainly does."

"But I never complain about the heat. No, sir. You know why? Because it's right now that I have my greatest appreciation for the crispness and excitement of autumn. And, of course, in the fall I can literally smell this day as well as I can standing here right now. It's a tremendous argument in favor of the changing seasons."

"Here's my pickup," Jack said, assuming the old man would totter off to his luncheon engagement. Instead, Cousins backed against the brick building, seeking the coolness of the shade. Jack walked closer to him.

"No, son, I can't tell you about the contents of the will. But I can tell you that I will read the will after the funeral Friday and that you're welcome to come. I suspect Kate might want to go to the services, anyway."

Jack cursed silently, while trying to maintain a pleasant smile on his face. Everyone knows, he thought. Everyone.

29

"I'd wager, though, that there will be more than a few people surprised by the will. Yes, sir, no doubt about that."

"Mr. Cousins, I know you need to get to lunch, but let me ask you one final question."

"No hurry, son."

"Was Gentry involved in anything controversial that you know of? Some deal in which he might have had serious disagreements with other people?" Jack was thinking of Beth Lacy's comments about the quarrelsome phone calls.

Cousins squinted at the sun. "Now, son, that's something worth your looking into. You see, if there was one thing that riled Geoff Gentry beyond anything else, it was the continued commercialization of this lake area. He thought there were too many resorts on the lake as it is. And he was very influential several years ago in persuading the state to tighten up its standards for sewage disposal into the lake.

"He was like a lot of us, I guess. When you get older, you don't appreciate change so much, because change is for the future and our perspective is on the past. Still, you have to admit that we've got to be close to reaching our capacity for hamburger stands on the lake." The old man laughed softly at his joke.

"That was the disagreement, then?" Jack asked, unable to hide his disappointment that the issue seemed so mundane.

"You should talk to a fellow by the name of Butch Banuchi. He can tell you all the details."

"Surely you can tell me more," Jack pleaded.

"Well, son, you gotta do something to earn your fee," Cousins said, unlimbering from the brick wall and beginning to walk off.

Realizing that Cousins had never answered his original question, Jack caught the lawyer's arm. "Mrs. Lacy said Gentry may have changed his will recently. Is that true?"

Cousins looked directly into Jack's eyes, and there was a sudden and deadly seriousness in the lawyer's expression.

"Geoff rewrote his will exactly one week before his death."

FOUR

"Christ, Kate, does everyone who lives anywhere near this damn lake know that we live together?"

"Probably, Jack."

He tried not to make it sound like an accusation. "Did you tell them?"

She looked at him with a bemused and tolerant smile. "No, but I don't deny it. Should I?"

"How in the hell did they find out?"

"We have neighbors. There are a dozen local fishermen who pass this place every day. People who live around here don't miss much."

"You can say that again."

But Jack couldn't stay mad, especially at Kate. She was the one who had saved him; breathed her joy of life into him when he had nearly drowned in self-pity and contemplated self-destruction.

He hadn't imagined he could be so happy in such modest surroundings. Kate's cabin was a rectangular structure with one small bedroom and a cramped bathroom off the main room, which served as kitchen, living and dining room and entertainment center. It was a precut house; the parts had been delivered to the building site, ready for

31

assembly. Jack could picture Kate—tan, curvaceous, but solid—helping her brothers cement the log walls into place and shingle the roof.

The cabin was located off the Y-Road, which ran east toward the lake from Highway 54, about five miles north of Camdenton. It was called a "second tier" lake home, which meant that it did not front directly on the water, although the lake was within view and sound. There was a rented space on a neighbor's dock where Kate kept the boat that Jack used all the time.

He crossed the room, encircled Kate's waist from behind and looked over her shoulder. He watched as she chopped vegetables on a cutting board beside the sink.

"What's for dinner?"

"A ham roast Mama gave me today, scalloped potatoes and wild greens."

"Wild greens?" he asked, pressing himself into Kate's behind.

"Wild lettuce, pokeweed, smooth dock and lamb's-quarters."

"Where'd you get that junk?" he asked, kissing her neck.

"It's not junk. Mama and me picked it behind their place. You just put the greens in some water and add enough salt to bring the bugs to the top." She paused, and turned to see his reaction. "Next I'll boil them and cook them in the drippings from the ham."

"Sounds terrible."

"Try it before you knock it, boy," she said, with a laugh, a turn of her head and a peck on Jack's nose.

"That's about what I said the first time I saw you."

"Bullshit."

"Honest Injun," Jack said, admiring Kate as she worked. She was tall, nearly his height. Her angular face was handsome rather than pretty. The coal-black hair was taking on a hint of gray, so that when the sunlight hit it just right it appeared to be inset with diamonds. There was something about the combination of her expressive eyes and perpetual smile that always gave Jack the impression he was about to become part of a conspiracy. Kate moved deliberately, as if she knew where she was going. She had a habit of saying outrageous things, which was delightful rather than irritating because she did it so naturally. He couldn't believe she didn't belong to someone else.

"Why do you wear your hair so short?" he asked. "Let it grow until it hangs in the crack of your butt."

"It's easier to keep this way," she said, pushing him aside to set the table. "Besides, it doesn't get in the way of *things*."

She was right, as usual. The greens, embellished with her homemade salad dressing, were delicious. That was Kate. She knew all kinds of things—how to troll for bass, shear sheep, prepare persimmon, make quilts, boil down molasses, butcher a hog and train hounds to tree coons. The first time she made love to him, he understood that her life was dedicated to the pure enjoyment of all things natural and enduring.

Jack pushed away the homemade apple pie, feeling stuffed. "I'm not sure what to do with this Gentry case. What's so confusing is all the doubletalk I seem to be getting. You always hear about country folk giving you the straight poop, but I'm having to interpret everything."

"Such as?"

"Take the widow Lacy, for example. She seems more convinced than I am that Gentry's death was an accident. Her main concern seems to be that the investigation doesn't bog down. She also said that lately Gentry appeared to be arguing with a person or persons unknown. Finally, like an afterthought, she says Gentry *may* have changed his will."

"Which makes you wonder if she's telling all she knows."

"Right. Then, there's this guy Cousins. Wow, what a courtroom lawyer he must have been in his prime. Devious. You never know where he's coming from. He won't tell me details of Gentry's will, but pretty much fills me in on his financial background. He doesn't give me any reason to think Gentry's death was anything but accidental, yet he backhandedly encourages me to stay on the case and 'earn my fee.' He even gives me the name of a guy I should talk to, and invites me to the funeral and reading of Gentry's will. Says the old man's last testament may turn some heads. Finally, he tells me Gentry changed his will a week before his death. You figure it out."

"I ain't the detective, honey. That's your game."

"Seriously, tell me something about the locals around

33

here. Are they really that close-knit a group? The widow Lacy says it's as bad as any small town, if not worse."

"No doubt about it," Kate said, with emphasis. "A lot of the people hereabouts are descended from the hill people of Kentucky and Tennessee, and they have that kind of clannishness about them. On parts of the lake, especially around Versailles, some of the original settlers were German Mennonites, and they've always kept to themselves. So you've got a core of what some people call the 'old stock.' They and their descendants have been here for generations. They socialize together, especially the older folks; they gossip together and usually marry among themselves. Not many people leave."

Jack thought he detected a wistfulness in Kate's statement. "And then there are what you'd call the 'new stock,' I guess?"

"Not by that name. But anyone who moved down here to retire or just live on the lake, or set up some tourist-related business—these are the newcomers and many of the old stock resent them."

"Why?"

"I guess it's mainly because of the differences in family income. Most of the folks who've always lived around here barely eked out a living before the tourist boom, which really started in the late fifties and early sixties. Before that, there was some logging, but that really died out in the thirties. People got by farming, but the land around here really isn't that good. Some raised mules, cows or hogs. There were a lot of vegetable gardens and chicken flocks. The old-timers call the chicken flock the mortgage lifter of the Ozarks."

"Then the new folks come along with enough money to buy nice homes and set up businesses."

"That's right. And it bred a form of resentment with some people. Of course, the side you don't hear too often is about the jobs that the resort atmosphere has created. A lot of folks that are making a decent living now would still be scratching in the earth without the tourist business."

"You're old stock, aren't you, Kate?"

She accepted the appraisal indifferently. "In a way, I guess."

"Does that bother you?"

"Yes and no. Sometimes it gets too close to breathe well,

34

but I left once for a couple of years and found out that I missed the place."

"Cousins—is he old stock?"

"He and his daddy and his daddy's daddy before him, at least."

"I got the impression that Gentry might have bridged that gap between the locals and the newcomers."

"About as much as is possible, I suppose. He was concerned about the lake, and that sits well with most people around here. Besides, he was an all-right guy." She paused, remembering. "I used to wait tables several years ago over at what's now Suzy's Place. Mr. Gentry used to come in for coffee in the mornings. He was tall, walked straight as an arrow, and was very dignified-looking. He had a stern face, a determined jaw. But when he cut loose with that big, booming voice, he was the friendliest guy in the world. And he learned something about everyone and their family."

Jack had a hard time thinking of the limp body and slack eyes he knew as Gentry as ever having had any vitality.

"So he and the widow Lacy were a hot number."

"You're crude."

Jack feigned indignation. "But she told me they were lovers."

"That's different."

"How do you think old people do it, Kate?"

"They do it slowly and enjoy it twice as long as you fast-on-the-trigger young boys," she said mockingly.

"Were the local folks scandalized?"

"About them, or us?"

"Them first."

"Oh, I suppose. Ma always mentioned it with a tsk, tsk, but I don't think Gentry and Beth cared much."

"Beth. You know her that well?"

"Everybody knows Beth well from the first time. Right?"

Jack chose not to answer the question. "Old man Gentry was loaded, according to Cousins. What about the widow Lacy?"

"Beth," she chided, "doesn't confide in me about her financial affairs, or in anyone else, I'd guess."

"You think Gentry was keeping her?"

"What if he was," she said, pinching her lips together.

35

Jack wondered if he should complete the statement: ". . . like you're keeping me." He did wonder how the widow could afford a hundred fifty a day, plus expenses.

Instead, he said, "I heard Gentry had two grandchildren. What do you know about them?"

"Too much. Alan's twenty-three, twenty-four. He's been in jail. He had a bad habit of taking things from other people's houses. Barbara, the granddaughter, had a bad reputation as a teenager. She was good at the three B's."

"The what?"

"Bumming, boozing and balling. But that was a few years ago. Maybe she's shaped up. She's about twenty now, and has been at the university in Columbia for the last two years. I think I've seen her recently in the family home on Turkey Bend, though."

"Her folks' place?"

"Used to be her mother's home. She married Mr. Gentry's only son, John."

"What happened to him?"

"He tried his hand at running several businesses in the lake area, but eventually left his family and drifted out to California. He was killed in a car accident several years ago."

"And Gentry's daughter-in-law?"

"She was an alcoholic, and drank herself to death about six years ago. Always resented her father-in-law; blamed him for driving her husband away."

"The grandson, Alan. Does he live on the lake?"

"Yeah, in a ramshackle cabin over on the west shore. He hangs out with the local riffraff in a bar north of Sunrise Beach."

"One other name I've heard, from Cousins. Banuchi."

Kate raised her eyebrows in surprise. "He owns all or part of several boat rental places, resorts, restaurants and some of the arcades and stuff on the Strip."

"He and old man Gentry involved in any business ventures that you heard of?"

"Don't know anything about that, babe." Kate rose from the table and began clearing the dishes to the sink.

"I don't have any clear idea of what to do next in this investigation," Jack said, renewing his interest in the pie as Kate poured more coffee.

"So why stay with it?"

36

He hesitated, searching for the reason. "I was there, and there's something about the way Gentry was killed. I can't put my finger on it all the way, but it bothers me. Then there's the money. I'm flat on my ass, you know."

Kate replaced the pot on the stove, folded her arms and leaned against the counter. "And your masculinity is starting to suffer because you're living here." It was a statement, not a question.

"Sort of."

"So start paying me rent," she said sarcastically.

He shrugged. "That's a possibility."

"Christ, Jack," she said, turning her back to him.

He remembered first meeting her in a local restaurant early in the morning. He'd had on the guard uniform, although they'd taken the gun and told him to return the clothes the next day. She'd struck up a conversation and wanted to know how he liked the job. He was blunt and told her what had happened. She took him home—whether out of pity or curiosity, he didn't understand at the time. But he was comfortable, even from the first. She treated him like a frayed but favorite coat.

What *did* she see in me? he wondered. Especially then. He remembered being drunk, reeking of liquor. He didn't even look the part of a macho cop. He was of average height for a man, wiry rather than muscular. And he didn't have a mustache.

"Kate, it's just that you've given everything, and all I've done so far is take."

"I'm getting plenty. You're forgetting the sex." Her back was still turned, and the sarcasm stung.

"C'mon, Kate." He regretted the course the conversation was taking. He owed her so much he could never repay. She'd given him more than a bed and three square meals. She'd put some brightness in his life, and he'd gotten off the sauce for the first time in ten years.

She turned to face him, hands on her hips. "You listen to me, Jack Olsen. I love you and I expect you to love me in return. If you do that, it doesn't make shit where the money comes from. So if you're going to leave me, do it for a real reason. Tell me you don't love me."

FIVE

Funerals are the pits, he thought, as he and Kate stood near the back of the crowd at the cemetery. Jack was surprised that Gentry had chosen to be buried near the lake, instead of in St. Louis or his boyhood home in Illinois. All the ritual, the comfort everyone took in the singsong words. Jack sensed the secret fear that forced them all to think about the possibility that this was the end, and not the beginning.

Kate wanted to go, as Cousins had surmised, and she said that as many of the old stock turned out for Gentry's funeral as would have for one of their own. He supposed it was a compliment. Mrs. Lacy and Cousins somehow got the word around that everyone was invited to lunch at the Gentry house following the funeral. And what Jack figured would be an uncomfortable trip down nostalgia road. But it turned out to be far more interesting than that.

Gentry's house was not as ostentatious as it might have been, considering his millionaire status. But it did have unique and striking features.

In many ways, it resembled a compound. Kate and Jack entered through ornamental iron gates, flanked by a long, pierced mansonry wall that joined a double-car garage opposite the main body of the house. The gates opened onto a roofed passageway about thirty feet from the front door of the sprawling ranch. Behind the masonry wall was a garden court featuring a beautifuly gnarled oak tree that seemed about to burst in its attempt to reach the heavens. Several people were in the courtyard, either seated beneath the shade of the oak tree or standing about as the vested waiter with his rolling service cart dispensed drinks and hors d'oeuvres.

Opening the door into the foyer, they were greeted by a wall-length Thomas Hart Benton painting. Jack almost expected to hear the commanding figure in the painting yell out orders.

Instead, they were met by Beth Lacy, who ushered them into a large living room.

"Kate *and* Jack, how nice of you to come," the widow said. Jack searched her face for signs of anguish and remorse, but all was placid and serene. Beth Lacy was directing traffic with consummate skill.

Jack and Kate walked farther into the elegantly furnished living room. The adjacent dining room area revealed a table laden with sandwiches and various snack items, and another waiter manning a rolling stock of soft drinks and liquor.

"It is noon," Kate said, almost apologetically. "Do you want a sandwich?"

"Sure—fix us a plate." Jack looked about the house. A double-sided fireplace divided the living room from what he soon discovered to be Gentry's study. Jack inspected several photographs and official-looking framed documents hanging on the wall. One proclaimed Gentry to be an outstanding citizen of St. Louis for 1953, another recognized his contributions toward building a new wing on a hospital.

"Nice, huh," Kate said, appearing with a plate of sandwiches, while balancing two drinks in her other hand. "I knew that experience as a waitress would come in handy some day. Try this stuff. I think it's caviar."

"Y'all kiddin'," Jack drawled, giving his best imitation of a Southern accent. "Ya mean 'at der funna l'il black and white spotted stuff 'at looks like bird droppin's?"

"Mind your manners, asshole. Remember that I'm a

39

daughter of the Confederacy and I expect at all times to be treated like a Southern belle."

They wandered back through the living room, which was now crowded with people, and then out the foyer into the courtyard.

Kate was greeted by several clusters of people, and she stopped at one group to chat and introduce Jack, who tried vainly to remember the rapid-fire sequence of names. Mainly because of Kate's reaction to him, one name stuck. That was Tom Wallace's. Jack was not so much annoyed by the friendly embrace between Kate and Wallace as he was by the coy way Kate then looked at everybody as if she expected them to be envious.

Disengaging themselves from the group, Kate and Jack strolled through the courtyard toward the pool, then to the back of the house where the yard sloped toward a boathouse and the lake.

Entering the rear of the house through one of three enclosed family porches, Kate pulled on Jack's arm and whispered in his ear. "You asked about Butch Banuchi. That's him right through the arched doorway."

Jack looked across the pool table and saw a portly man in a black suit. He had wavy black hair, thinning slightly on either side of the widow's peak, and the clearest, rosiest complexion of any man Jack had ever seen.

"I guess that's what an Italian cherub looks like," Jack said, feeling the pain of Kate's elbow digging into his rib cage.

"What about the grandkids," he said. "Any sign of Bonnie and Clyde?"

Kate pointed them out in the crowd. Alan was a gangly kid with greasy brown hair. He was the only one there wearing a string bow tie. Barbara, on the other hand, looked as if she had stepped from the cover page of a fashion magazine. The shiny blond hair, parted in the middle and flipped up on the ends, framed a perfectly proportioned face. The pink summer dress traced a luscious figure.

Jack's appreciation of Barbara Gentry was interrupted by a sudden awareness that flowed through the crowd and directed everyone's attention toward the foyer. There stood Roy Cousins, leaning on his cane, his left hand trembling slightly as he signaled for the attention of those inside and outside the house.

"Folks, it was Geoff Gentry's desire, as expressed in written instructions that accompany the will, that anyone living in the lake area who so desired might attend the reading of his will." Cousins's voice and countenance suggested authority. Jack noticed that he was resplendent in a dark-blue pin-striped suit. "So those of you who are interested can gather in and about the living room. The rest of you continue to take advantage of the food and drinks. Don't feel like you have to hurry off."

Jack guessed close to seventy people crowded into the living room, the library, the family room, the dining room and even the kitchen. People leaned against the hallway walls leading to the back bedrooms, and others stood outside in the passageway to listen through the opened windows. He noticed and smiled perfunctorily at Sheriff Davis.

Jack and Kate were near the foyer, just inside the living room. Cousins stood under the arched doorway bracing himself with the cane, yet with an aura of confidence and command that could be felt throughout the room. He was, obviously, going to stand to read the will. Mrs. Lacy sat immediately to Cousins's right, while others throughout the living room, including the grandchildren, had drawn up chairs to face the old lawyer.

"Now these are rather unusual circumstances befitting an unusual man," Cousins began.

"I don't know for certain, but I suspect there are provisions in Geoff Gentry's will that he wanted to be widely known. Knowing the local grapevine in this area, you might conclude that he wanted the news to come from the horse's mouth, so to speak, and not get colored by retelling four and five times." Knowing nods and a ripple of laughter spread through the crowd.

"Now I don't intend to read this will verbatim. It would only confuse most of you with all those fancy lawyer terms like whereas, hereby, devise and bequeath." Cousins was clearly enjoying his role as master of ceremonies. The only one in the room who seemed nervous, Jack thought, was the grandson, Alan.

"Geoff Gentry hired me to help him write this will," Cousins said, the smile now perfunctory and businesslike.

41

"I can tell you that it's valid beyond question. The witnesses to the will have impeccable credentials." He paused, as if allowing time for objections.

"Later today I will file Geoff Gentry's will for probate in the Camdenton County Court. That means simply that the court will determine the validity of the will and oversee the efforts of the executor in carrying forth its provisions. I'm pleased to announce that I was named executor of the estate of my dear friend, Geoffrey Gentry the second." The smile was gone from the old man's face and a respectful silence fell over the crowd.

"It will be my job to get the estate in order," Cousins continued. "It will be necessary to do an inventory, determine the debts and assets, pay taxes, collect rent, and generally get everything shipshape so it is possible to distribute the proceeds of the estate according to the last will and testament of the deceased."

Cousins coughed, signaling that he would begin detailing the provisions of the will. There were several general and specific legacies, including five thousand dollars to Lloyd McGinnis, Gentry's groundskeeper, and twenty-five hundred dollars to his cook, Mrs. Anna May Scott.

The Thomas Hart Benton painting in the foyer, along with other specified art works currently held elsewhere for safekeeping, were willed to the State of Missouri to be properly displayed for public viewing.

Gentry left twenty-five thousand dollars to each of the hospitals serving the lake area, and one hundred thousand dollars to the Washington University medical school in St. Louis for research related to heart disease and cancer. Finally, twenty-five thousand dollars was given to the St. Louis Symphony.

"All of Mr. Gentry's personal effects in this house are left to Mrs. Elizabeth Lacy, to dispose of as she sees fit," Gentry concluded. The old man paused and surveyed his audience for several seconds. Jack noticed that Cousins had yet to actually consult the will he held and frequently waved at the audience for emphasis.

"The remainder of Geoff Gentry's estate is to be held in trust, with Mrs. Lacy designated as trustee. In the unfortunate event of her death or disability, I would become trustee."

Jack noticed a perceptible look of consternation on the face of Alan Gentry, as he fidgeted nervously in his chair.

Cousins continued, more quickly than before, "There is a detailed list of investments recommended by Mr. Gentry and designation of several individuals to serve as investment counselors to Mrs. Lacy in her capacity as trustee.

"According to the provisions of the will, monthly stipends are to be paid from the income of the estate as follows: one thousand dollars each per month to Alan Gentry and Barbara Gentry, grandchildren of the deceased. The trustee is empowered, however, to consider extraordinary expenses of these natural heirs."

The grandson was now standing, pale as death. He turned to look at those behind him, as if searching for a face. Jack tried to be unobtrusive as he moved slightly to his right so that his line of sight coincided roughly with the direction in which Alan was looking. The face that stood out belonged to Banuchi, although Jack admitted to himself that it might only appear that way because Banuchi was one of the few faces familiar to him. Alan's questioning look was fleeting. Then he left the room abruptly, absentmindedly shoving people aside as he made his way out the door. Jack noticed that the granddaughter, on the other hand, still wore the same unyielding smile.

Cousins, ignoring the slight confusion that resulted, began reading from the will. "Also to be paid out from the receipts of the trust is twenty-five hundred dollars per month for the operating expenses of a Lake of the Ozarks Development Council, whose duties generally are to relate to maintaining and improving the quality of the lake. The will prohibits any payment pending incorporation of the council. It is required that the council employ a full-time director and make provisions for an adequate staff."

Cousins explained that the Council's duties would include efforts to develop a multi-county zoning ordinance for future residential and commercial development on the lake; establish a fish hatchery, parks and wildlife refuges on the lake; and, establish a museum.

The old lawyer shifted his stance a pace to the left. "Finally, the will provides that this testamentary trust can be dissolved at any time if it is the opinion of the current trustee that the decedent's grandchildren possess sufficient maturity and judgment to capably administer the estate. In no event shall the trust exist beyond the year 1990. In the event of the dissolution of the trust, a sum of two hundred and fifty thousand dollars shall be given to the aforementioned lake association for its continued support." The reading of the will was over.

While Kate went outside, Jack lingered after the departing crowd. Cousins talked briefly with Mrs. Lacy, then saw Jack and crossed the room to stand at his side.

"Well, that's over, thank goodness," the old lawyer said, producing his pipe. Jack thought he looked exhausted.

"Like I said, son, there were a few surprises in Geoff's will."

"Yes, and the grandson seemed most surprised of all."

The old man was noncommittal. "Still, no one benefited from Mr. Gentry's death or his will in any way that seems unusual," Jack suggested. "Wouldn't you agree?"

"Yes," Cousins drawled, staring vacantly through the open door. " 'Course, some folks may have been expecting something entirely different from what they heard."

The old man then tottered off, leaving Jack to mull over his parting remark.

SIX

Beth Lacy was sunning herself near the water's edge when Jack arrived. He thought of how his mother would have disapproved of an elderly woman wearing shorts, let alone the bright-yellow tank top the widow sported.

He had called before coming, just in case Mrs. Lacy was too emotionally exhausted from the funeral the day before. But she had sounded fine on the phone, and she actually seemed chipper when he arrived.

"Most people lie in the sun to get a tan," she smiled, reaching out to touch him even though he was too far away. "But I do it for its healing qualities. I find if I lie in the sun for at least a half hour every day it has great therapeutic value. I try to relax, think positive thoughts. It helps me heal myself from within. So you see, Jack, the sun's really best for what it does on the inside, not the outside."

She did have a good tan, though, and Jack remembered that he had first thought she was naturally dark-complexioned. Although Beth Lacy was basically a thin person, he noticed the folds of skin that sagged along the inside of her thighs and upper arms. The fullness of her hips had dissipated with age, and what Jack assumed were once full and robust breasts had succumbed to the forces of gravity.

As if sensing his thoughts, she said, "At my age, there's no other reason to have a tan."

"I think it's very becoming," he said, feeling sorry for his critical appraisal of the widow's body.

"Come in the house with me," she said. "I've got a pitcher of lemonade cooling in the refrigerator."

He followed her indoors.

"Mrs. Lacy," he began.

"Beth," she corrected, handing him a glass of lemonade.

"Beth, I wondered if you still want me to keep track of the investigation into Mr. Gentry's death now that the will has been made public."

"Why would that make any difference?"

"I thought the funeral, the finality of it all, might persuade you to simply let the local authorities go ahead with the investigation at their own pace."

"The finality of it all," she repeated, as if tasting the words. "Yes, there's certainly that realization. We fight it to the bitter end, I can assure you. Even when your age makes death a distinct possibility at any moment, you still have a tendency to deny the obvious. Do you know why?"

"No, ma'am."

"Because, as I think you will discover in time, we all stay young in mind and heart. We simply get trapped inside a body that is growing old."

She was right. He didn't care to think about it.

"Yes, Jack, I do want you to continue investigating Geoff's death. Actively investigating it. It's very important to me—to everyone, I hope—to find the persons who are responsible for his death. It's a question of seeing justice done."

Jack felt relieved; he wanted to stay on the case.

"Go ahead, ask your questions," she said, patting his arm reassuringly.

"Did you know the contents of Mr. Gentry's will before it was read?"

"No, it was a surprise to me."

"But when we visited before, you told me that you suspected he had changed his will."

"Yes," she said, smiling tolerantly, as if humoring a not-too-bright student.

46

"So you knew Mr. Gentry planned to change his will, but you didn't know any details of the proposed changes?"

"Exactly. Geoff told me several weeks ago that he was planning to change some aspects of his will. I never thought too much about it or asked him any questions."

Jack considered that response for a moment as he drank some of his lemonade. Was it reasonable to assume that she would ask Gentry no questions at all? He told her he was going to change his will, and she just shrugged? Was Gentry a man to leave his multimillion dollar estate in the hands of his closest companion, yet never consult with her about how to manage it?

"Perhaps it seems logical to you that he would have talked to me about it," she said, again surprising Jack with her perceptiveness.

"Yes."

"But that would only make sense if Geoff anticipated dying in the near future," she replied. "Besides the fact that we naturally don't like to talk about these things, Geoff couldn't have anticipated what was going to happen to him, especially so soon after changing his will. Maybe he did *plan* to talk to me later."

Jack shrugged, finding the explanation reasonable, if not totally convincing. "If you were surprised by the will, obviously others were, too. What were the general provisions of the first will, or at least the one previous to this last will?"

"I haven't the faintest idea," she said, pausing to think. "But, given the way the final will read, one possibility is that Geoff planned originally to divide the estate between his grandchildren."

"Did he ever tell you that specifically?"

"No."

"Did he ever say that he had talked to his grandchildren about the contents of his will?"

"Not that I remember."

Jack tried to think about a way to be diplomatic about the next subject, but then characteristically tackled it head on. "How'd Mr. Gentry get along with his grandchildren? What did he think of them?"

"Having heard the will, it won't come as any surprise to you when I say that Geoff thought his grandchildren immature, and lacking in good judgment. Naturally, they

47

had disagreements. I'm certain you've heard of Alan's troubles with the law. And Barbara, she has been, ah, how should I say it—indiscreet in her relationships with others, especially men.

"But, as the will demonstrates, Geoff hoped they would both overcome these faults. The proof of Geoff's love for his grandchildren is that they will eventually receive everything."

Jack smiled. "I'd guess from Alan's reaction to the provisions of the will that patience isn't one of his virtues."

"Which only further justifies the will."

"How would you characterize the feelings of Alan and Barbara toward their grandfather?" Jack asked.

Beth Lacy laid her head on the back of the sofa and stared thoughtfully at the ceiling. "The children's mother, Linda, was very resentful of Geoff. She believed—and I'm certain this was not the case at all—that Geoff was responsible for driving off her husband, John."

"Why would she think that?"

"She believed that Geoff drove his son too hard by demanding that John be a success in business. It is true that Geoff set John up in several businesses here on the lake."

"Did he drive him hard?"

"John left about the time we moved down here, so my knowledge of their relationship is based on what Geoff told me."

"Which was?"

"Geoff hoped John would be a success, yes. But Geoff wasn't the type of man to belittle his son for his failures. The truth, I'd guess, is that John was lazy. He would have deserted his family eventually under any circumstances. But Linda couldn't accept that. She found it easier to blame others, and she turned to the bottle for comfort. She also poisoned the minds of her kids about their grandfather."

Jack summed up the situation, thinking aloud. "So the grandkids didn't think highly of their grandfather. If they got wind of his plans to not let them inherit his estate right away, they might have considered doing him in before he got around to changing his will."

He expected her to be horrified at the suggestion; instead, she eyed him coolly, her smile strained.

"Jack, I hired you to make certain that the investigation of Geoff's death is thorough and complete," she said, mak-

48

ing an effort to be precise and controlled. "If, in the course of your investigation, you explore other possibilities, that is understandable. I have no reason, however, to think that Geoff's death was premeditated. Do you?"

Jack rose from the sofa to again inspect the figurines in the glass case. He answered her question with a question. "Mrs. Lacy, do you receive any pay for being trustee of the estate?" He noticed that she didn't correct him to a first-name basis this time.

"Yes, Roy has told me that I will receive a fee, which is set by state law, and is based on a complicated formula partly involving income earned by the trust."

"Got any idea of what it'll come to, say on a monthly basis?"

"None whatsoever."

"Tell me if you think I'm being too personal, but do you need the money?"

He thought she seemed amused at the question, but the widow answered with warmth and sincerity. "My husband left me this beautiful house, which is paid for. He worked thirty years for the same construction company, and there is an ample retirement benefit, along with my social security benefits. I worked most of my life, too. Perhaps you didn't know. So I have more than enough money, Jack, and I'm far too old to covet fame or fortune."

"Only one more question," Jack said, returning to the sofa. "Did Mr. Gentry say anything to you about any dealings he might have had with Butch Banuchi?"

"Only that Mr. Banuchi had approached him about buying some land Geoff owned off the Y-Road, not too far from Kate's place."

"What did Banuchi want the land for?"

"A resort, apparently. Geoff wasn't specific about the details. As you might have guessed by now, Geoff wasn't high on more resorts on the lake. He said no to the offer, and that was it, as far as I know."

"The quarrels over the telephone that you mentioned. Were they possibly with Banuchi?"

"Maybe. I do know that most of the conversations seemed to be concerned with development on the lake. Maybe quarrels is the wrong word. I had the impression Geoff was twisting arms."

49

"You're saying that the calls involved more than one person, then?"

"I really didn't try consciously to eavesdrop. But, yes, I think he talked to several people."

"Do you have any other names? Some of the people he may have been talking to?"

"No," she said, then seemed to remember something. "Tom Wallace. You might want to talk to him."

The athletic-looking man at Gentry's funeral, Jack thought. The one who had kissed Kate and smiled. He rose to leave, but stopped short of the door. "Mrs. Lacy, what are your thoughts about dissolving the trust and letting the estate pass to Mr. Gentry's grandchildren?"

"Only time can answer that question, Jack. Obviously, Geoff didn't think now was the time, and I have to respect his wishes. He wanted me to use my judgment. And that's what I'll do."

"Pardon me again for my bluntness, but what would happen if both you and Mr. Cousins were deceased?"

"I asked Roy that question myself, because it is a natural consideration. After all, Geoff didn't exactly put a couple of spring chickens in control of his estate. As I understand it, the courts ordinarily would appoint a trustee when all the trustees named in a will are dead. But Geoff had other ideas. If all the trustees are dead before the year 1990, the will specifies that the trust is dissolved, and the grandchildren inherit."

Jack was astounded. "Why would he do that?"

Beth Lacy smiled broadly. "Maybe he thought Roy and I would live forever. Maybe *he* planned to outlive both of us. Seriously, I don't know. If I were to guess, I'd say it had to do with Geoff's desire to see his grandchildren inherit his estate whenever they were capable of managing it. And he wanted his friends to make that decision, not the courts."

The explanation sounded logical, but something about the provisions of the will bothered Jack. By virtue of Gentry's achievements in life, Jack imagined him as intelligent, perceptive; the kind of man who would provide more elaborate safeguards to ensure that the fruit of his life's labor was not misspent. But perhaps Mrs. Lacy was right. Maybe he was forgetting to credit Gentry with a universal human trait: the tendency occasionally to let the heart overrule the head.

"Mrs. Lacy, would it be possible for me to look through Mr. Gentry's home?" Jack asked. He hoped she wouldn't ask why, since he had no particular purpose in mind.

But Beth Lacy offered no objections and handed him a key from her purse.

He strolled idly through the house, looking in all the rooms, inspecting the bric-a-brac. He went out onto the porch and looked at the lake. Briefly, he considered what it would be like to live in such a house—one probably worth two hundred thousand dollars. But it was only a fleeting thought; Jack had never coveted a large amount of money and the headaches it brought. Lately, his passion was to uncomplicate his life.

There was a four-drawer filing cabinet in Gentry's study, which Jack discovered to contain folders alphabetized according to their headings. He thumbed through the folders, not knowing exactly what he was looking for. He did discover that most of the information in the files was descriptive. The actual insurance policies, deeds, stocks and bonds were obviously kept elsewhere.

Jack looked through the correspondence folder, hoping to find some reference to the proposed resort that Gentry opposed, but there was nothing. Most of the letters were to friends, to lawyers and stockbrokers about financial dealings, or to state and national government agencies regarding environmental issues in the lake area. These he examined superficially.

He hoped the file on property would pinpoint the old man's holdings on the lake, but the descriptions by township and sections, as well as metes and bounds, were only confusing.

In one drawer containing a box of Kleenex, Jack found a stack of calling cards rubber-banded together. He shuffled through them, separating out those of a sorority housemother, a resort on Lake Taneycomo, a St. Louis architectural firm and an excavating company in nearby Warsaw, Missouri.

He wasn't certain why he kept those cards. Jack slumped back in the swivel desk chair and considered his generally unproductive search of Gentry's home. But, then, what had he expected to find? Some clue that would point to the fact that Gentry's death was other than accidental?

But that would have been too easy, too much to expect. All he had to go on was a *feeling* about the way Gentry was killed, as if the men in the boat had deliberately beat the old man to death with baseball bats. Then, there was the business of Gentry revising his will only days before his death. Coincidence? Mrs. Lacy painted a picture of Gentry being at loggerheads with his grandchildren; involved in some sort of controversy with unknown persons. Did this information amount to anything? Jack didn't know, and that gave him a feeling of dissatisfaction.

SEVEN

The more Jack thought about it the more he could appreciate Gentry's opposition to more resorts on the lake. As Cousins said, it seemed a saturation point had been reached. The east side of the lake had lost much of its natural beauty as it was overwhelmed by buildings, concrete and bright lights. The numerous pleasure craft created an oil and gas slick on the water that was pervasive in many areas of the lake. According to Kate, commercial development on the east shore had stalled briefly at Turkey Bend, but was picking up and marching south toward Camdenton. The proof of that was that Banuchi wanted to put in a resort off the Y-Road, which still was largely undeveloped.

The next day after talking to Mrs. Lacy, Jack planned to stop and see the sheriff, but when the courthouse came into view, he made a right turn and kept going. It was early in the day and he could stop on the way back. He considered going fishing for a few hours.

As he crossed the lake before entering Hurricane Deck, Jack recalled being told that the bridge was considered one of the best steel structures built in the country in 1936. As he glanced quickly to the left and right, there were few homes or resorts on the Osage branch of the lake. The forest grew to the shoreline and presented a weaving carpet of greenery for as far west as he could see. If he wanted to recapture part of his youth in the forested hillsides of central Wisconsin, this was the place to stay and build a home.

It was only when he drew near to the bar located north of Sunrise Beach that Jack knew why he had come that way. It wasn't to go fishing, it was to see Alan Gentry. This was where the grandson spent his time, according to Kate.

The Stables was a remodeled two-story house with rectangular flat-roofed wings added on both sides. The effect, Jack thought, made the second story of the old house resemble a church spire. Rough cedar boards had been nailed vertically to the exterior of the old house to match the decor of the wings. The porch of the house had been retained, however, and several men were sitting at the tables and drinking beer. Even at ten o'clock in the morning, the parking lot contained more than a few pickup trucks, with the customary rifle racks visible through the rear windows.

Jack had several reasons for wanting to talk to Alan Gentry. Jack was curious about Alan's reaction to the reading of his grandfather's will. Was it natural disappointment, or had he expected something different? Although Jack had seen Alan only once before, and then at a distance, there was something familiar about the grandson. But he couldn't immediately put his finger on it.

Inside, he could see little until his eyes adjusted to the darkness. He felt the glances thrown his way by the dozen or so men in the bar. His blue jeans and checked shirt, plus his arrival in a pickup, would put some of the patrons at ease. On the other hand, they didn't know him, and that was reason for uneasiness in any local tavern.

Jack stood at one end of a long bar in the south wing. He ordered a beer he didn't plan to drink. He couldn't get used to either ordering a coke or standing in a bar with his hands in his pockets.

He smelled it immediately, the pungent odor of marijuana. Someone was smoking grass. He hadn't expected that; not in a rural area with conservative values. Most of the patrons were gathered in the darker recesses of the bar, away from the door. Jack looked there for the smokers.

At that end of the room, a single shaded light bulb illuminated the green baize of a pool table, and Jack could hear the click of the balls. But the light was too low to reveal any faces, so he moved closer.

One of the pool players was Alan Gentry. In addition to faded blue jeans, Gentry wore a T-shirt that was cut off at the top of his rib cage. Jack remembered him as tall and thin, but his bare arms and stomach gave Alan Gentry the appearance of being emaciated. His stringy hair looked as if it had been washed in motor oil. Jack thought Gentry looked like a teenager, rather than a man in his early twenties.

When Gentry sat at a table awaiting his turn to shoot, Jack joined him.

"What's happenin', man," Jack said, trying to sound like one of the brothers in a South Side Chicago bar.

"Everything's cool, baby," Gentry replied, a knowing smirk on his face. Jack had figured it right; Gentry had done enough time in the joint to ape the lingo.

"I know you from somewhere?" Gentry asked, giving Jack the once-over.

"No, man. I just wanna watch you guys shoot."

"That's cool. It's eight-ball. A fiver on the game. You wanna play the winner?"

"Maybe."

Jack suddenly recognized the characteristics; it was what seemed familiar about Gentry. He was a junkie of some kind. Gentry appeared to be wired to a small electrical charge. When he rose to take his turn with the cue stick, he walked on the balls of his feet. He floated, then jerked like a puppet on a string. Amphetamines, maybe, Jack considered.

"Hey, Spider," Gentry said to his partner, "this fella needs some persuadin' to get into the game."

Spider was aptly named. His hairline was nearly joined with his eyebrows and his face was covered with a dark stubble; matted hair sprouted in clumps from his arms and torso.

Spider put forth his hand, which Jack shook reluctantly. "Name's Spider. What's yours?"

"Jack."

"Got a last name, Jack?" Gentry asked, as he cued the ball aimlessly.

55

"Olsen."

"Olsen. I've heard that name somewhere before." Jack could almost hear the wheels turning in Gentry's head.

"You from around here?" Spider asked.

"Been here a coupla months. Just drifting through."

"Olsen, huh?" Gentry repeated, scratching his head with a clawful of dirty fingernails. "Hey, I know about you. The sheriff said you were the one who fished Gramps outta the lake. Guess you weren't quick enough though, huh?"

Jack felt the color rise in his face as he watched Gentry cue another poorly aimed shot. "He was dead before I got to him."

"Say, you wouldn't be around looking for a reward, maybe, huh?"

"From what I heard at the funeral, you ain't got much money to give away," Jack shot back, taking a perverse delight in zinging Gentry. He watched as the smile left Gentry's face and his eyes narrowed.

Gentry sat on the edge of the table, the cue stick in both hands. Jack tensed, automatically feeling for the absent nightstick. He'd been swung at with cue sticks before. The reaction was right from the cop's unwritten street manual; a block with the nightstick and a swift kick in the balls. He'd seen many a drunken poolroom bully gingerly make his way to the patrol car holding his swollen family jewels.

"Know what else I hear about you, Olsen?" Gentry said, the smirk back on his face. He'd raised his voice to command an audience.

"You're the ex-cop who shacks up with ole Kate Carter." Spider laughed aloud, and Jack heard snickers from other areas of the bar.

Jack was trying vainly to control his temper when the tension was broken by the tapping sound of high heels. The girls came from the upstairs portion of the old house. Both wore hot pants and had puffed-up hairdos. The blond wore a skimpy halter, the brunette a flowered shirt that was unbuttoned, with the shirt tails tied together just above her belly button.

It was the brunette who sashayed the length of the bar, using a bored frown to brush off the various lewd proposals. But her face brightened when she saw Jack.

56

"It's about time we got some new blood in here," she said, walking over and sitting down beside Jack. The loose-fitting blouse gaped so that he could see one of her breasts.

"Whatcher name, honey?" she asked.

"Margo!" The voice boomed from behind the bar. "Get your sweet ass over here with Sally."

For the first time Jack looked closely at the bartender. With a pair of hams for forearms, he could have passed easily for the village blacksmith.

"Forget it, Willy," Margo said playfully. "Sally can't do anywhere near as much for me as goldilocks here can." The brunette batted her false eyelashes at Jack, revealing eyelids covered with several layers of purple shadow.

"Do like the man says." Gentry's voice was a hiss, and it wiped the smile from Margo's face. She looked back at the bartender, who had moved in front of the bar. Suddenly, she beat a hasty retreat to the other end of the room.

Jack looked around the room. A pervasive silence settled over it. Most of the men had drinks in front of them, but many glasses, like Jack's, were full. It was predominantly a young crowd. Jack spotted the group of grass smokers. He was distracted briefly by the arm-waving antics of a man who appeared to be hallucinating. In the shadows along the walls sat at least a half dozen men who were making no pretense at drinking. They appeared drunk, but had none of the characteristics of boozers, who weave, bob, talk loudly, slur their words and frequently fall face down in their own vomit. Instead, Jack noticed that these men were quiet, relaxed and loose; their only movement was a slight nodding, as if they were keeping time to silent music. Heroin? Barbiturates? He was in a bar full of hop-heads. Those who were able were staring at him.

Jack rose slowly, smiled broadly and walked toward Alan Gentry. He leaned against the scrawny youth, whispering into his ear. "Beth Lacy sent me to talk to you. She said that if you don't listen, not to bother her again until 1990."

Gentry's smirk was replaced by the same look of horror that was on his face during the reading of the will. He turned slowly and placed the cue stick on the table.

"Hey, Willie, everything's cool," Gentry said to the

still watchful bartender. "Bring us a couple of beers over here. Margo, play something on the jukebox."

Gentry, a wary look on his face, sat opposite Jack.

"So what's she want?"

"*She* wants you to answer all my questions."

"Shoot, man, I'm clean."

Jack nodded sarcastically, looking around the bar. "Sure you are, kid. Now tell me where you were the afternoon your grandfather got run over on the lake."

"Hey, man, I was right here," Gentry protested. He rose, holding his arms straight out in supplication. In a loud voice, he solicited confirmation from everyone in the room. "Hey, everybody, I was here all afternoon the day my granddaddy got himself killed. Right?"

There was a muffled chorus of agreement, and the smirk returned to Gentry's face. He blew his nose into an ever-present handkerchief.

"I can vouch for him every minute of the day," Spider said, coming to the table.

"Beat it, creep," Jack said, watching the hairy half-man back away.

"Don't be so rude to my friends, man," Gentry said.

"I learned about your kind the hard way, sonny. You treat shit like shit. Now tell me where you live and if you have a boat. Before you answer, let me tell you that I'm going to personally doublecheck everything you say."

"I live near here, off the five-thirty-five lake road," Gentry said, feigning indignation, "and I don't own a boat right now."

Jack considered wiping the smirk off Gentry's face with a quick backhand. He was the kind of kid who smirked when they first caught him shoplifting, Jack thought, and then looked to his companions to help protest his innocence.

"You live in one of your grandfather's houses?"

"It's just a rundown cabin. Not even on the lake."

"You poor devil. How much did your grandfather give you for spending money when he was alive? You're not the kind to work for a living."

"Hey, it was peanuts, man. He gave me a few bucks each month and acted like it really hurt him."

"I'll bet."

58

"It's hard to find a job when you gotta record," Gentry protested further. "Lotta people don't want to give a person a second chance."

"Sure," Jack snorted. "You and your grandpa argue about your being in jail, the fact that you don't have a job and that you're just generally a fuck-off?"

"I don't have to take this shit off you, man."

"Answer the question, or I'll get up and walk. Did you and your grandfather argue?"

"Sometimes, man, but nothing serious."

"You argue recently?"

"No, man, not for a long time."

Jack sensed that everything Alan Gentry said was a lie. "What did you do when your grandfather told you he was going to disinherit you?"

"Nothing. I mean, he didn't tell me. Besides, I ain't disinherited. I still get the money."

"Your kind doesn't like to wait until 1990," Jack said, returning the smirk. "Why did you get up and stalk out during the reading of the will? Who were you looking for in the audience?"

"No one, man. I was upset, the funeral and all. You know."

Jack laughed. Like most chronic liars, Gentry had an answer for everything.

"You see much of your sister?"

"No. She hangs out with the college kids."

Maybe the sister did have some class, Jack thought. "What are you going to do now, Gentry? Just draw your thou per month and shoot pool?"

Gentry smiled. "Not much else to do, man."

As Jack continued to stare, Gentry blew his nose again. That's when it occurred to Jack. Gentry was obviously using some kind of uppers, and at first Jack had assumed it was amphetamines. But the constant sniffling was characteristic of heavy cocaine users. Was that possible? The Cadillac of drugs, in the Ozarks?

Jack stood, fixing a hard stare on Gentry, who was soon unnerved and fidgety. Then Jack walked deliberately toward the bar, committing to memory the faces of those he passed.

He stopped in front of Margo and Sally, as Gentry caught up.

"Hey, man, what are you going to say to the widow?"

Jack smiled and continued to look at the two hookers. "Take care of your cold, sonny. You better button up too, Margo."

EIGHT

Jack had been waiting about ten minutes when the sheriff and another man came out of a door next to the area where the switchboard operator and dispatcher sat.

"Now, if you arrest any tourists, Bob, just make sure they ain't nobody important," Davis joked, repeatedly clapping Bob on the back.

"I sure do thank you, Mel," Bob said, his gnarled brown thumbs hooked into each side of the bib of his overalls. "I been wanting to be an honorary deputy ever since Jake Schneider got to be one. You remember that time last fall when Jake was having all kinds of problems with the kids in his pumpkin patch. He sat out there one night with his shotgun, flashed his badge at 'em and said as how he would turn 'em over to you next time he caught 'em. That was the end of his troubles." The farmer beamed contentedly.

"Just remember one thing, Bob," Davis replied, chewing steadily on his gum. "I only trust a few men enough to give away these badges. So don't you abuse the privilege any. Know what I mean?"

"Sure do, Mel," Bob agreed seriously. "You can count on me."

"That badge makes you part of a network of law and order here in the county," Davis continued. "That's why I been able to rid this county of crime. That's what you people elected me to do. Right?"

Bob left, still thanking the sheriff profusely on his way out the door.

Sheriff Davis then turned and stared briefly at Jack before speaking. "You ain't here looking for a job, are you, Olsen? We don't have any vacancies."

Jack considered being sarcastic and asking for an honorary badge, but thought better of it. "Just wanted to have a short talk, sheriff. About Gentry's death."

Davis, a powerfully built man despite the protruding stomach, regarded Jack appraisingly. "Sure, I got a few minutes. Come on back."

Jack followed the sheriff down a carpeted hallway. The sheriff's department occupied the first floor of a new wing that had been added to the rear of the old courthouse.

"In here," the sheriff said, motioning to an office at the end of the hall. Jack took a seat with his back to a picture window, which gave the sheriff a commanding view of the hallway and other offices.

"So what can I do for you, Olsen?" the sheriff asked, speaking to the door on Jack's left.

Jack was uncertain how to proceed, although he knew he had to overcome the sheriff's obvious hostility.

"Mrs. Lacy asked me to find out how the investigation is going," Jack said, searching carefully for the right words.

"What's the matter? Don't she think we can do our job?"

"It's not that. She just has a natural concern, and most citizens don't understand the way a law enforcement agency undertakes an investigation."

"But you do, huh?"

The question didn't require an answer, and Jack sat silently.

"She paying you, or are you just being her errand boy out of the goodness of your heart?" Davis stared directly at Jack, who remembered the sheriff's habit of letting a conversation drift and then abruptly dropping in a loaded question or accusation. It wasn't a bad tactic for a cop.

"Yes, she's paying me."

"That's the problem with a lot of the people who move

down here from the city. They think we're just a bunch of hicks and don't know as much as those big city cops. Well, let me tell you something, fellow. Our arrest and conviction record down here is better than it is in Chicago."

"I don't doubt that at all," Jack said sincerely. "Look, I came to see you because I want to cooperate with you."

"You mean you need our help. Just like the state police. They got jurisdiction in this thing, but they can't get involved in local investigations. They don't have the manpower. So they come to me."

"I understand. And then they'll want to take credit for your work," Jack said, hoping to seize an opportunity.

"That's right," the sheriff said, again looking out the door.

"But I don't want any credit. No one needs to know I'm involved except you. Everything I do dig up, I'll share with you. In fact, I can be an unpaid, honorary deputy."

"Before we do any cooperating, what happened to you at Tan-Tar-A?" Davis asked, again boring in on his suspect.

Jack nodded affirmatively. "I was hired as a security guard on the four-to-midnight shift. The second night I brought a bottle to work, got drunk and passed out against a wall in one of the underground parking garages. Some hotel guests saw me and thought I was dead. The supervisor came along and fired me."

It was the truth, and Jack hoped that his honesty would exact a modicum of begrudging respect from the sheriff.

While the sheriff again assessed the door, Jack remembered an incident in which he and his partner, Jose Ramirez, were cruising around the near west side of Chicago, working on a quart of bourbon. They responded to a call reporting a holdup in progress and arrived just as the stickup men were emerging from the front door of a liquor store.

He and Ramirez both stumbled from the car, first cursing at the holdup men and then opening fire on them with their service revolvers. But they missed, and in the ensuing car chase they failed to negotiate a turn and plowed the squad car into the front of an old brownstone. They were both diagnosed as drunk by the attending physician at Cook County hospital.

In the subsequent investigation, though, they were suspended only for failing to exercise proper restraint in the use of their firearms. In fact, they had almost gunned down an elderly couple on the sidewalk. But no one mentioned that both cops had been drunk. The force had protected them.

They hadn't been that understanding at Tan-Tar-A.

"That what happened to you in Chicago, too?" Davis asked, seeming to read Jack's thoughts.

"They never fired me," Jack said, and that, too, was true. He was on an extended leave of absence for medical reasons. "I was a Chicago cop for ten years, and I can still go back. Look, sheriff, let me be honest. I agreed to look into Gentry's death mainly because I can use the money. So far, it looks like an accident to me. If that's what it was, then I'll tell Mrs. Lacy and go about my business. In the meantime, I may be able to find some evidence you can use. After all, someone did run over Gentry."

It wasn't exactly the truth, but Jack hoped it would loosen up the sheriff. Finally, Davis said, "The water patrol and the state boys think they know the make of the boat, based on your description. They're checking through the registration records up in Jeff City to see what they can come up with. 'Course, that's a big job, and even if the computer kicks out several boats that fit the description, they can't be totally sure that they have the right make and model. Just because a fellow on the lake has such a boat doesn't mean he ran down Gentry. If it was someone from out of state, or if the boat wasn't registered properly, then that's a different ballgame altogether."

The sheriff smiled at Jack and shrugged to express the complexity of it all.

Jack waited.

The sheriff didn't disappoint him. "We're checking around for a boat that matches the description, too. This is a good example of where my honorary deputies can play an important role. I've passed the word for them to be on the lookout. A lot of those boys are on the lake every day. I've contacted all the boat repair shops in the area to watch for such a boat with damages to the hull or prop."

He looked pleased with his recital.

"It looks like you're being very thorough," Jack said pleasantly, struck by the total emphasis of the investigation

64

upon the boat and not its occupants. "So you think it was probably an accident, then?"

"Well, couple of drunks or wild kids. Whichever, they committed a crime, that's for sure. But, in my opinion, there's nothing to indicate that there was any premeditation. You got any evidence to the contrary?"

"There's nothing really solid," Jack said, "except some curious coincidences."

"Such as?"

"Gentry changed his will about a week before his death."

"Roy Cousins tell you that?"

"Yes."

"Just like him. Never said nothing to me. 'Course, I ain't surprised. Cousins put time and money into my opponent's campaign during the last election."

Jack continued. "Then, there's the fact that Gentry was overheard having several telephone conversations in which he appeared to be arguing with someone, or perhaps several different people."

"Do you know who they are, these people he argued with?"

"No," Jack said, feeling intuitively that he shouldn't reveal to the sheriff the names mentioned by the widow or Cousins.

"Anything else?" the sheriff asked.

"Somebody apparently wanted to buy some of Gentry's land for a new resort on the lake, and Gentry evidently opposed such a development."

"That sounds like him," Davis said sourly. "Who was wanting to buy the land?"

"Don't know that, either," Jack lied. "Maybe you can make something out of it all."

"Well, I appreciate your telling me what you know, Olsen. I'll keep it all in mind and see if it fits in anywhere during our investigation. 'Course, I think we'll find out that it was a couple of drunks. Seen it happen before."

The sheriff began shuffling through a small pile of papers. Jack recognized the signal that the conversation had come to a close.

"One more thing, sheriff, just out of curiosity. The grandson, Alan Gentry. He seemed to be real upset during the reading of the will."

"Well, that's understandable, I guess," the sheriff responded. "He thought he was going to get all that money."

"Yeah, and then to get only twelve thousand dollars a year and not have to work for it. That's a shame."

Davis smiled and laughed for the first time during their conversation. "It's the truth. He's worthless as teats on a boar."

"I hear he's been in some trouble with you," Jack said, not at all sure that Davis had arrested Alan Gentry.

"Yep, we caught him with his fingers in the till, so to speak. A few years back someone reported suspicious goings-on one evening and we arrived just as Gentry and one of his buddies were loading a TV set into a van. When we searched his cabin, we found enough evidence to solve over fifty burglaries on the lake. God knows how many he was really involved in. They'd been fencing the stuff in K.C. and St. Louis. The police in both those cities jailed a couple of fences on account of us. They were real appreciative for our information." The sheriff beamed in self-congratulation.

"How long has Gentry been out of jail?"

"He put in nearly three years, and he's been back for about eight months."

"Keeping his nose clean?"

"Guess so. He ain't come to my attention. Why? You think he's somehow involved in the old man's death? That don't seem likely."

Jack couldn't believe the sheriff was as naive as he pretended. Alan Gentry had all the motive in the world, especially if he knew his grandfather had planned to change his will.

"You know where Alan Gentry hangs out?" Jack asked innocently.

"Nope. Haven't been keeping track of him. Might try his probation officer."

So Davis denied knowing anything about Alan Gentry and his hangout. Yet Kate knew about it. Surely a few of the honorary deputies frequented the local bars and gathered information for Davis.

"What about Gentry's granddaughter?" Jack asked.

"Well, the only thing I know her to be guilty of is being a nympho." The sheriff sneered. "And as long as she doesn't charge for it, that ain't no crime."

That at least squared with what Jack had been told by Kate and the widow, although it didn't seem to have any relevance to the case. Unless Barbara knew that her grandfather was going to change his will.

"There's some scandalous incident in every family, though," the sheriff added. "For example, people hereabouts were shocked when the widow Lacy took up with Mr. Gentry, especially so soon after Mr. Lacy died. Now, that was a strange death."

"What do you mean?" Jack asked, intrigued by Davis's desire to discredit the widow Lacy.

"Eldon Lacy went for a walk one winter evening during a snowfall and never came back. They found him two days later in a wooded area about a half mile from his house."

"What was the cause of death?"

"The autopsy was inconclusive. All the coroner could say for sure was that he died of exposure."

Jack had to admit that it was a strange tale. He rose, shook hands with Davis and turned to leave. "Oh, one more thing, Sheriff, if you don't mind. The autopsy on Gentry. How did he die?"

Jack thought Davis looked flustered for a moment. But when he answered, the sheriff looked Jack straight in the eyes. "Gentry died from either a broken neck or a blow to the head, according to the coroner. Either one was enough to kill him."

"He didn't drown? There was no water in his lungs?"

"The coroner says he was dead before he hit the water. I suppose the boat hit him."

Instead, Jack had a mental picture of a man in a boat, bracing an oar.

Kate explained that the Stables had always been a rough hangout.

"And it's no great secret that a few chippies hang out at the place," she said, "and that for a price a man can spend some time with them in an upstairs bedroom."

"Prostitution?"

"Yep, right here in River City."

"They ever raid the place? Run in the girls?"

"Not that I know of."

"The sheriff just shuts his eyes to it?"

"Sure, but not just Davis. It's been going on for a long

time. People have come to accept it. It's the place where all the boys go for their first experience. Dad even used to kid Ma about taking Ned, Latham and Walter over there. May have for all I know."

"Where do the girls come from?"

"They're usually from the city, and they drift in and out. Sometimes, in the past, there's been some local talent involved."

Jack wondered if it was organized—girls who made their way from Chicago to Houston, with predetermined stops in between.

"What about drugs?"

Kate thought for a moment. "They're around, all right. Every now and then someone gets busted for smoking pot, or growing it, or having a lot of brightly colored pills. I've never heard of drugs being sold at the Stables, but then I've never asked, either."

"Don't you think it's funny that Davis didn't know the Gentry boy hangs out there?"

"He's funnin' you, all right. He knows. Everyone does."

"Why would he play dumb then?"

"I don't know, pussy cat, unless he doesn't want you to know that he knows what goes on at the Stables."

"Check it out for me."

"What?"

"See if anyone knows that drugs are for sale at the Stables."

"Okay. In the real estate business, I get around and see a lot of people. Those that know me will give me the straight dope."

Jack ignored the pun, thinking hard about his conversation with Davis. "The sheriff said he didn't know anything about a new resort. Do you think he was telling the truth?"

"Maybe. I didn't know about it until you mentioned it, so it obviously hasn't made the local grapevine."

Jack smiled. "You know what?"

"What?"

"I'm warming up to this investigation."

"Why?"

"Because I know drugs are passing hands in the Stables and that Alan Gentry is somehow in the thick of that scene."

"And?"

"And the old man could have been killed deliberately, according to the autopsy and what I saw. Let's say Alan has an expensive habit. His grandfather finds out about it and threatens to change his will and prevent Alan from getting his hands on all that money. Maybe the old man is not specific about the changes at first; maybe he's angry and threatens to totally disinherit Alan."

"Alan would have been desperate."

"Yeah, just as desperate as he was after the funeral, when he found out his grandfather *had* changed his will."

NINE

Driving out the Turkey Bend peninsula made Jack think again about his experience at Tan-Tar-A. At first he had been overwhelmed by the size of the 550-acre resort. Not only were there the hundreds of rooms and suites in the main building, but numerous studios and cottages with direct access to the lake. There were indoor pools, a health spa, tennis courts, a bowling alley, a shopping mall, an ice-skating rink, restaurants and bars. Outside were the golf course, stables and riding trails, marina, tennis courts, playgrounds, pools and, for the winter, a ski slope.

Other than habit, there hadn't been any particular reason for his drinking on the job at the hotel. He was still on the tail end of a period of depression that had raged for years. And he was depressed by the resort. It seemed unreal to him, in much the same way he felt the slums of the city to be unreal.

Jack wondered how another resort could compete with the likes of Tan-Tar-A. Why did anyone think there would be enough tourist trade in the future to justify another large resort? Was it to be just a fishing place? Or would it offer some specialized activity that he couldn't imagine? What could be added to the lake that wasn't already there?

Following Kate's directions, he first glimpsed the house where Barbara Gentry lived by looking across a narrow cove. He traced a U-shaped course around the edge of the water, following a red clay road overlaid with sand and gravel. The house, one of the many older two-story frame structures that dotted the lake, was relatively isolated. There were no other houses around the cove, and the forest was thick for at least a hundred yards around the house.

Meeting Barbara Gentry at the door, Jack was even more impressed with the young woman's classic proportions, especially since she was wearing a skimpy white crocheted string bikini that left little to the imagination. She could be just as modest naked, he thought.

"Mr. Olsen, I saw you at the funeral," she said, extending her hand. "How nice of you to come."

To the funeral, or her house? She moved slowly, but with practiced precision, as he followed her through the house to a family room just off the kitchen.

Jack was greeted by the sight of a thickly muscled blond giant languishing in a chaise longue, sipping a tall drink filled with skewered fruit. He too was attired in a bikini—black briefs that again left little to the imagination.

"This is Hank Loomis," Barbara said. "Hank, this is Jack Olsen. He telephoned, remember. Said that Mrs. Lacy was sending him."

The giant grunted inaudibly at Jack, shifting his weight and sending a ripple through a bulging pectoral. The girl lowered herself to the floor beside her friend and gave Jack a half-amused, half-expectant smile.

Jack remembered sitting in the precinct coffee room when his fellow cops were discussing how to deal with a muscle-bound weightlifter like Hank, if the guy was bent on tearing you apart. Several policemen testified from personal experience that nightsticks were of little use against such rock-hard muscle. But Ramirez had the answer that satisfied nearly everyone.

"You don't fuck around trying to duke it out with those guys," he said. "That's why you got this gun." He pulled out the .38, twirling it around his finger cowboy-style. "Bang. Shoot the sonofabitch, man. That'll make him *your* size." Jack couldn't believe how easily he had accepted that reasoning, then.

71

Jack gave Barbara and Hank the same spiel he had used on Sheriff Davis, telling them the widow had hired him to make certain that the investigation of Mr. Gentry's death proceeded as rapidly as possible, and that nothing be overlooked. Jack believed in watching facial expressions and listening to voice inflections. In the face, the tipoff showed first in the eyes and the mouth; expressions of love, hate, pity, indifference. On that basis, Mr. Muscles obviously didn't care about Jack's new job. Barbara Gentry, on the other hand, had the same stoical look on her face as when the will was read. It was a beautifully sculptured blank; there was nothing to be read.

This one really has ice water in her veins, he thought. He'd have to try harder. "Mrs. Lacy said your grandfather was having arguments recently with someone on the telephone. Do you know anything about these conversations?"

"I know nothing about my grandfather's private or business life, Mr. Olsen." Jack detected a haughtiness in her voice. Or was it irritation?

"What about Mr. Gentry's opposition to a new resort on the lake? Did he ever talk to you about that?"

"He never talked to me about anything, Mr. Olsen. He just dictated terms. As far as his opposition to a resort, all of us in this family have been bored a thousand times with his monologue about preserving clean water and virgin forests. He was a little hypocritical about it. Resorts were all right up to a certain point, which is to say that they were all right for those down here early, like Grandpa, but not now."

She spoke in a fairly dispassionate manner, but Jack detected a little fire in her eyes. He decided to see if he could get her to unravel.

"Didn't your father run a resort for a while?"

A muscle twitched in her face. "Yes, my father ran a resort, but only after Grandpa had insisted that Daddy be a bank teller, then a grocery store manager, then a restaurant manager, and so on. Grandpa broke Daddy's spirit by requiring high standards that no one could meet. In Grandpa's book, you weren't trying hard enough if you weren't a millionaire."

"So your dad went to California to live his own life?"

She nodded agreement. "That's right. He would have

72

taken Mom and us with him except that Grandpa would only support us if we stayed here. He wanted to force Daddy to come back."

Jack wondered about that. He supposed the old man might have refused to support his wayward son, but would support his daughter-in-law so that he could be near his grandchildren. But then the widow had a different story. Hers suggested that the son deserted his family. Jack knew he would never know the whole truth, since they were all dead now.

"But before Daddy could get his feet on the ground, he was killed," Barbara continued. Jack remembered the widow saying that Gentry's son had been in California for several years before his death.

"So you grew up here, in this house?"

"Grew up is about all we did here," she replied, with bitterness. "Mother was so unhappy she drank herself to death. Everyone knows that."

Jack could imagine the rest of the scene. A drunken mother, an absent father, two wild, unsupervised kids. It was a tragedy replayed tens of thousands of times across the nation.

"So you see, Mr. Olsen, my grandfather was a bastard," Barbara said, regaining her icy composure.

"Did you argue with him?" Jack asked, noting that her opinion of her grandfather didn't prevent Barbara from staying in the family home and continuing to accept his money. Wealth has a way of creating hangers-on, he thought, who come to hate their dependency.

"Oh, yes, we argued numerous times. You see, he didn't care for my *life-style*, as he liked to put it." She moved closer to the beach boy and ran her hand over his thigh.

"Hank and I live together," she said, "just like you and Kate Carter do. That's our business. But Grandpa thought I was promiscuous. Then, after Grandma dies, he turns around and shacks up with Beth Lacy. More hypocrisy."

Jack conceded that the girl might have a point. Maybe the old man had pontificated a bit, and maybe he had had a double standard in some areas.

"You knew, then, that your grandfather planned to change his will and put you on a monthly budget?"

"No, I didn't know that," she said sweetly. "But it really

73

doesn't matter to me. A thousand dollars a month is ample for me, and my college costs will fall under the category of extraordinary expenses, I assume."

"You're going to the university in Columbia?" Jack asked, thinking Kate had said that Barbara had been in the area for several months.

"Yes, but I was ill in the spring and came here to recuperate. Doctor's orders. It was the only place I had to go. Besides, I consider it *my* home, not his."

"So you were down here the day your grandfather was killed?"

The muscleman stirred from his chair. Jack tensed.

"Going for another drink," he said. "Anyone else?"

Jack declined, warily.

An amused smile on her face, Barbara said, "Yes. In fact, we were out in our boat and evidently drove by the cove where Grandpa was killed."

"Mr. Gentry was killed about four-twenty," Jack said, startled at the frankness of her admission. "What time were you in the area?"

"We went to a party at a place on the tip of Horseshoe Bend that afternoon. One of my sorority sisters. I believe we arrived right at four. Isn't that right, Hank?"

Hank stood on the landing in the hallway, looking to Jack to be twice as big as himself. "Yeah, that's right, Barbie. They were starting the games at four and we were a few minutes early."

"You've heard the description of the boat that struck and killed your grandfather?" Jack asked.

"Yes, Sheriff Davis told us."

So the sheriff had talked to her. Jack wondered when that conversation had taken place. More important, had the sheriff also gone to tell Alan Gentry of his grandfather's death? If so he had lied to Jack about not knowing where Alan hung out.

"Did you see a boat on the lake matching that description?" Jack rose and walked to the back of the room.

"No, we didn't," she answered.

"Great view you got here," Jack said. The family room opened onto a screened porch at the back of the house. Doors leading off both the porch and the back of the kitchen opened onto an outdoor dining patio, secluded by a

74

shoulder-high brick wall and planter. A rock path led to the boat dock.

"Why don't you go down and look at it?" Barbara said, coming to stand beside Jack.

"Look at what?" he asked innocently.

"Our boat. You do want to make sure we didn't run over Grandpa, don't you?"

"Oh no," Jack protested, laughing. "Listen, it's been nice chatting with you, but I've really got to go."

She called his name before he reached the steps leading from the room. "Why don't you stay awhile? Have a drink with us."

Hank rose from his chair and came to stand beside Jack. He put a huge hand on Jack's shoulder and said, ever so slowly, "We can do some swimming, Jack."

Barbara, now all quivering seductiveness, snuggled close to Jack, holding his arm. He could see the nipples of her firm breasts as she pressed close to him. "Hank's got a lot of little swimming suits you could wear," she said, her eyes laughing.

"Yeah, and we're gonna watch some naughty films later," Hank said enthusiastically.

Jack backed away, both hands in front of him, like a traffic cop signaling for a car to stop. "Thanks, just the same," he said, "but I promised Kate a movie tonight. We're going to see an animated version of *Bambie*. One movie a day is all I can stand. Hard on the eyes, you know."

On the other side of the cove, he parked on the side of the road, walked to the front of the truck and adjusted the binoculars to bring the boat into view. Barbara was right. It wasn't the one.

The sound of the gunfire and the explosion of sand and rock as bullets peppered the road near Jack's feet was simultaneous. He dove instinctively for the cover of the pickup, scrambling to press himself against the tire and fender for maximum protection. The bullets continued to rip away at the road, only inches in front of the tire. Jack identified the gun as a .22-caliber rifle, an automatic, given the rapid fire.

Suddenly the gunfire stopped. Jack's first thought was that the gunman was reloading. The gunfire was coming from the west. Jack moved to a standing position behind the cover of the truck cab. He peeked carefully around the corner of the cab, but could see nothing in the forest.

The renewed gunfire caused Jack to flatten himself against the pickup once again. For a moment, he worried about his feet being exposed below the line of the pickup before concluding that the gunman's angle of fire prevented him from shooting under the truck.

The bullets ripped bark from the trees on the east side of the road before the gunman sighted on a large rock. The whine of the ricocheting bullets caused Jack to panic. He didn't have a gun; he couldn't fight back. If he stayed, he could be hit. Jack looked about wildly, trying to decide where to run, and when.

The latter question was answered by another lull in the shooting. Making his decision, Jack jerked open the pickup door and slid across the seat on his stomach. He turned the ignition key with one hand and used the other to depress the accelerator. The truck in gear, he turned onto his back so he could reach the gas pedal with his left foot. The pickup lurched forward as he tried to remember the turns in the road. He then scooted into a sitting position, keeping his head behind the edge of the window. With a clear view of the road, he soon had the truck at top speed.

After he reached the blacktop and encountered other traffic, Jack pulled over to the side of the road. He lit a cigarette and tried to control his trembling hands. His mind filled with questions. Who was shooting at him? Why? If they (he?) wanted to kill him, why not try driving him into the open by shooting at the pickup? And why hadn't the gunman shot at the pickup when Jack was making his getaway? Unless the gunman didn't want to leave any evidence of the shooting.

Jack thought about the shooting site—bark chipped off a few trees, chips off the rock, maybe a few slugs that could be found near the road. Nothing conclusive. Was someone trying to scare him? Play with him? Was there any connection with the shooting and his visit to Barbara Gentry's house, his employment by Beth Lacy?

As Jack drove toward the main highway, he wondered if others had heard the gunfire. Barbara and her boyfriend, for example. Would they call the sheriff? Jack wasn't sure about what to do, but he had a strong impulse to do nothing for the moment.

76

TEN

When he thought of the best years in his life, Jack remembered his boyhood in Wisconsin, or the time he spent in college, or his early twenties, when he was finally on his own and life seemed an everyday adventure. But sitting in the pickup truck with Kate, on a turnout at the end of the Grand Glaize bridge, Jack knew he was living the best of times.

"Is that the proper dress for a real estate lady," he teased, looking at her cutoff jeans and tank top.

Kate leaned against the door, her long legs spread in unladylike fashion. "This isn't my selling uniform, Charlie, although it would be okay if I was peddling this luscious body."

"Oh God."

"No, this is really my private eye outfit," she said, feigning seriousness. "You know. For snooping around among the tourists, so I won't be recognized."

"I'm just glad you wore a bra."

"You're right. None of the tourists will be wearing one. I can take it off."

"Later," Jack replied, casting an exaggerated look at Kate's bustline.

She had worked during the morning, but came home at noon, announcing that she was going with him for his afternoon appointment with Butch Banuchi. He couldn't think of any reason not to take her, especially since he enjoyed her company. He hadn't told her about the shooting.

During lunch at a nearby restaurant, Kate began to tell him what she had learned about drugs being sold in the lake area.

"While we were having coffee this morning at the office, I brought up the subject of drugs. Casually, of course." She used a newspaper to fan herself against the muggy midday heat. "Charlene Potter, the office gossip, started talking a mile a minute. She says she has a neighbor kid who hung out in the Stables all the time. His parents were worried sick because he'd come home stoned every night. Charlene said the boy's dad went down to the Stables to drag the boy home a couple of times. The father also complained to the manager."

"Who's that?"

"A local tough named Clyde Lewis."

"But he's not the owner," Jack guessed.

"No. I asked my boss who owned the Stables, and he said it sold about a year and a half ago to some lawyer or a corporation."

"What happened when the guy complained to the manager?"

"Nothing, I guess. Lewis apparently said the kid was bringing drugs into the Stables. According to Charlene, Lewis then banned the kid from coming there anymore."

"That made the parents happy, I suppose."

"Probably. Anyway, the boy left town shortly after the incident, according to Charlene. The scuttlebutt is that he's somewhere in a detoxification program."

"But, like you say, this is just hearsay," Jack said uneasily.

"Yes, but I also talked to my brother Ned, who really keeps up on what's happening in local politics. He was elected county clerk once. Anyway, he said it's going to be an election issue this fall. Apparently there are people who know what is going on at the Stables."

"Including Davis," Jack mused aloud, "and he had to know that Alan Gentry hangs out there."

78

"I'd guess so."

Jack wondered why the sheriff had been so coy about the subject. He made a mental note to ask Roy Cousins about the Stables and the drug problem in the lake area.

The temperature was crowding a hundred. Because of the lack of a breeze the heat hung oppressively in the air, creating water mirages at a distance.

As they started down the steep concrete steps leading to the marina and Banuchi's office, a helicopter thundered off its pad on the cliff above them, giving its passengers the aerial view of the lake.

"Does Banuchi own all this?" Jack asked.

"The helicopter ride? Sure. And the marina and all the rental boats. This is the biggest place of its kind on the lake. Brother Latham sometimes works here as a fishing guide when things get slow."

Jack had discovered that Kate's brothers, like a lot of people who were permanent residents of the lake, strung several jobs together to make a living. The work was often seasonal, varied; as a life-style, many persons preferred it to a less flexible schedule.

"Banuchi's got his finger into quite a few places on the lake," Kate continued. "He doesn't make any secret of it, though. He just lets everyone in real estate know that he's interested in anything that comes on the market—residential or commercial."

"Where's he get his money?"

"That I don't know, sweetheart. He showed up down here about three years ago and bought this place. It does real well and he's been expanding ever since."

"Do you know where he came from? He's not retired. He can't be that old."

Kate shrugged. "I heard he's from Chicago. Some say he was in business up there and got tired of the city. Sold out and came down here. He's in his mid-forties, I'd guess. A bachelor. Travels a lot in the winter."

She stopped on the stairs, blocking his way. "Personally, I'm like a lot of the hillbilly gals down here. I get the hots for that baby-smooth skin of his. Wanna squeeze it. You know?"

The stairs opened onto a landing that led in one direction to the marina, which was a beehive of activity. Jack could smell the water and the fish. Employees were busy

79

instructing customers in the use of speedboats, and the wisdom of wearing a life vest. Boats roared in from the lake, dropped into the no-wake zone and queued up for the gasoline pumps. A tall, tanned youth was showing a group of teenage customers how to operate the jet skis. Along a roofed area with several permanent boat slips, a man painted the trim of a cabin cruiser called *Belle's Folly*.

Jack and Kate followed a walkway leading in the other direction from the marina to a double wide mobile home that had been set on a concrete block foundation. They were greeted by two attractive young ladies wearing yellow blazers who offered to provide information about the varied activities and rentals available through Banuchi Enterprises. Kate and Jack found Banuchi in a master bedroom that had been converted to an office.

He was dressed impeccably in a blue summer suit. The stocky man gave Jack a surprisingly strong handshake and inquired solicitously of Kate whether she objected to his cigar.

"Would you care for one?" Banuchi asked Jack, having received the green light from Kate. "They're one of my bad habits. I have them imported from the Caribbean. It's a special blend I discovered several years ago."

"No, thanks," Jack said. "I'm trying to kick the habit."

"Good for you," Banuchi said. His manner of speech was precise, his voice gentle and smooth. He seemed a pleasant man. Jack had expected more of the entrepreneur.

"Now what can I do for you two good people? Kate, you don't happen to have a hot piece of property for me, do you?"

"Not today," she laughed. "But I'm working on it."

Banuchi's dark eyes darted inquisitively to Jack.

"Mrs. Lacy asked me to help in the investigation of Mr. Gentry's death," Jack said.

"Ah, yes, that's a splendid idea," Banuchi said, shaking his head decisively. "Such a stalwart man. It was a tragedy the way he died. Anything you can do to find those who are responsible will certainly be appreciated by those of us who knew and respected Mr. Gentry."

Jack searched for a way to broach the subject of the proposed resort. Although he was curious about Banuchi's involvement with Gentry, he wanted to be careful not to offend Banuchi.

Jack asked, "I wonder if you've heard the description of the boat that struck Mr. Gentry?"

"Yes, certainly. Sheriff Davis stopped by to provide it. It's ironic, but Sheriff Davis and I were chatting here in my office the afternoon Mr. Gentry was killed, bless his soul."

Banuchi glided so smoothly over the alibi that Jack was uncertain whether or not it was mentioned purposefully.

"Anyway, we don't carry any boats that fancy in our line of rental equipment. I have had a written description of the boat posted down by the gasoline pumps, and all the employees have been instructed to report to me immediately any boat that fits the description. And I've seen that the description has been posted elsewhere on the lake where I have business interests.

"This is the best approach we can take at this time, and I have hopes that it will pay off in the near future. It's obvious that whoever is involved in this hit-and-run has either pulled the boat off the lake or is keeping it hidden in some boathouse. But we might expect they will come out of hiding eventually. These criminal types, they're careless. They won't expect us to continue watching for them, but we will."

If Banuchi's concern wasn't sincere, he had fooled Jack, who could now understand why Banuchi Enterprises had expanded. The man who puffed intently on the pale green cigar could undoubtedly be very persuasive in his business dealings.

The telephone rang. Banuchi answered, and then listened.

"Excuse me for a moment, please," he said, rising from his chair. "I hate to interrupt our conversation, but the cashier from the marina has a check he wants me to okay. I'll be right back. Can I have one of the girls get us something to drink? Some coffee? A soft drink maybe?"

Kate and Jack declined, and Banuchi left the room purposefully, his cigar leading the way like a lantern in the dark.

"This guy should have been an army recruiter," Jack said. "He could persuade a pacifist to join up."

"I just hope he remembers my legs the next time he wants to buy real estate," Kate said wickedly.

Jack stood to stretch his own legs, glancing idly at the

81

items on Banuchi's desk. His eye was caught by a card tucked into the side of the desk blotter. He reached across and pulled it out. He was certain it matched one he had taken from Gentry's desk. There was something familiar about the distinctive red and blue lettering. He put the card in his pocket.

"You detectives just take what you want!" Kate exclaimed in mock indignation.

"Just like the Huns."

"Do you rape women, too?"

"I feel the urge coming on right now. How about on top of fat boy's desk?"

Banuchi returned, apologizing for the interruption.

"Now we can continue our conversation," he said eagerly.

"Mr. Banuchi, we're assuming the odds are greatly in favor of Mr. Gentry's having been the unintended victim of some drunken boaters or wild kids," Jack said. "But just on the wildest chance that he might have been run down intentionally, we're trying to find out about Mr. Gentry's social and business contacts in the few months preceding his death. Could you shed any light?"

Jack was pleased with the way he had opened the door on the subject of the resort, and he sensed that Banuchi understood his purpose. The black eyes bulged slightly.

"The only contact I had recently with Mr. Gentry concerned an offer I made to buy some of his land," Banuchi said. Turning to Kate, he added, "Kate, you know the land. It would be the second turn off west of your house, back toward the north shore. A very nice piece of property. About six hundred acres."

Jack couldn't think of six hundred acres as a *piece* of property.

"Yes, I know the area," Kate said. "I've often wondered why no one has built there. It's a lovely location with an impressive rocky promontory."

"Yes, it is," Banuchi agreed emphatically. "I predict that it will be the next growth area on the lake."

"Mr. Banuchi, what did you plan to do with the property?" Jack asked innocently.

"I and other investors planned to build a resort hotel on the land. A hotel complex we hoped would be better than any existing resort on the lake."

Jack arched his eyebrows questioningly. "But Mr. Gentry said no."

Banuchi nodded. "He did, unfortunately. We talked about his concerns at some length, but I, was not able to convince him that ours was a sound proposal."

"What did you argue about?" Jack probed.

"Argue?" Banuchi replied, waving away the suggestion with his cigar. "Never. This was business, Mr. Olsen, and that's not my approach. Mr. Gentry's concern was that the lake was at the point of overdevelopment; that there was a danger to the lake from increased sewage disposal and oil and gasoline discharges from boating. Also, he feared that the natural beauty of the lake would be scarred by too many structures and roads leading to the water's edge."

"But you don't agree?"

"Not totally," Banuchi said reflectively. "Mr. Gentry had a point, of course. But I think he exaggerated it."

"How so?" Kate asked.

"This lake has approximately thirteen hundred miles of shoreline. Do you realize that is more shoreline than there is in the entire state of California?

"No, we're nowhere near the point of being overdeveloped on this lake. There are vast areas on the west shore, especially up toward Warsaw, that are relatively untouched. It might appear we have overdevelopment because there is such a concentration of commercial establishments in this area. But overall, it's simply not true.

"As far as the lake itself goes, we have new and rigid state standards for discharges into the water. The state environmental experts have concluded, as a result of recent studies, that the lake is clean and safe. Also, we have an environmental protection plan for the proposed resort.

"Finally, I believe that people should enjoy our natural resources. That means using them. There's no question that people want to use this lake. You see, businessmen like myself don't build hotels and create a demand for them. We react to the demand that already exists."

While Banuchi produced a gold lighter and relit his cigar, Jack asked, "Isn't it a mixed blessing to have so many people down here?"

"Why?" Banuchi responded. "If they want to come and visit, who is going to say that they shouldn't? The federal Department of the Interior promotes the Lake of the

Ozarks as one of the ten best vacation areas in the country. There are many local benefits of the tourist trade. Land prices, as you know, Kate, increased twenty percent last year. Retail purchases were up seventeen percent. The total volume of business exceeded one hundred million dollars. New jobs open up all the time. Do you know that the family income in this area increased nearly ninety percent over the last decade?

"So you see, there is a demand by people to use and enjoy the lake. I think we can allow that and still protect and preserve the lake. But Mr. Gentry and I simply had a gentleman's disagreement over this point."

"Mr. Banuchi," Kate asked, "does it mean that your plans for the hotel have to be dropped since Mr. Gentry's land is held in trust and can't be sold at this time?"

"Oh, no," Banuchi said softly, smiling. "That is a nice property Mr. Gentry owned, but we weren't wedded to it exclusively. There are no zoning restrictions on the lake. We can build anywhere. We'll just have to keep looking for the right property. You keep your eyes open, Kate. There'll be a nice commission on this deal."

"Mr. Banuchi, what did you do in Chicago before moving down here?" Jack asked.

"Import-export business," Banuchi answered briskly.

They took their leave of Banuchi, who graciously gave them free dining passes at an elegant lake restaurant he owned.

"Well, that blows one theory," Jack said, as they climbed the stairs.

"What's that?"

"That Gentry's death might have been related to bad feelings that came about because he squashed the idea for a new resort. What this guy Banuchi said is that he intended to build the resort all along, whether Gentry liked it or not."

ELEVEN

Of the four calling cards Jack had taken from the desk of
Geoffrey Gentry, the one that matched the card from
Butch Banuchi's office was that of a St. Louis architectural
firm, MacMillan and Company. Except that a different
architect's name was listed in the lower-right-hand corner
of each card.

Acting on a hunch, Jack called Alfred E. Wright, the
architect listed on Gentry's card, and asked if he could
see the drawings for the resort hotel to be built on the
Lake of the Ozarks. Jack told Wright that Gentry, before
his death, had recommended that Jack see the drawings
as an example of the firm's work.

Wright was properly sorry about Gentry's death, which
had been reported in the St. Louis newspapers. He was
hesitant, though, to show the drawings to Jack, since there
was a company policy about such things. And Wright al-
lowed that he really hadn't worked on the project for
Banuchi Enterprises. He had only agreed to show the
plans to Gentry when Gentry prevailed upon a family
friendship. To be precise, Wright's father and Gentry had
had business dealings dating back a number of years.

With that information, Jack felt he had found the necessary lever. Jack said that he was involved in settling Gentry's estate, a white lie he hoped Cousins would endorse, if necessary. Jack lied again by telling Wright that Gentry's will stipulated that funds from the trust be invested in the Banuchi hotel project, if it seemed financially sound. Jack implied, not too subtly, that Wright's father would surely be interested in seeing a proper execution of Gentry's will. Wright relented, and an appointment was made for one p.m. on Friday.

Jack thought it interesting, although not extraordinary, that Gentry obviously had gone out of his way to view the drawings of the proposed resort hotel. He doubted that he would be able to make heads or tails of the drawings, but a trip to St. Louis would be an outing for him and Kate. They talked about it and made plans to do some late afternoon shopping and have dinner at a nice restaurant.

When they were finally on the road, leaving the lake area made Jack remember the day he had arrived in late April.

He'd left Chicago with no particular destination in mind, although he thought vaguely about driving to Acapulco. Anywhere would do, just as long as it was out of the city. Driving down Highway 54, his spirits had lifted when he saw the cliffs at Louisiana, Missouri. Crossing the Mississippi River there, he left behind the cornfields of Illinois and entered onto a gently rolling terrain that gave way, in turn, to the forests of the Ozark Highlands.

The leaves of the trees were not yet fully developed, so it was easy to look into the forest and see the brillance of the "understory" trees; the dazzling white of the dogwood, the sparkling brilliance of the redbud.

In his first days, before the Tan-Tar-A fiasco, he had rented a cabin. He went for walks in the early mornings, listening to the wind rustle last fall's leaves, and the sounds of squirrels, birds and other forest animals as they scurried about. He began to relax there, and the thoughts and sounds of the city gave way to a quieter, introspective existence. Then he put back on a uniform and a gun and had nearly lost it all.

"You know what I liked best about the spring down here?" he asked Kate, as they crossed the Missouri River at Jefferson City.

"Meeting me."

"Besides that. It was all those beautiful little violets that grow wild beside the road."

"Which kind?"

"What do you mean? The purple kind."

"Were they Johnny-jump-up, bird's-foot, or dog's-tooth?"

"Hey, to me a violet's a violet."

"You probably think the same thing about women. You're an indiscriminate person, Olsen. I don't know what I see in you."

They entered the city on Highway 40, because Kate said it would take them to Memorial Plaza, where they could eat the sandwiches she had brought, and then walk to their appointment.

Turning east onto Market Street, they came to the west end of the plaza, across from cavernous old Union Station. In the distance the Archway to the West was visible above the buildings of the inner city.

Kate parked the bus on Chestnut Street between 14th and 15th, across from Keil Auditorium. To stretch their legs, they walked past the front of the columned War Memorial Building, crossed the street and stood near the sunken entrance to the memorial.

They were stopped by a young man, drunk and unkempt, who was panhandling.

"Hey, buddy," he said to Jack, "can you spare some loose change for a sandwich?"

Jack reached for his billfold and handed the drunk a five-dollar bill.

"Say, buddy, that's real generous," the drunk slurred.

"Forget it," Jack said.

"Why'd you do that? Give him five dollars. He'll only spend it on booze."

"Probably. But he may have enough left over to actually buy a sandwich."

"He can get food free at a mission or the Salvation Army."

"Okay. I did it out of a feeling that there but for the grace of God . . ."

"Was it really that bad?" she asked.

"Yes, it was," he said, looking for the drunk, who had disappeared. "I just hadn't sunk that far yet. The police surgeon sent me to the police psychologist, and they both agreed I was an alcoholic. They were going to force me into a rehabilitation program. But I couldn't see that it would work. So I took a medical leave without pay. I don't think they expect me back."

"Why wouldn't you enter the rehabilitation program?"

"Because I would have had to stay on the force, and continue to work my eight-hour shift every day."

"You couldn't do that?"

He shook his head. "Not and stay sober."

"Maybe it's time you told me about it," Kate said, reaching for his hand.

"It was because of this," Jack said, taking the city in with a sweep of his hand. "The drunken stumblebums, the pimps, the murderers, the drug pushers, the rapists, the stickup artists, the wise guys. The whole fucking, dirty stinking mess.

"Every day I swam in the sewer, and after a while I began to think that I stank myself. When I was off duty, I couldn't bear to socialize with decent people. I was afraid for them, or of them. I don't know which. Anyway, I wasn't sure I could recognize decent people. I'd run across too many guys who looked like upstanding citizens but who turned out to be child molesters.

"Besides, decent people couldn't imagine my experiences, let alone talk about them. The guys in the suits who ride the train home to the suburbs after work—they're clean, almost sterile. They don't really know what goes on in the city. They can't imagine the vermin that live there.

"So I did what most cops do after work. I'd go to a policeman's bar and we'd relive the day while we drank ourselves blind. Then, after a while, I started drinking on duty. Pretty soon, life was just an alcoholic haze. I really don't know how I did that, especially the last three or four years. It's a wonder I didn't get canned. A miracle I didn't get killed."

Jack searched Kate's face for the aversion he hoped wouldn't be there. It wasn't.

"What happened to your marriage, Jack?" she asked kindly. "I'd like to know."

"What you would expect. Joyce couldn't understand why I couldn't leave my troubles at work, come home and enjoy the family. Of course, she was right. I should have been able to. When I couldn't leave my troubles at work, Joyce told me to get another job. Right again."

"But you stuck with being a cop for so many years," Kate said. "Why?"

"I've thought about that a lot. In many ways the answer is back in Wisconsin. I was raised on a farm. My dad milked cows. I thought life was just that simple until I went off to college in Madison. I wasn't prepared for a campus of twenty thousand students. I certainly wasn't prepared for the studies, the ideas. I began to learn that the world was complex and that there weren't answers for many problems. I liked it there, but still I left to join the army. The police shrink said I was searching for order and precision in my life."

"Did you like the army?"

Jack nodded. "Yes, in many ways. It was simple, predictable. I was an MP."

Kate smiled, encouraging him to continue. "So you became a cop after the army."

"Yep. I believed in it, too, and the dream died hard. I thought we could get rid of crime if we just locked up the bad guys. But it doesn't work that way. Not all the bad guys get locked up, and two come along to replace every one that does. What happens is that you don't reduce crime, you *police* it. You try to keep it inside some boundary, whether it's FBI statistics or a few square miles in the city. If crime doesn't slop out of those boundaries too often, the people don't care. It took me too long to learn that lesson."

"That's very cynical," she said, "but I can understand it."

"What happened, Kate, was that cynicism turned to depression and depression turned to despair. I couldn't help myself, so I started to destroy myself. I know it doesn't sound logical, but that's the way it happened." He paused, remembering. "I began to drink to relieve the tension. And that worked for a long time. Then something changed. The booze started to depress me. I had developed a great tolerance for booze. All of a sudden, four or five drinks would send me off the deep end. I had blackouts. I hated myself, but I took it out on other people. Booze owned me then. It cost me my wife, my kids, my friends and my job."

The anguish showed in her face. "But you took the first steps to help yourself. You got out of a bad situation. You're sober."

"But what do I do now, Kate?"

"What we do now is start over. But we don't worry about reforming the world. We start with simple goals: to be decent people, to enjoy every day, to help someone else when we can. Both you and I will be thirty-five this year, John Eric Olsen, and we both know that's not a bad time to start anew. We're battle-scarred. We know what we are and we know what's worthwhile. That gives us a leg up on the younger generation."

Kate looked at the uneaten sandwiches drying in the sun.

"I've had my share of troubles too, Jack," she said. "You know about Bert. We'd been married seven years when he was killed in Vietnam in 1969. We were high school sweethearts. Those five years before he left for the army were good times. I loved him deeply. I wish we could have had children.

"I moped around for a year before coming here to St. Louis. Worked at the telephone company for a while, then took some courses and got a job as a secretary.

"I was big into the swinging singles life, trying to forget everything. I was at a nightclub every other evening and ran through boyfriends like fire across the prairie. I even persuaded myself that Mr. Right had come along. Luckily, before I made the final plunge, I looked around at what I had and what I was buying for the future—a slick apartment, swimming pool, sports car, a lot of nice clothes, a lot of plastic people."

She sighed, tears welling in her eyes. "That's when I went home, nearly three years ago. I knew I needed some work, that I didn't want to be a waitress or hotel maid, so I got into real estate. I help people find a home where they can be happy with their family and friends. Maybe it doesn't sound like much, but I get a good feeling from it. I live one day at a time, trying to squeeze as much enjoyment out of each one as I can.

"So when I saw you that first time in the café, drunk on your ass, my head was screwed on right. But I knew what hurtin' was, and I could see that you hurt. I wanted to help. My surprise, after I took you in, was that I'd found the man I was going to live with for the rest of my life. And I wasn't even looking for you. Isn't that funny?"

She sought him out in a strong embrace and they wept together in each other's arms. He hadn't cried since Wisconsin.

Alfred Wright was a sparse man, about fifty, who had a nervous habit of wringing his hands. He told Jack and Kate repeatedly that it was unusual to show plans and drawings—especially incomplete ones—without a client's approval. Spies were not unknown in the trade, he whispered, and it was possible that a competing architectural firm could profit from knowing what MacMillan and Company was doing on this particular project. With such inside information, they could present a plan that might be more attractive to the client.

"Why, then, did you agree to see us?" Jack asked.

The architect wheezed, and his furtive eyes darted about the room. "My dad and Mr. Gentry were in business together several times throughout the years. Dad owns part of this firm. He said Mr. Gentry could look at any of our drawings. Dad's kind of crotchety in his old age. I don't like to bother him too often. Since you're involved in settling Mr. Gentry's estate, and making investments from the trust fund, I figured Dad would want me to help in any way possible."

"If we can see the plans, then?" Jack prompted.

"Certainly," Wright said, moving to a drafting table. It appeared that Alfred Wright was a working partner, which fitted Jack's image of the man.

"I had the plan view and the perspective drawings delivered to my office in anticipation of your visit," he said. "You understand that Mr. Givens is the supervisor of this project."

The name on Banuchi's MacMillan and Company card.

"What are plan views and perspective drawings?" Kate asked.

"A plan view is the view you'd get if a structure was sawed in half and you were above it, looking down," Wright explained.

"What are perspective drawings?" Jack asked.

"It's an artist's rendition of what various rooms or areas of a structure will look like once in use," Wright explained.

"Great," Jack said. "I think that's just what we want."

91

"To visualize the lay of the land on which the hotel is to be built," Wright said, "imagine that you nearly touch your thumb with your forefinger, so that you have a nearly completed circle with an outlet. This corresponds to a secluded cove. The forefinger area is much fatter than the thumb area. In fact, the forefinger area looks much like the side view of an eagle's head." Wright paused to see if they appreciated his similes.

"As you can see from the plans, the land area that appears as the forefinger, or eagle's head, would have at its center a thirty-story, circular-shaped hotel. Radiating out from this building like spokes of a wheel are covered passageways leading to luxury units located near the shoreline. There are ten such passageways that can be completely enclosed, or there are side panels that can be removed during mild weather."

Wright handed Jack and Kate a perspective drawing that showed a side view of a passageway flanked with rose bushes and blooming flowers.

"Once you reach the end of any passageway, you can turn left or right into another passageway. Follow this outer passageway and you come to the various luxury units. It's unique, wouldn't you say?"

Before Jack or Kate could answer, Wright launched into a second phase of his descriptive tour. "Of course, the most unusual aspect of this plan may be the thumb area. This is rocky land, rising precipitously toward the lake. Private condominiums will be constructed on the cliff face. Because the cliffs in this area are primarily shale, a support structure will be built from the top of the cliffs to the beach area. It will be at a slight angle, so the condominiums will be tiered as they rise—like stadium steps."

Kate nudged Jack, whispering in his ear. Banuchi might have said he wasn't committed to any particular site for his hotel, but, Kate pointed out, the plans were tailor-made for Gentry's land. Jack muttered to himself; the people who had lied to him were a mounting number.

Wright maintained a discreet silence during their whispering. Jack motioned for him to continue.

"The marina will be located along the landward side of the cove," Wright said. "The condominiums will be joined with the main hotel complex by a suspended walking bridge. Also, there will be a ferry service for the less energetic. Or you can ride an apparatus like a ski lift from the top of the cliffs to the restaurant on the thirtieth floor." Again, the pregnant pause by the architect. "You must admit, this is a novel plan, the likes of which you've never seen before, I'd gamble."

Kate was first to respond. "I thought there was everything on the lake. But this . . . this is something entirely new."

Wright was pleased and continued rapidly, lest the dazzling nature of the broad perspective overshadow the brilliance of the detail. "To the right of the road approaching the main hotel is an outdoor sports area. Golf course, tennis courts, go-cart track, that sort of thing. The passageways extending from the main building form pie-shaped wedges that create private areas, not only for gardens, but outdoor swimming pools, shuffleboard, a dance pavilion, miniature golf and lounging."

"What will this all cost?" Jack asked, overwhelmed by the scope of the project.

"Millions, I suspect," Wright said nonchalantly, as if that was a minor concern alongside the architectural brilliance. "But this is just the overview. The detail is even more fascinating."

"Show us," Kate said eagerly.

"The main hotel has nearly six hundred luxurious rooms. Each room, given the circular nature of the hotel, has a magnificent view.

"The first and second floors consist of registration, administrative offices, a restaurant, bar, coffee shop and small shopping mall.

"On the roof of the building is an outdoor pool and lounge area. The very top floor is a revolving restaurant, which connects to the sky lift from the cliffs. Dining in this restaurant will provide an unparalleled view of the lake. The twenty-ninth floor is a bar and disco dance floor, constructed so as to be virtually soundproof."

Wright explained that the tenth and twentieth floors would contain indoor swimming pools and lounge areas, the pools serving the additional purpose of providing dead weight against wind sway. From the drawings, Jack could see that the pools would be kidney-shaped and dovetail around the elevator bank, taking up about half the floor. The ninth and nineteenth floors would be for additional structural support and storage for room service equipment and supplies.

"Above the two swimming pools, on the eleventh and twenty-first floors, would be a health spa, with exercise and massage areas," Wright said. "These would be accessible by elevator and by the stairway from the pool areas."

"Can we see a perspective drawing for these areas?" Jack asked.

"No, not really," the architect said, pondering the situation. "You see, the clients were vague about these areas, other than to say that there should be about fifteen small but private massage rooms on each of these floors. Uniquely equipped massage rooms, I might add—television, refrigerator, studio couch."

"Interesting," Jack said. "Who are the clients besides Michael Banuchi?" Jack tried to be casual, hoping that Wright would automatically supply additional names.

"Actually, Banuchi Enterprises *is* the client," Wright corrected. "I suppose various investors will be involved, but we don't require such information."

"How do you know if the company is solvent?" Kate asked.

Wright sniffed. "Mr. Banuchi paid in advance for our services. Whether his corporation can afford to construct the hotel is not our concern."

"So Mr. Banuchi relayed to you personally all the ideas for the hotel?" Jack asked.

"Remember, again, that I am not the project director in this instance. I do know that two gentlemen accompanied Mr. Banuchi to our offices, however, and that one of them actually presented most of the hotel concepts. Mr. Jacoby was his name, as I recall."

Kate, who was leafing through the perspective drawings, said, "This hotel appears to have an orientation to a younger set, or at least couples, as opposed to families. Would you agree, Mr. Wright?"

"In a way, Miss Carter," the architect said deliberately. "The emphasis certainly seems to be upon sports, swimming, exercise, dining, dancing. Let's say the hotel would appeal to the young at heart, regardless of age."

Kate nodded, graciously accepting the gentle rebuke.

"I've really saved the most unusual feature of the hotel for the last," Wright said.

94

"What's that?" Jack asked.

"This is a perspective drawing of the fifth floor," Wright said. "Do you know what it is?"

"No," Jack said.

"It looks like a computer to me," Kate ventured.

"You're right," Wright exclaimed, beaming at Kate as if she were a pupil who had recited correctly.

"Our instructions are to have one floor set aside for a computer such as a small IBM 370. This area, of course, requires several unique supporting features. For example, this floor has an isolated electrical system so that electrical surges from other areas of the hotel will not affect computer operations."

"What's it for?" Jack asked.

Wright stroked his chin. "Oh, the computer can be used in a host of ways. Registration and room assignment. Billing. Monitoring supplies. It could run the heating and cooling plant. But I can tell you one thing that it definitely will be used for. Here is a perspective of a typical hotel room, although the same feature will be available in luxury units and the condominiums."

"Closed-circuit TV?" Jack guessed.

"Close," Wright said, wagging a finger. "It's a computer terminal with an attached lens that magnifies an electronic image onto a screen mounted on the wall."

"Wow, this is blowing my mind." Kate laughed, and Wright looked exceedingly pleased.

"This is a feature that should appeal to the gaming enthusiast," the architect said. "The developers of the hotel are obviously trying to cater to those people caught up in the electronic game craze. With this feature, hotel occupants can play electronic tennis, hockey, squash, soccer—any of those games that can be computerized. Because these terminals have an input feature, hotel guests can play each other or the computer. Tournaments with prizes are obvious possibilities, I would guess."

As they walked toward the VW bus, Jack asked Kate, "What did you think of all that?"

"My first impression was that it would be the kind of hotel I'd go to if I wanted to get laid."

"Yeah, but the real key to that setup is the computer. Nobody goes to all that trouble just so hotel guests can play Ping-Pong in their rooms. I bet that if we find out more about the computer, we'll also find out why Gentry opposed the hotel. And I don't think it had anything to do with environmental issues."

Wright watched them from his office window and then stared off into the distance for several minutes. Having made his decision, he dialed the operator and placed a long-distance call.

through ...

TWELVE

Before six o'clock in the morning, the forest reverberated
with the sound of the old motorcycle Jack had bought
from one of Kate's friends. The sun was struggling to
break through the clouds and disperse the light rain; soon,
the heat of the day would call forth rising columns of
steam from the watersoaked ground. Kate and Jack roared
away from the cabin, Kate cursing his driving when she
lost her egg sandwich trying to hang on through a sliding, gravel-tossed turn onto the blacktop road. She punc-
tuated her directions with painful jabs into Jack's ribs
that made him wince and left him sore, but happy, as
they sought out the site for the Banuchi hotel.

When they reached the area after a short ten-minute
ride, Jack was disappointed. He struggled to visualize
the land fully developed with a thirty-story structure of
brick and mortar.

"There's nothing here but trees and bushes," he complained, as they pushed the bike off the road and started
through the forest.

"You expected a road maybe," she chided him.

"C'mon, Mudball," Jack shouted at the panting, rain-soaked Labrador. "Get out front there and scare off the varmints."

"You city boys are all alike," Kate said, striding out purposefully. "Afraid you'll fall into a pit of vipers that'll take all day to kill you."

"The thought had occurred to me."

For a half mile they struggled through the woods, and when they finally emerged at the cove, Jack couldn't visualize the thumb-and-forefinger illustration suggested by the architect. But he could see the rocky cliff jutting into the lake and was awed by the possibility that condominiums could somehow be chiseled into its face.

"Well, Jack, my boy, this is it," Kate said. "The future home of Willy the computer and a retreat for the girls from the St. Louis massage parlors."

"Great. Now we have to walk back."

"Not before we take a swim."

"Christ, Kate, it's six-thirty in the morning. It's raining. We're already wet. We'll freeze to death and catch pneumonia."

"Whoever heard of pneumonia at the end of June," she replied mockingly.

"Yeah, well, just wait until we go flying down the road with our clothes soaked even more than they already are."

"Okay, let these dry over there under that pine tree," she said, dropping her jeans to the ground and kicking them through the air.

"All right, goddammit," Jack yelled, stripping off his shirt.

The sand and mud sucked at their ankles as they advanced slowly into the water, shivering against the chill. The dog splashed ahead confidently. The intermittent rain gently drove nailholes in the water.

They swam vigorously, outdistancing Mudball, who retreated to the shore to go prowling into the woods. They admired each other's bodies in the distorted view of the clear green water. Jack struggled against the firm arms that threatened to dunk him, and then submitted to the softness of Kate's breasts and stomach as she overrode him and pushed him deep into the water.

They made love in the squishy mud near the shoreline, in full view of two blue jays and a scarlet tanager.

"I'm cold," he said, "and filthy."

98

"So we'll swim out and clean off."

For a moment, Jack lay on his side, his head propped with his hand. He was semi-serious. "This morning ought to be recorded for posterity, like an old newsreel. So it won't die with us."

"Oh Jack, sweet Jack," Kate said, burying him in the mud with the weight of her body. "We'll know. And we're forever."

There was the inevitable huddle of people when they arrived at the Camdenton County courthouse; townspeople and farmers who were persuaded to linger awhile and talk, either before or after they had concluded their business.

Kate planned to go to her office after she helped Jack sift through records in the county recorder's office. They wanted to determine the exact dimensions of the land owned by Gentry, as well as the owners of any land adjacent to the proposed hotel site.

"Surprise, surprise," Kate said, comparing land ownership records with a plat of the area.

"What's the matter?" Jack asked in a low voice so the clerk couldn't hear.

"Gentry did own most of the land. The so-called forefinger area. About five hundred acres. But the area with the cliffs, someone else owns that."

"Who?"

"Tom Wallace."

"That name's familiar. Mrs. Lacy mentioned him." Jack snapped his fingers in sudden recollection. "We met him at Gentry's funeral."

"Yep. I went to school with him."

"So he owns all the thumb area?"

"That and a strip back to the road. According to the description, it would be a hundred acres or slightly more."

"It would be interesting to know if he was also opposed to the hotel."

"Sure would. And I know how to find out."

"Me, too. I go talk to him. You go to work."

"Oh, no you don't, ace. I wouldn't miss this for anything."

As they drove north of town and then east on State Road A, Jack noticed that business was picking up at the many roadside fireworks stands.

"Tell me something about this guy Wallace," Jack said.

"He's got a hog farm, almost directly south of the state park. It's not much of an operation. It was the family homestead that he inherited when his dad died of a stroke a few years ago. He lives with his mother."

The weather-beaten house listed slightly. Its lawn was overgrown, neglected, while several sections of a once-proud white picket fence lay broken on the ground.

Mrs. Wallace held back a vicious-sounding coon dog as she explained to Kate that her son wasn't home. She was short and plump and smoothed her tangled hair as she cast self-conscious glances at Jack.

As had become his custom lately, Jack appraised the boat sitting on a trailer near the barn. It was a two-seat fishing boat that didn't faintly resemble the killer boat.

"We ain't seen you out this way as often as we used to Kate," Mrs. Wallace said nervously.

"I've been meaning to stop by and see you, Bertha. But with work and all . . ." Kate shrugged helplessly.

"Yes, I reckon so," the old woman said. "Tom, he's gonna be plumb mad that he missed you. I'll be sure and tell him you were here."

"We'll try and catch him some other time," Kate said.

"God, this place stinks," Jack said, after they got into the car. "And I thought cows were dirty and stupid. Look at all those pig shacks. There's an ocean of mud out there."

"Remember this morning?" Kate asked with a broad smile. "You didn't know pigs had so much fun, did you?"

On the way back to town, Kate told Jack about a man who had worked with computers, or so she'd heard, before buying a shop in the area.

"His name is Leon Radimacher. Here, I wrote down his address. He's a potter; the shop's down on the Strip."

She parked the car beside his pickup in front of the courthouse. Jack had driven in separately, so as to have transportation when Kate went to work. Preparing to kiss him goodbye, Kate suddenly registered surprise and pointed across the street.

"There's Tom Wallace."

Jack didn't need any identification of the man Wallace was talking to in front of the bank. The expensive suit. The cigar. The gleaming complexion. It was none other than Butch Banuchi.

100

"What do you suppose they're talking about?"

"I don't know, but Banuchi is leaving. Let me go stop Tom before he gets away." Before Jack could reply, Kate was out of the car and double-timing across the street. He saw no choice but to follow.

Kate introduced the two men again, and Jack looked up at Wallace. He had a strong face with sparkling teeth. He had broad shoulders and narrow hips. Jack could easily envision him as an athlete.

"Can't say that I'm glad to see you." Wallace smiled at Jack. "Haven't seen much of Kate since you came to town."

Suddenly, Jack understood Mrs. Wallace's comments. Kate and Tom had been seeing each other. Kate had that coy look on her face again, just as she had the day of Gentry's funeral. He felt a sudden emptiness in his stomach.

"Tom, Jack has been hired by Beth Lacy to look into Mr. Gentry's death," Kate said.

"I'd like to ask you a few questions, if you don't mind," Jack added.

"Sure," Wallace replied. "Why don't we go into the café here and get out of the heat."

Wallace took Kate's arm and led her through the door while Jack followed, begrudging the taller man's graceful movements.

"I'll bet you want to know about the hotel," Wallace offered, as he seated himself beside Kate in a booth. "I was just talking to Banuchi about it. Suppose you saw us out front?"

Neither Jack nor Kate answered the question, although Jack noticed that their silence didn't do anything to wipe the gleaming smile off Wallace's face.

"I guess the resort's not going to be built in the area where it was originally planned," Jack said.

"Looks that way," Wallace shrugged, offering Kate cream for the coffee that had been served.

"Were you in favor of selling your land to Banuchi?"

"You bet. That land has been in the family even before the lake. Never was worth anything. I always hated paying the taxes on it."

"You weren't too happy then when Gentry refused to sell his land."

"I was damned mad and told Gentry so," Wallace answered. Despite the ever-present smile, or perhaps because

101

of it, Jack wondered if the hog farmer might not have a short fuse.

"You two argue about it?" Jack asked.

"Sure did. I called him on the telephone several times and tried to persuade him to change his mind. When he wouldn't do that I called back and gave him a piece of my mind. Got it off my chest, anyway. He could afford to hold onto his land. He didn't need the money. I do."

"What was Banuchi offering an acre?" Jack asked, hoping that Wallace would be more apt to provide that figure as opposed to an overall price.

Wallace laughed. "That was open to negotiation, I figured. Let's just say that I wouldn't have let him get it cheap."

"What's land like that go for in this area?" Jack asked Kate, not to be deterred.

"Ordinarily, maybe a thousand or fifteen hundred an acre, although a good lake lot might bring ten to fifteen thousand." Kate smiled at her high school classmate. "I'd guess Tom could have held out for a good price."

Especially if he knew that Banuchi was so set on the site that he'd had architect's plans prepared, Jack thought, calculating that twenty-five hundred dollars an acre would have made Wallace a quarter of a million dollars.

"Did you ever see the plans for the hotel?" Jack asked casually.

For the first time, Wallace didn't smile. "Didn't know they even had any drawn up," he said.

"So you didn't know anything about the details of the hotel?"

"I figured it'd be a fancy one, about the same as the others on the lake," Wallace said, focusing his attention on Kate and ignoring Jack.

"Where were you the day Gentry was killed?" Jack asked, annoyed.

"Fishing. Just like Gentry was. Only I was over in the area south of the state park."

"By yourself?"

"Yes, but you can look somewhere else, private eye," Wallace said. "First, I don't have the kind of boat that killed Gentry. Second, it wouldn't have done me any good to kill him no matter how mad I was. Anyone who'd ever met the old man could guess that Gentry would have something in his will to prevent any commercial development on his land."

Wallace insisted on walking Kate to her car. When he left, Jack asked, "What's with you two?"

"I used to date him."

"When?"

"Before you came."

"Seems like an asshole to me."

"C'mon. Everyone can see he's a real stud."

Jack looked hurt.

"But I live with you, not him," she consoled. "And that's by choice, honey."

The potter had a heavy beard, but was bald except for the sides of his head. While Radimacher waited on customers, Jack admired his work, especially several small ceramic wine glasses.

"I get four dollars apiece for those," Radimacher said, "and a lot of people think that's high. It takes me several hours to make one. When I was a computer consultant, I got two hundred fifty a day, plus expenses. This society has its priorities all screwed up."

"Mr. Radimacher," Jack said, "I hate to impose, but you may be the only computer expert in the lake area, and I have a few elementary questions that need answers."

Radimacher shrugged indifferently. "Actually, I think of myself as a potter now that I've left my old life behind. But I'd be glad to help a new neighbor."

Jack said, "I'm not so interested in how computers work as I am about what they can do."

"Eventually, they may be able to do more than we can presently imagine," Radimacher said, "including some aspects of what we call thinking."

"I know you can use computers to project various games on a TV screen," Jack said.

"Yes, although you don't need a programmable computer for those games. In fact, it wouldn't be cost-effective unless there were a situation in which the players affected the game by interacting with the computer."

That's insightful, Jack thought. "What other kind of games can computers play?"

"There are really no limits. Games with finite possibilities or infinite possibilities. Let's take chess, for example. A very complicated game with virtually unlimited options. Sixty-four squares, thirty-two pieces, several having the capability of moving up to seven spaces in any direction.

"A group at MIT programmed a computer to play chess. They've worked for years and still haven't computerized all possible chess moves. Card games, on the other hand, are easier. The number of playing options are strictly limited by the number of players and the number of cards remaining to be played."

"So a computer can play cards," Jack said.

"Sure. The computer 'deals' in the sense of randomly selecting different cards and assigning them to the players. Any card game is possible, as well as dice or roulette."

"Let's take blackjack as an example," Jack said. "Each player has a computer terminal, and he can see his hole card, but no one else's. A player can ask the computer for a hit or signal that he's going to stay or fold?"

"Precisely. Same with poker. Your down cards would show only on your terminal screen. Of course, you can imagine how both games would be open to manipulation. Two players in the same game could set up a communications system between themselves, especially if the players were dispersed."

"Like in different rooms."

"Yes," Radimacher agreed. "And the dealer, in this case the computer, would be difficult to beat."

"Why?"

"One reason is that the computer could almost instantly calculate the odds on drawing any card at any point in the game. Over the long run, even if the game was played fairly, the computer should win. It would never bluff. Just play the odds. Furthermore, there could be blatant cheating by the house. The computer would know all hole cards and could be programmed to calculate its odds for winning. Or, as another example, you could program the computer to fill inside straights only when the house is already a loser."

"What about horseracing?"

"Oh, it's possible. It would be similar to the computerized boxing matches, in which a champion of the past, like Gene Tunney, fights Muhammad Ali. The problem is that you can't adequately program a computer to take into account intangibles. Like a boxer's state of mind, or a horse's indigestion. These things affect real fights and races. But the computer would assign a numerical value to every characteristic of a horse race. For example, the horse's track record, weight, leg length, the jockey's record, the track condition, etcetera. The results would be fairly predictable. That is, anyone with access to the program could analyze the data beforehand and predict how the computer would react. Or, if you had the program and your own mini-computer, you simply run the race before it is officially run."

Jack thought about Radimacher's last comments before speaking. "But Joe Blow off the streets wouldn't know that. He'd think the race or fight was still up in the air until the very end."

"You're probably right," Radimacher conceded. "The majority of people really don't understand computers and, until they do, they're going to get ripped off. Especially as computers come to do more and more things."

It could be about to happen, Jack thought. Right here. Not too many months down the road.

THIRTEEN

The old man's long white hair fanned out on the pillow and matched the color of nearly everything else in the hospital room. Jack hadn't gotten pneumonia, but Roy Cousins had. It was a complication of a broken hip. They found him near his home in a ditch, where apparently he had lain all night, the victim of a hit-and-run driver.

Cousins had lost weight; it showed especially in his face. And he looked frail, holding out a trembling hand to welcome Jack. But though his voice had an unusual raspy quality, it still commanded attention. "It was nice of you to come, son. I wanted to talk to you before they put me in one of those confounded oxygen tents. Then I'll just be able to breathe and not talk. It's an ignoble end for a lawyer, I assure you."

"Is it serious?" Jack asked, concerned. "You seem in good spirits."

Cousins shrugged. "Pneumonia's a tricky thing, especially for an old man of eighty-three."

Jack was not surprised. He had a tendency to judge old people younger than their actual years. Somehow, old was sixty and all beyond that was relative.

"On the other hand, illness has little to do with the

state of the spirit," Cousins continued. "Mind still prevails over matter."

Jack thought the old man brightened with the opportunity to dispense a few pearls of wisdom.

"I've been watching you, son," Cousins said. He pulled Jack closer, never having let go of his hand.

"Not that I've been watching you personally, but there are other eyes that let me know what you're up to."

"What do you think?" Jack asked, remembering that Cousins had said he must earn his fee.

"I think you're doing fine. Exceptional, in fact. I hadn't expected that you would work out so well."

Jack frowned. "Why?"

"I thought maybe you were too down on yourself and other people to take a real interest in finding out why an old man died."

Jack's feelings were hurt, temporarily, but he also recognized the truth of Cousins's statement.

"I think this case has been good for you," Cousins said. "It's given you something to do. You've met some interesting people, I'd venture, and learned a little more about the lake. And I think the Gentry case has proven to be more interesting than you first thought."

"Yes, it has," Jack agreed.

"You met the grandchildren," Cousins said, stating a fact, not asking a question.

"Yes."

"Lovely pair, aren't they? Now do you understand Geoff's reluctance to split a few million dollars between them with no strings attached?"

Cousins rolled his head away from Jack, coughing and then gasping for air.

"The nurse said I wasn't to stay long," Jack apologized. "What are they giving you?"

"Oh, antibiotics of one sort or another. I wouldn't attempt to pronounce the name. Doctors are the natural successors of the Indian medicine man. No one understands their rituals. And everyone overestimates their power. Of course, some people say the same of lawyers."

Jack shivered, imagining he could see the pallor of death spreading over the old man.

"You met Banuchi also."

"Yes."

"And?"

"My first impression was that he was strictly on the up and up. He wanted to build a resort on Gentry's land, but he could, and would, build it elsewhere if necessary."

"You sound as if you had a second impression. Why?"

"I saw the architect's drawings for the hotel. Banuchi's more committed to that site than he let on."

The old man went into a prolonged coughing spasm that left him weak and drawn. Finally, he forced out the words. "That's the initiative that's really impressed me. In just three weeks' time, you've made such progress. It took Geoff months."

Jack was pleased. It had all happened because he'd stolen brightly colored calling cards. Like a bird that gathers ribbons and diamonds and doesn't know the difference. Only later did Jack wonder how the old man had found out about the trip to St. Louis.

"I've never seen the plans," Cousins said, his strength seemingly renewed by a sip of water. "Geoff gave me his impressions. Let me hear yours."

"There are a lot of things impressive about the hotel, such as who's putting up the big money that's involved," Jack said, unsure how to put his other impressions.

"Go on," Cousins urged.

"Gambling," Jack blurted, feeling both ridiculous and excited.

"What else?"

"Sex for hire, maybe," Jack said, remembering the "massage" rooms that seemed designed for more intimate liaisons.

"Those were Geoff's impressions, too." He rose onto an elbow with difficulty.

Jack pulled up a chair and sat down. The nurse would have to run him out.

"You know about Wallace?" Cousins asked.

"Yes."

"He's a hungry one," the old man said grimly.

Jack bristled, remembering the possessive way the hog farmer had looked at Kate.

"I heard you were in the Stables," Cousins said, grinning.

"Yes."

"What did you think?"

"Drugs."

108

"Now you have the key," Cousins said, reaching again for the water. "Follow the drugs and you will solve everything."

"What do you mean?"

"The mystery of who killed Geoff Gentry," Cousins said, so furiously that he spat water on the sheets. "Not accidentally, but premeditated, cold-blooded murder." With greater composure, he added: "The same ones who left me to die in a ditch."

"Why?" Jack asked, although his gut told him Cousins was right on all counts.

"The Lake of the Ozarks is about to enjoy an ignominious distinction," Cousins said. "It is to be a testing ground. The object, I suspect, as Geoff did, is legalized gambling. Which, in turn, will provide a natural environment for even more profitable illegal activities in drugs and prostitution."

"Could it happen?" Jack asked, not wanting to recognize the possibility.

"Oh yes," Cousins replied, his eyes blazing. "In every state, the people are tired of taxes. Taxes on their income, taxes on their property. But, at the same time, they want more and better government services. They won't accept the idea that government can only do for you if you give to the government. The idea of the free lunch is alive and well, my boy."

Cousins paused, trying to draw strength through the hinged straw that protruded from the water glass.

"The campaign will take place on many different levels," he continued. "The hotel won't openly allow gambling at first. They'll just whet the customers' appetites with their innocent, but intriguing, computer games. They know the customers will initiate gambling among themselves, and then the hotel can discreetly intervene and take over the *burden* of administering the gambling.

"I suspect there'll be a well-financed, slick PR campaign throughout the state, telling the people that their taxes are too high and that taxes can be reduced with revenues gained from legalized gambling. They'll get more than a few converts. Many people will shut their eyes to the obvious for the right price."

Jack nodded. "Sheriff Davis."

"I'd guess he's in their pocket already," Cousins confirmed, "although he probably thinks he's just ignoring a little drug traffic at the Stables. He's not smart enough to see the whole picture."

Jack wasn't sure he agreed with Cousins's assessment of Davis's abilities. There was a shrewdness about the sheriff that Jack instinctively respected.

"I know Mel Davis has ambitions to be a state representative," Cousins added. "They'll finance him, and others like him, to get the political clout they need. The weak part of their plan is that they can't buy honest people, who will rise up and tell the truth and throw the scoundrels out of public office."

Jack wasn't so sure Cousins was right. "Who are *they?*"

"The people with the money for this type of campaign? Don't worry about them. You can never get to them. You can only stop this thing, even temporarily, by picking off their front men here in the lake area."

"That's got to be Banuchi."

"That's my guess, too, but you'll have to prove it. Geoff made a tactical error, in my opinion. He concentrated on the hotel. Not only was he going to stop it on his land but he attempted to establish new zoning regulations that would stop Banuchi's hotel, period. That's what he was trying to do before he was killed. That's why he made a provision in his will for an area development council, hoping it would carry on the effort even if he was gone."

"Do you think Gentry anticipated someone killing him?"

"I've mulled that one over quite a bit," the old man replied. "I don't know."

"Why do you think Gentry's approach to stopping the hotel was wrong?"

The old man lay back, looking at the ceiling. "Maybe I'm being too unkind to an old friend as a result of the benefit of hindsight. But Geoff's approach would only have resulted in a battle of charges and countercharges. There was no way he, or anyone else, could prove that the hotel was being built to serve ultimately as a gambling casino. Also, I doubt that Geoff could have organized that much opposition. Banuchi is a worthy opponent."

"But you think he was killed because of his opposition to the hotel?" Jack ventured.

"I'm pretty sure that's true as far as it goes. But there may be more than one motive involved."

110

Cousins sank into the pillow, closing his eyes. Jack saw that he was exhausted.

"You're the only one who can beat them now, Jack. Remember, follow the drugs. Don't get sidetracked trying to investigate anything like my *accident*."

Jack knew he couldn't ignore what had happened to the old man. He rose. Cousins opened his eyes, struggling for a last measure of strength.

"A final note of caution, Jack. I doubt Banuchi would soil his hands with murder. There are others involved. Be careful. The person you least expect may do you the most harm."

Jack shuddered as he remembered that so far the old man had been right on target with his observations and hunches.

For a woman pushing seventy, Beth Lacy looked vivacious. She wore cool white cotton slacks and a matching sleeveless blouse decorated with purple and yellow flowers. Unlike so many gray-haired elderly women, she didn't wear her hair in tight curls; it was full and straight and recently had been shampooed and shaped.

She greeted him with her usual effusiveness and he joined her at an outside table shaded by an umbrella. The heat of the day was dissipating as the late afternoon sun dipped low in the sky.

She offered Jack a beer, which irritated him slightly, since he was certain she knew he didn't drink anymore. They knew everything else about him, he thought.

"How is Roy?" she asked.

"He was weak and tired when I left," Jack answered. "But, then, we talked a good deal and I suppose that's not good for him."

"I plan to visit him this evening," she said, "and I dread it so. Somehow I fear the worst. Pneumonia in the summer can be so bad, let alone a broken hip at his age."

As always, Jack had called before coming. He thought she might expect him to pay a social call after his visit with Cousins. And she was his employer. He should bring her up to date about his activities; yet he was reluctant to do so. He felt more comfortable confiding to Cousins. The widow seemed too naive. Or was she just purposefully vague? So many things she had told Jack raised more questions and doubts in his mind.

"How has your investigation been going?" she asked.

"I've been to several marinas on the lake, making certain that they have a description of the boat," he said, stretching the truth.

"That's an excellent idea," she said. "Keep reminding them and they won't forget about it."

"And I've been to see Sheriff Davis to find out what he's doing."

"That man needs someone to ride herd on him," she said pointedly. "First Geoff is killed in an accident and now Roy Cousins is severely injured. There are some irresponsible and careless people in this area that should be put in jail. And he's doing nothing."

Irresponsible and careless people, he thought. Did that mean she thought that Gentry and Cousins were victims of accidents? Even after he had hinted several times, not so subtly, that premeditation was a possibility. Was she simply naive, or was there calculation in her remarks?

"I've been talking to anyone who had any contact with Mr. Gentry," Jack said, "to determine any possible conflicts, and to find out where they were on the day he died."

She was politely incredulous. "You're checking alibis?"

"Yes."

"I was visiting a friend who lives at the nursing home in Osage Beach."

Jack joined the widow in laughing at the idea of her needing an alibi. Inwardly, he was relieved to have acquired the information so easily.

"As you know from the last time we talked, I'm not ruling out the possibility that someone with a grudge against Mr. Gentry may have killed him."

She pursed her lips and nodded negatively. "I just find that so hard to believe, Jack."

"Just as background, Mrs. Lacy, when again did Mrs. Gentry die and what was the cause of her death?" Jack smiled broadly. Sometimes it was an effective way to mask a serious question.

"Elsie died nearly five years ago, in September of 1973. It was a heart attack. Very sudden. She was dead on arrival at the hospital."

"You knew her well?"

"Yes. We were neighbors for over seven years. When she and my husband were both alive, the four of us would play bridge at least once a week, and we got together frequently for cookouts."

"I imagine Mr. Gentry was very lonely after his wife died."

"Yes. Eldon and I would invite him over at least once a week so he wouldn't ramble around that big house all by himself."

"I don't mean to dwell on depressing events, Mrs. Lacy," Jack said, hesitating, "but I did hear of your husband's unfortunate death."

She looked at him keenly for a moment, but then began to talk in a conversational tone. "Yes, it was tragic, the way Eldon died. He was seventy at the time, six years older than I. He had hardening of the arteries. The doctors gave him medication, but he was still prone to lapses of memory, when he often didn't recognize people. Also, he began to wander off by himself. Usually if I left the house to go into town and shop, I'd have someone stop by and watch him. But the night of his death, he left the house after midnight, while I was asleep." She stopped, shrugging helplessly.

Jack lowered his eyes, sorry for her as a human being and feeling guilty that he had made her talk about her husband's death. But he couldn't help thinking of Mrs. Lacy, a vigorous woman, strapped with a senile husband. And robust Geoffrey Gentry, recently widowed, only two houses away. They must have started dating soon after Eldon Lacy died.

"I want you to come into the house a moment," Mrs. Lacy said brightly.

Inside, she disappeared momentarily, telling him to look at the porcelain birds she was painting. Returning, she sat at the coffee table, opening a checkbook.

"Jack, I want to pay you for what you've done so far. Before his accident, Roy said you were making great progress, and I've been pleased with what you've told me."

"That's not necessary," he said. "We can settle later."

"Nonsense," she replied emphatically. "You have two accidents to investigate now. It will take more of your time and money. I don't expect you to pay out of your own pocket." He remembered how she had represented the job

113

as part-time, when he had first talked to her. Now she had expanded his duties without giving him a choice—not that he hadn't planned to look into Cousins's "accident."

"Now, let's see," she said, making calculations in the air with a pencil. "It's been three weeks since we first agreed that you'd work for me."

"I haven't worked all those days, though," he said, self-consciously.

"How many then?"

He calculated roughly. "A dozen full days at the most."

"All right. And your expenses?"

"None," he said, not wanting to mention St. Louis, although he had planned to.

"There's gasoline, surely," she protested.

"Don't worry about it. The daily rate is exorbitant, anyway. Let's cut it back some."

"No, we won't. Here's a check for twenty-five hundred dollars, which includes an advance."

Jack was stunned. It was more money than he had ever made during any comparable period.

"And here's a key to Mr. Gentry's house, in case you want to look around there again. I think that's everything."

She paused, biting a fingernail in contemplation. "You see, I'm going to leave tomorrow morning on a plane for New York. There are some friends and relatives I want to visit. I need to get away and think clearly for a while." She smiled at him. "I'll be gone about ten days to two weeks. Is there anything else you'll need?"

Realizing what the widow had been saying to him, Jack shook his head negatively. He had been mesmerized momentarily by an ashtray on an end table across the room, which contained cigar butts that he recognized immediately.

FOURTEEN

Everyone knows that things are never quite what they appear to be on the surface. For that reason, Jack was always cautious, sometimes slightly fearful, of the lake. What was below the surface? How deep was the water? Where was the barely submerged tree or rock that could rip a gaping hole in a speeding boat? What kind of reptiles really lurked under the water?

Jack, an enthusiastic if not accomplished water-skier, jumped the twin white water peaks created by the prop and swung even with the boat by pressing hard on the left ski. Waving with one hand, Kate turned the boat sharply to her left, whipping Jack to a faster speed as he tried to hang on through the arc. He crouched low, knowing that the water would not receive him gently when Kate succeeded in toppling him.

"You whore," he said, as Kate helped drag him into the boat. "I nearly lost my trunks when I went down."

"You're lucky that snapping turtle didn't see you with your pants down. He woulda went for that worm."

"It's a snake, woman."

"No, I've seen snakes before. That's a worm."

As she threw back her head in uproarious laughter, Jack pushed her over the side of the boat.

"You prick," she screamed, thrashing to the surface, sputtering water.

He smirked. "That's more like it."

In addition to skiing, Jack wanted to be out on the lake for other reasons. He wanted to check some alibis, and he wanted to look into a few coves near the area where Gentry was killed on the off chance of spotting the red boat with the gray lightning stripes.

Jack secured the camera case and took out the binoculars as Kate throttled the boat out of the water. They had skied from Kate's boat dock nearly to the tip of Turkey Bend. The fifteen-foot fiberglass boat was so old that the green-colored hull had faded to an off-white as a result of the combined actions of sun and water. But the new eighty horsepower Mercury outboard motor made the old boat fairly fly.

Jack scanned the coves idly as the boat skimmed along on top of the smooth water. It was a Wednesday morning, June 28, and traffic on the lake was light. Kate pointed out Barbara Gentry's house first, although Jack had been searching the shoreline with the binoculars. From the lake, the shoreline was a tangle of look-alike trees and homes.

Kate slowed the boat as they dipped slightly into the cove, not far from the dock where Barbara Gentry's boat was moored. As agreed beforehand, Kate set the throttle so that the boat leveled out at thirty miles per hour. Jack recorded both the time and the odometer setting on a piece of paper before returning to the binoculars. In addition, he kept on the lookout for markers along the shoreline indicating the distance from Bagnell Dam. By this measure, Barbara's house was between the twenty-two-mile and twenty-three-mile marker.

Just opposite the Grand Glaize bridge, Jack made a time and mileage notation. Rounding Shawnee Bend and turning back west, they soon came to the area where Gentry had been killed. Kate swung the boat into the cove and Jack had a curious sense of *déjà vu*. He felt as if he were reliving the event from the perspective of the killers. He shivered, wondering what must have been going through their minds at the time. Were they nervous? Frightened? Angry? Uncaring? Who could understand the workings of such minds? Minds bent on murder.

"It's about eight miles from Barbara's place," he said.

116

"Traveling at our speed, it would have taken them sixteen minutes to get here."

"Yes, but they could have traveled faster, especially in the boat you saw," Kate said. "Or there could have been a lot of traffic to slow them down."

Jack shook his head. "It was a Monday, remember. There wouldn't have been that much traffic. But then, again, they wouldn't have wanted to attract a lot of attention by zipping across the water at a high speed. I think we have a good average at thirty miles per hour."

"Of course, if it was Barbara and her boyfriend, they would have arrived at the party on Horseshoe Bend in that boat," Kate said, "and someone would remember that."

"But what if they had a prearranged plan to switch boats. That's something we have to keep in mind."

From where Gentry was killed to the tip of the Horseshoe Bend peninsula was seven miles, or another fourteen minutes, Jack calculated after they made the run.

"Barbara said they arrived at the party right at four," he told Kate. "But suppose they ran over the old man, covered the distance to the party in five or six minutes so that they were there by four-twenty, four-twenty-five."

"Later, they could have said they arrived at four and no one would have noticed the difference," Kate agreed.

The channel between Shawnee Bend and Horseshoe Bend was up to a mile wide in spots. Barbara and Hank could have hidden the fancy speedboat in any one of a dozen coves and returned to get it later. Or maybe they had hoisted it into a nearby boat storage shed. In either case, that would have delayed their arrival at the party until four-thirty or later. Someone should have noticed that difference. Jack made a mental note to talk to someone who was at that party.

As they started back east, Jack had another idea. He unfolded a lake map, comparing it to the shoreline.

"Over there," he said, pointing to the Shawnee Bend shoreline around the ten-mile marker. "Let's time it from there to the spot where Gentry was killed."

It was five miles.

"Why from there?" Kate asked, shutting off the motor and allowing the boat to drift.

"Because that would have been convenient to Alan Gentry. He leaves the Stables, picks up the boat and trailer at

117

his cabin or someplace nearby. It takes only a few minutes to get to a boat launch. From the time the boat hits the water, it takes them ten to fifteen minutes at top speed to do the whole job and have the boat back on the trailer."

"He would have had to be gone from the Stables for an hour," Kate said. "Somebody should have noticed."

"Not necessarily. Time's a fuzzy thing for some of those boys. And I have a feeling that some of the others have acquired a bad memory for certain events. What we can check are the boat launches in that area. Maybe somebody will remember seeing the boat."

They retraced their way back to the Grand Glaize bridge and Banuchi's marina, where they docked the boat and told the boy to gas it while they were getting something to eat. While eating Jack figured the distance and time from Banuchi's place to where Gentry was killed.

"Round-trip, it would be about twelve miles. Banuchi could have done it in ten to fifteen minutes if he was flying. I'll have to check and find out exactly what time he and the sheriff were together that afternoon."

"He didn't do it, sweetie," Kate said.

"Banuchi? How do you know?"

"You've met him. Do you think that's his style?"

Kate's question triggered Jack's remembrance of Cousins's remark about Banuchi not being the kind to soil his hands. Jack knew that assessment was probably right, and mentally he scratched Banuchi as the killer. But not as the guy who might have hired it done.

Tourists are always taking pictures in the Lake of the Ozarks, especially if they rent a boat. So Jack snapped away with the new thirty-five millimeter camera he had bought with his "largesse," as Kate referred to the fee he had received from Beth Lacy. He didn't know exactly what it was he wanted, but he concentrated on taking pictures of all the employees at the marina.

Back in the boat, they wound their way down the snake-like Grand Glaize channel until they were floating in front of the shale cliffs south of the state park.

"This is the kind of scenery I imagine in a James Fenimore Cooper novel," Kate said. "A wide river bordered by forests. Cliffs. Maybe a waterfall."

"There aren't any waterfalls around here."

"In my mind there are. Along with a large tribe of the

118

mighty Osage Indians. A proud people. Intelligent, but fierce when someone bugged them."

"How do you know there were Indians here?" Jack asked, preoccupied with figuring the mileage from the bridge.

"I've lived here all my life," Kate answered. "I know about this area. Before the dam, the big and little Niangua rivers used to join the Osage near here, and then the Osage flowed on another eighty miles to join the Missouri. The rivers were like highways for the French and Indian trappers."

"Who were looking for beaver, no doubt," Jack said with a leer.

"You crude bastard," Kate replied.

"Your boyfriend made damned sure he was as far away from the scene as possible," Jack said, switching subjects. "Over seventeen miles from here to where Gentry was killed. Of course, that doesn't mean Wallace was really here. He didn't say that anyone saw him."

"We can check that, too," Kate said. "I know several old boys that fish in this area. I'll ask around."

"I'm not sure we've accomplished a whole lot."

"Sure we did. Don't be such a pessimist."

"Alan Gentry's the best bet. He could have got that boat in and out of the water in just a few minutes."

"Banuchi appears to have an ironclad alibi," Kate offered.

Jack grunted noncommittally.

"Barbara Gentry's alibi should be the easiest to check," she continued. "With all the people at that party, someone was bound to see them arrive and remember the time and their boat."

"Wallace has the weakest alibi," Jack said, unable to hide his dislike of the man. Still, he wondered if they weren't forgetting someone. Banuchi's motive for wanting Gentry out of the way was to remove any opposition to the proposed hotel, regardless of where it was built. That was a strong motive if the hotel was to be used for gambling. Wallace, on the other hand, could have wanted Gentry dead, hoping that his heirs would be agreeable to selling the land for the hotel site—a prerequisite if Wallace's land was to sell. Alan and Barbara Gentry could have feared being disinherited, in which case they might have

119

wanted the old man dead before he had time to change his will.

There might even be two separate tracks of motives, he thought, as Cousins suggested. Or were different motives related in some way? And there was Cousins's admonition to trust no one. Was he excluding someone? There was Mrs. Lacy. He remembered the cigar butts in the ashtray. She had talked to Banuchi, and the hotel developer was in up to his eyeballs as far as Jack was concerned. Then there was Sheriff Davis. But why? Was there yet someone else?

Jack was startled from his thoughts by a surge of the boat, which nearly dumped him from his seat.

"What are you doing?" he yelled, and then saw that Kate had swung the boat around so that the bow was heading into waves created by a fast-moving pontoon boat.

"This thing is light," she said. "We could have been swamped if those waves had hit us broadside."

Jack admired the way she had maneuvered the boat—executing a slight curl, nearly a pivot on the stern, that plopped the boat on top of the first advancing wave. It suddenly occurred to Jack what an expert boat handler she was. He tried to remember what Kate had been doing the day he and Gentry were fishing in the cove, and then sheepishly put the thought out of his mind.

As they came in sight of the marina, Jack had Kate slow down while he focused the binoculars on the dock area. He saw Banuchi standing outside the supply building, talking and gesturing to another man. Beside them was a girl in a floppy hat, whose face Jack couldn't see.

"Get in a little closer," he said, fumbling in the camera bag for the telephoto lens. "Get some gas."

"We just filled up, ace."

"Buy a couple of quarts of oil."

Near the gasoline pumps, Jack brought Banuchi into clearer focus. After a half dozen shots, Jack was contented. They paid for the oil and headed for home.

Under a covered dock, behind a tall cabinet containing oars and life jackets, Barbara Gentry watched Kate and Jack speed away. When she had been standing beside Banuchi, Barbara had not been paying attention to the conversation. That had been when she'd first noticed the binoculars staring in their direction.

Moving around the walkway toward the mobile home-office, Barbara and Banuchi were stylistically impeccable—she in a vanilla-colored sun dress with spaghetti straps and flounce, and a matching picture hat with a slightly rippled brim; he in a white Panama suit, open-necked yellow silk shirt, and white patent leather loafers.

"It's not wise for us to be seen together, Barbara," Banuchi said, as they were seated in his office. "I hope it is important."

"Do you know Jack Olsen was taking pictures of you a few minutes ago?"

"Maybe he admires my new suit," Banuchi chuckled softly, lighting a cigar.

"I think he'll be trouble," she said, taking a seat opposite Banuchi's desk. "He struck me as not too imaginative, but tenacious."

"Tenacity is a virtue for a bulldog, Barbara. But it won't do Mr. Olsen any good as far as I'm concerned, because he has nothing to chew on."

"Not yet," she said coyly, sliding the hem of her dress to mid-thigh length. "But wait until he leans on my brother a few more times. Guys with big habits have big mouths."

Banuchi raised his eyebrows questioningly.

Barbara rose and walked to the window, looking out toward the lake. "Unpleasant as it was, Hank and I went to Alan's shack last night. He lives like a pig, you know. I wanted to find out just what Alan had told Olsen. But brother dear was too stoned to remember anything. Offered us coke from a sugar bowl sitting in the middle of a table." She smiled sympathetically. "That's not smart."

Banuchi nodded. "Your brother will certainly come to trouble if he continues to be so careless about his drug habits."

"What do you think needs to be done, Butch?"

"Observe and be patient," Banuchi said pleasantly. "I don't think Mr. Olsen will stick with his investigation much longer."

Barbara sat on the edge of Banuchi's desk, leaning toward him to provide a better view of her breasts. "You're the coolest, Butch baby."

Banuchi smiled benignly. "It's imperative that we all be

121

calm and collected, Barbara. Our main business is to get a hotel built. All these other things are minor distractions."

"You're right." She rose from the desk and pulled her dress over her head in one deft movement. Wearing no underclothes, she stood naked and regarded Banuchi with her pouting, naughty look.

Banuchi appraised her classically sculptured body and couldn't help but linger over the slightly rounded belly, the deep navel and the triangle of golden curls. He began to breathe deeply, and beads of sweat collected high on his forehead.

Barbara walked slowly around the desk and sat on his lap. "You're really gonna smoke now, baby," she said, taking his cigar.

FIFTEEN

It was nice to wake up without a hangover. Jack busied himself about the kitchen, slicing a grapefruit, making toast, watching over the egg poacher. He remembered the days when he would stay out drinking until two or three in the morning, after working the four-to-midnight shift. Then he usually slept until noon. When he got up, he would be grouchy, having slept fitfully as a result of the combined effects of nicotine and alcohol. At first, he had taken a lot of aspirin as a morning-after cure; in time, he had discovered the medicinal effects of a Bloody Mary.

But now he was into the habit of waking daily at six. Kate was equally punctual, awakening promptly a half hour later. He had learned to relish that half hour that belonged to him totally. He could stay in bed, watching Kate or slowly waking her up in his own fashion. Sometimes he took walks; other times he read. It was the best time to write to his children, and he reserved at least two mornings a week for doing that.

He missed his children—Harold, ten, and Samantha, seven, who recently had sent him a short note in her neat but labored handwriting, asking when he would be home from vacation. Harold had a better understanding of the situation. Jack was always cheery in his letters, and in his most recent had proposed that he and the children go see their grandparents in Wisconsin in late July. He had mentioned a separate package of fireworks that should arrive shortly after the letter. Jack tried to be philosophical about the misspent years during which he had been a father in name only. There was only himself to blame. He remembered sitting on the bed one morning in his shorts, delirious with drink and inner rage. Suddenly, Harold was standing in the doorway and Jack realized he was pointing his service revolver at the boy. He hadn't even known he had the gun in his hand. That was the day before he left.

The pictures Jack had taken at the marina had been printed. He sent them along to a detective he knew in the narcotics division. The man worked undercover most of the time and knew by heart the Chicago Who's Who in dope. The drugs showing up in the Stables had to come from outside the area, and Jack figured Chicago was a good place to start. Besides, it had been Banuchi's town. In time, Jack hoped to send the lieutenant pictures of the Gentry kids and Wallace. Organized crime had its fingers deep into the drug scene and the lieutenant had ears within the organization. He could circulate the pictures of the principals in the Gentry case and find out if any of them had been in the city making drug buys. On an outside chance, Jack also asked the detective if he had ever heard of a Mr. Jacoby, the man who had accompanied Banuchi to the St. Louis architectural firm.

In the meantime, Kate was checking the alibis of Tom Wallace and Barbara Gentry. In the case of Wallace, she enlisted the help of her brother Latham, who went fishing nearly every day. So far, he had been unable to find out much, other than to validate the fact that Wallace was known to fish often near the cliffs in the park area. Whether he had been there when Gentry was killed was open to question. Kate was unable to find out anything about the party Barbara Gentry said she had attended. Jack saved Alan Gentry and Butch Banuchi for himself.

First, he wanted to visit Gentry's home again. It might be worth his time in light of what he had discovered since being there the first time.

McGinnis, the groundskeeper, didn't seem concerned

when Jack told him he would be in the house for a while. Jack asked if anyone else had visited the house, and McGinnis volunteered, over the roar of the lawnmower, that Mr. Cousins had visited once or twice.

The only sign that Cousins had been in Gentry's den were neat piles of cancelled checks on the desk. From what the old lawyer had told him about the role of executor of the estate, Jack assumed that Cousins was determining the incidental bills owed by and to Gentry.

Jack thumbed idly through one stack of checks before going through the file cabinet again. He skipped the alphabetized folders and searched through a lower drawer that he found to contain, among other things, several copies of the book written by Gentry, and a high school yearbook. The graduating class of 1918. It was in mint condition, and Jack took a chair and began to look through it.

The *Hurkaru* was dedicated to a classy-looking faculty lady pictured from the back, with her head turned inquisitively, as if she had just heard someone walk up behind her. The oval-shaped faculty photographs were of bygone days. Pretty women. Handsome men. Mostly dust now. Then the class pictures. The seniors were pictured individually, like the faculty; the other classes were grouped together in rows, with many girls dressed in navy suits, or wearing long skirts and white blouses with a large, crossed tie. Pictures of athletic teams, musical groups.

Jack sought out the picture of Geoffrey Gentry II, a proud-looking youth who was class treasurer, a member of the chorus, the Latin club and the basketball team and a participant in the senior class play. Distinguished, it said, by his booming voice. Elsewhere, Jack read that Gentry was seen most often in the company of Alice Fricke; that he had won an apple-bobbing contest; that the class prophecy for him was that he would become a famous auctioneer; and that his fondest wish was to drive a car from New York to San Francisco.

Jack had a sense of the man that he had lacked before. Gentry had been an ordinary high school boy whose wishes had come true in large part, although Jack suspected tribulations along the way, despite the wealth. Gentry had, after all, buried a wife and a son. His grandchildren were a disappointment.

125

Would the boy from the yearbook have stepped forth down life's path with so much vigor had he known the fate that awaited him, inevitably, on June 5, 1978? The answer was clear, Jack knew. Of course he would have.

Suddenly, Jack wanted very much to find the killers of this man; to put behind bars those who were responsible for snuffing out a life before it had run its natural course. That was a crime.

This time when he looked through Gentry's correspondence file, Jack attached greater significance to one letter. Although there were more than a dozen letters addressed to different people in the lake area, they were all variations on a central theme. Jack took one for reference:

April 10, 1978

Cecil Hanrahan
Chairman, Camdenton County
    Board of Commissioners
1211 Main Street
Camdenton, Missouri 65020

Dear Cecil,
    As you know, I have long harbored a concern that the ecological balance of the lake area be preserved at some minimally acceptable level. I am talking about the relationship of man and his environment. Rather than tax your patience with many far-flung analogies such as the passing of the buffalo herds and the demise of Indian culture, simply let me say that when the lake bed is finally covered with three feet of beer cans, when all the fish have died from ingesting pull-top tabs, when the shoreline is entirely ringed with buildings so that it appears to be one long, continuous string of neon lights—then we will have lost something very valuable.
    Now there are those who say bluntly that I am an old fuddy-duddy who has made his money and wants to make the lake area an exclusive club by barring all future commercial or residential development. I also have been accused of being a carpetbagger of sorts, not having lived here all my life.

126

I hope you know that these are not the facts. Although I have been on the lake only since 1962, it has been the primary orientation of my life, and that of my family, since the late 1950s—nearly twenty years. In that time, I have pushed aggressively for two causes. One, as you know, was to lobby at the state level for the creation of an environmental protection agency with the authority to establish reasonable and acceptable standards for clean air and water. That goal was accomplished through the work and efforts of a great number of individuals, including yourself. I hope you will agree that the lake has benefited greatly from these regulations, while at the same time business ventures have in no way been unduly limited, nor have capital investments been subjected to unreasonable restrictions.

Similarly, I now respectfully call upon you to lend your considerable talent and the prestige of your office to a second campaign to benefit the lake area in which we work, live and play. That is the establishment of a multi-county zoning code to encompass all the lake area. Without question, there are few if any other areas in the state, or the Midwest, that lack zoning regulations given such a high density of homes and population.

While it is true that such development as has occurred to date has been accomplished with a high degree of common sense—often due to subtle, behind-the-scenes pressure and guidance by you and others—it is nevertheless true that anyone can build any structure anywhere on the lake with minimal restrictions and no prior review by responsible, locally elected or appointed officials. I submit that we have reached a point of development that demands such a review in the form of zoning restrictions. My opposition is not to development per se, but only development that is unwarranted and unwise. While this latter category encompasses environmental concerns, it should also relate to projects *socially or morally abhorrent*. I will be talking to you more about this subject in the near future.

I realize the problems of coordination that are presented due to the fact that there are three county boards involved. It is my intention to present to each board in the near future an identically worded resolution expressing the desirability of a multi-county zoning code, and advocating the appointment of an ad hoc task force to draft appropriate regulations.

Based on my experiences in board rooms, and my firsthand impressions of politics, I have no intention of moving to this point unless the votes are there. Accordingly, I plan to spend some time on the telephone in the coming weeks to test support for such a resolution.

I sincerely hope that you will be with me on this issue.

With deepest respect

Now Jack understood the telephone calls which Mrs. Lacy had overheard and characterized as argumentative. Some, perhaps, were instances in which Gentry ran into opposition to his proposal. Then there was the admitted telephone argument between Wallace and Gentry. Banuchi couldn't have helped knowing of Gentry's efforts, which must have caused the developer some concern. Gentry was not only refusing to sell his land, but he had proposed that all building on the lake be subject to closer scrutiny. Had Gentry been successful, he would have attempted to use zoning regulations as a tool to block Banuchi's hotel, wherever it was to be built. Clearly, Gentry must have been a thorn in Banuchi's side.

It took Jack a while to fathom the procedure Cousins had used for categorizing the checks. Finally, he determined that they were separated according to regular living expenses. Then there were the regular monthly checks to Alan and Barbara. Checks to a St. Louis bank had the notation "loan" in the memo space, and finally, there were checks Gentry wrote to a St. Louis stock and brokerage firm.

Jack looked over the summary statements from Gentry's local bank for the last six months. Regular monthly deposits of four thousand dollars had been made but there was no indication of the source of funds. As he thumbed through each pile more carefully, two checks immediately aroused his curiosity. One was fifteen hundred dollars to Mrs. Lacy; the other was eleven hundred thirty-two dollars and sixty-seven cents, made out to the Stoner Clinic in Columbia, Missouri.

Jack had wondered about the financial arrangement between Gentry and Mrs. Lacy, and this check was his first clue. Jack recalled that the granddaughter had been ill which might relate to the bill from the clinic in Columbia. Slim leads but the only new ones Jack had. He decided to check them out.

It was a slow day anyway, with Kate planning on going to dinner with a St. Louis couple after they looked at lake property all day. Besides, Jack had never been to Columbia.

On the outskirts of the university town, he filled the pickup with gasoline, retrieved a can of pop from the machine and dialed the Stoner Clinic from a phone booth. He said he wanted to inquire about the details of his bill and was switched to the business office. He told the woman who answered that his name was Geoffrey Gentry, and he felt relieved when that revelation didn't faze her. After giving her the number of the check that had been cashed by the clinic, he told her gruffly that the bill was unsatisfactory because it didn't break down the charges. In clipped tones she replied that eleven hundred thirty-two dollars and odd cents was the standard fee for a vacuum aspiration. What! he bellowed. For a minor operation. Jack didn't have the slightest idea what a vacuum aspiration was, and the clerk wouldn't tell him.

Jack drove until he spotted the student union on the university campus. He looked up Barbara Gentry's address in a student directory and then asked directions to the sorority house.

Jask presented the card he had taken weeks ago from Gentry's desk, but the house mother wasn't there. The girl answering the door indicated that he could talk to the "chairwoman of the house council." In the basement area, Jack waited to be introduced to Ms. Debbie Myers while she finished a spirited point at table tennis. A dozen other girls lounged about in the cool recreation room, reading, playing darts and listening to records. All but two were wearing the latest youth uniform—track shorts with colored trim and solid-colored T-shirts featuring a current slogan.

"What can I do for you?" Ms. Myers said. She was a tall, willowy blonde with thin lips.

"My name is Jack Olsen. I work for Roy Cousins, a lawyer in Camdenton, which is south of the Lake of the Ozarks."

"I know where it is," she said, lighting a cigarette. Several of the girls moved within listening range. Jack noticed that some looked at him warily, while others appeared amused. One seemed to be doing an inventory of his body.

"Mr. Cousins is executor of the estate of Geoffrey Gentry, who, as you may know, just died."

"We heard," Ms. Myers said. Jack thought he heard someone mumble the phrase "money bags."

"Mr. Cousins is trying to get the estate in order of course," Jack continued, "and I'm helping to catalog Mr. Gentry's financial obligations. Can you tell me if there's any outstanding debt for Barbara Gentry's room and board this year?"

"You could have written," she answered, "but since you're here, leave an address. The treasurer isn't here, but I'll have her send you a full accounting."

"Thanks. That'll help a lot. We can't pay any bills from the proceeds of the estate until we know who was owed. You understand."

"Sure, man," Ms. Myers said, blowing smoke in Jack's face.

"Nice house," he said, looking around the room. "I suppose Miss Gentry's bill will not include the month of May, since she was sick."

"No way," the blonde said emphatically. "Room and board's for the whole year, whether you stay or not."

Jack figured it was his turn to stare. After a few seconds, the blonde began to fidget nervously.

"No proration, huh?" he asked finally. "Not even for unexpected illness." He appeared forgetful. "Refresh my memory. What was Miss Gentry's problem?"

"I don't know," the blonde said.

Jack turned to the other girls, an exaggerated look of disbelief on his face. He raised his voice, tinging it with sarcasm. "Barbara Gentry lives here for eight months and has to leave suddenly and no one bothers to find out her problem. This is a sorority?"

" 'Pendix," someone said.

"What?" he shouted, cupping his ear.

"She had her appendix removed," Ms. Myers said coolly. "Thanks for dropping by, Mr. Olsen."

He sat in the pickup puffing on one of the few cigarettes he rationed himself. The trip had been worthless, the meeting with the sorority girls exasperating at best.

As he was about to start the engine, however, a pigtailed head wearing glasses thrust itself through the open window on the passenger's side.

"There's a park bench in front of Waters Hall, around the corner from the union." she said, pointing. "I'll meet you."

Three left turns and he was in front of the building. The girl was sitting on the bench. She didn't look at him at first, and he stood rather than sit down beside her. She had freckles and was plump, but still attractive.

"I don't particularly like being a snitch," she said finally. "But I don't like being quiet when lies are told, either. You see, that makes you part of the lie."

She looked at him for the first time, and he sat down beside her. "What's the lie?" he asked softly.

"It wasn't an appendectomy. It was an abortion."

"How do you know?" Jack asked suspiciously.

"She bragged about it. She's that kind. So are most of the rest of this group. At first I thought it was cool, and I tried to be one of them. But they had a party recently on the lake, and I wasn't about to do some of the things they did. That's when I knew I didn't belong."

"Was that the party on June fifth?"

"Yeah. How'd you know?"

"Barbara was there. With some guy named Hank."

She nodded. "Right. The party's another reason I know she didn't have an appendectomy. There's no way she could have hid a scar with what she had on."

"Is that what a vacuum aspiration is?" Jack asked, self-consciously. "An abortion?"

131

"Yes. The clinic specializes in them. No questions asked if you're in the first trimester of pregnancy. Whoosh, it's all gone."

"Why are you telling me this?"

She stabbed at her glasses, pushing them higher on the bridge of her nose. "Like I said, I don't like being part of a cover-up. Besides, you said you worked for the Gentry estate. Right?"

Jack nodded affirmatively.

"I met Mr. Gentry once when he came up for a family day. She snubbed him all evening, but he went around and talked to everyone. I thought he was real nice."

Jack remembered that Kate had felt the same way about the old man.

"You don't happen to remember what time Barbara got to the party on the lake?" Jack asked, more interested in Barbara's alibi.

"I remember exactly. They came at three-fifty-nine."

"How can you be so sure?"

"They marked down the time of everyone's arrival. Later, they drew several three digit numbers. If they matched the time of your arrival, you got to pick a slave who had to do as you asked. Hank picked me. Believe me, I remember what time they arrived."

Recalling the muscle-bound beach boy, Jack appreciated her discomfort. "Did you see them arrive? Did they come by boat?"

"I didn't see them arrive, but I did see their boat."

"Was it red and black with gray lightning stripes on the side? A very striking boat."

She thought for a moment. "No, I don't think that was the color. It was just a regular boat."

They sat without speaking for a while, and Jack was about to take his leave when she spoke. "She didn't have any idea who the father was. And she didn't care. That was bad enough. But what really got me was how much she enjoyed telling about Mr. Gentry's reaction."

Jack was amazed. "You mean she told him she was pregnant?"

"And that she was going to have an abortion, too. She said he cried and she thought that was the funniest thing in the world. The poor man."

It fitted Jack's image of Gentry. He had had high standards, had cared about what happened to people, the land and the things that lived and grew on it. Yes, he would have cried about wasted lives—both Barbara's and that of the innocent fetus.

SIXTEEN

The night of July Fourth, Kate and Jack went to Camdenton to watch a fireworks display. Two days had passed since Jack's trip to Columbia. In talking over the situation with Kate, it looked as though they had run up against roadblocks in trying to substantiate or disprove the alibis of all the principal suspects.

Jack's trip to Columbia confirmed the fact that Barbara Gentry hated her grandfather. He remembered her referring to her grandfather as a bastard. And she obviously tried to humiliate him publicly about the abortion. It seemed entirely possible, even likely, that Gentry had told his granddaughter that she would not receive her full inheritance until she demonstrated greater maturity and judgment.

But had she killed him? Her recorded time of arrival at the party seemed to preclude that possibility. Unless Jack was missing something. Perhaps she and her boyfriend, Hank, had killed the old man on the way to the party and somehow had doctored their time of arrival.

Tom Wallace's motive for killing Gentry was also outstanding. With Gentry out of the way, he might have expected that the heirs would be more receptive to selling the land for the proposed resort, hence making it possible for Wallace to reap a profit of close to a quarter of a million dollars. While Barbara's alibi was at least plausible, Kate had not been able to substantiate Wallace's.

Alan Gentry and Banuchi had already established alibis. Although Jack didn't believe Alan at all, he had unearthed no evidence to contradict the grandson's alibi. Also, Jack had failed so far to link Banuchi even indirectly to the killing. Jack had checked and Mrs. Lacy had been visiting the nursing home at the time Gentry was killed. He still couldn't dismiss her as a possible co-conspirator. He knew she had at least been talking to Banuchi.

Jack knew he had to dig deeper than just checking out alibis. He needed something to point the way. There was the boat; that would certainly do it if he could find it. Then there was the drug trail; Cousins was convinced it would illuminate everything.

Those would be his next two priorities, but first he wanted to follow up another lead that could sharpen the focus on Banuchi's motive. It involved Gentry's efforts to tie up the Banuchi hotel project anywhere on the lake through the use of zoning codes.

The day after the Fourth, Jack was in the business establishment of Cecil Hanrahan, chairman of the Camdenton County Board of Commissioners. Hanrahan was a pharmacist by trade and, along with his wife, owned and operated a local drug store. Jack leaned against a refrigerator behind the prescription counter as the businesslike pharmacist continued his work, straining to read ingredient labels through thick glasses.

"The resolution Mr. Gentry proposed," Jack asked, recalling the letter. "What happened to it?"

"It never came about," the pharmacist said briskly.

"Why?"

"Geoff didn't have time to work out the politics," he said, snapping the hem of his white smock so that it was as tight as a dress uniform.

"People were opposed?"

"Not necessarily," Hanrahan replied. "You see, the resolution that Gentry proposed had to be passed simultaneously by three county boards. That isn't easy."

"No, I suppose not," Jack agreed.

"Each board wanted something in return for passing the

135

resolution," Hanrahan continued. "That's the politics I was talking about. Geoff, though, might have managed enough trade-offs to please everyone."

"If he'd lived long enough," Jack finished.

Hanrahan shrugged. "Even if the resolution had passed, appointing the task force to draft zoning regulations would have been a doozy. Everyone for and against zoning would have wanted to be on it."

"Do you think zoning regulations can be adopted?"

The pharmacist divided a pile of pills and filled an amber-colored bottle. "Anything's possible," he said, "I doubt it now, though."

"Why?"

"Two reasons. First, folks down here like the free enterprise system. They want to buy and sell land for whatever purpose pleases them. I'm not sure I cotton much to a board of appointed bureaucrats telling us how we can use the land hereabouts. I sure wouldn't go for the politicians doing it. Second, too many people were beginning to think that the zoning idea was the result of a vendetta Geoff had against Banuchi. Seems like Geoff would have done anything to stop Banuchi's hotel. In fact, he told me that he planned to speak out publicly against the hotel."

"Do you know anything about the hotel Banuchi was to build?" Jack asked.

"Only what he's told me, and, frankly, it seems like a sound proposal. Wish I had the money to get in on it."

Maybe Cousins was right, Jack thought. Trying to block the hotel through zoning regulations would only have resulted in a war of words, unless Gentry could have proved his suspicions about gambling. And that would have been difficult to do before the fact. On the other hand, Butch Banuchi wasn't the type to savor a public debate that could generate questions and suspicions about the hotel. That could have been the final straw that made him decide to get rid of Gentry.

As he had done on several previous occasions, Jack was checking for concealed boathouses located between Sunrise Beach and Hurricane Deck, both on the lake and away from it. Alan Gentry lived in the area and hung out there. If he had killed his grandfather, Jack was certain that he

136

had launched the boat from the west shore and that it probably was still hidden there.

Standing beside his truck on a high point overlooking the lake, Jack used the binoculars to check out the only stretch of shoreline he had missed so far. On his map, he made several landmark notations for the covered boathouses. He planned to come back by water and check them with the hope that the lakeward doors would be open so that he could see inside. He wanted to avoid having to knock on an owner's door and ask to look inside the boathouse. He had been turned down a few times with that request, and his persistence once had nearly gotten him shot.

The search for the boat continued to prove futile, and Jack sat in his pickup outside the Stables, trying to work out his next move. He sensed that it was time to *do* something. He had discovered a cast of characters, all of whom appeared to have had reason enough to want Gentry dead. Now he needed to confront them, to break down the one alibi that was concocted; to get someone to confess would be the best he could hope for.

Just as Jack was working himself into a stew, Gentry emerged from the Stables, in the company of Tom Wallace. The lanky youth was staggered by the blazing July sun, and Wallace steered him to a shady area near the north end of the building. While Gentry leaned against the wall, frequently blowing his nose and occasionally scratching his scraggly hair, Wallace talked to him, gesturing with his hands. Jack watched as Gentry shrugged and ambled back inside the bar. Wallace stood with his hands on his hips, shaking his head as he watched Gentry retreat inside. Then Wallace started for his pickup. Except that he found Jack standing in his way.

"You're keeping bad company," Jack said.

"Why don't you go away, then," Wallace rejoined, flashing a mouthful of ivory.

"You hang out here often?" Jack asked, gesturing toward the bar.

"That's none of your business."

Jack's lip curled in a snarl as he hissed, "I'm making it my business, and you're going to answer my question."

Wallace moved sideways a step, and Jack half expected the taller man to take a swing at him.

"Let's get some things straight between us," Wallace said, squaring away in front of Jack. "You don't have any legal authority to hound me, Olsen. I figure the only reason you're bothering me is that you're afraid I'm going to take Kate away from you. And you got a right to be scared. She was mine before you came, and when she's tired of you, she'll come back to me."

Jack fought an urge to send a roundhouse right in search of a few of those beautiful teeth. "We'll see about that, pig farmer," he said instead. "Now let me lay a few facts on you. First off, Gentry was murdered, and I'm going to prove it. Second, you're a prime suspect in my book. You had a reason to want the old man dead."

"Hold it!" Wallace interrupted, clearly shaken.

"Hear the rest," Jack snarled, pushing the bigger man against his pickup. "With the old man gone you figured the dope addict in there would inherit the land. You figured Alan would be easy to deal with. But you didn't count on the old man's will, did you? You said yourself Banuchi is looking for another building site. I'd say you lost out all the way around, asshole."

"Wait a minute," Wallace said, ashen-faced. "I didn't kill Gentry."

Jack sneered. "You don't have a good alibi. Nothing but your word that you were fishing alone."

Wallace regained part of his composure. "You're wrong about that, Olsen. I got a witness who can place me near the state park at the time Gentry was killed."

It was Jack's turn to be surprised. "Who's that?"

"I don't have to tell you. I'm not a suspect. Nobody else believes Gentry was murdered except you."

"Suit yourself, buddy. But mark my words, I'm going to find out who did it. And you're near the top of my list. If you want to wait and tell a grand jury where you were that day, it's okay with me."

Jack measured the impact of his bluff on Wallace.

"You contact Bo Youngman. He knows where I was."

"It'd better be convincing," Jack said, "or you're still in trouble. Now, I want to know what you're doing here. This place deals in dope, and someday soon the shit'll hit the fan and it's going to splatter a lot of people."

"I wanted to see if Alan Gentry had talked to Mrs.

138

Lacy," Wallace mumbled, kicking at a rock with an over-sized cowboy boot.

"Why?"

"You heard the will. She could dissolve the trust any-time and give the estate to Gentry's grandkids."

"So you wanted to persuade Alan to go calling on the widow, hat in hand, telling her how he's turned over a new leaf and is now a good boy." Jack smiled broadly, enjoying Wallace's discomfort. "You want to sell that land of yours badly, don't you, pig farmer. Makes me wonder just what you would have done in the first place to get all that money."

For some time, Jack had wanted to look through Alan Gentry's cabin to see if he could find any clues that would lead him to the boat. It was more shack than cabin and looked as if it had been moved from its original location. It sat on a foundation of several strategically placed con-crete blocks. The effect was reminiscent of slum housing in the deep South. The siding had fallen off in several places, revealing holes punched in the black fiberboard sheathing.

Jack parked the pickup about a mile away. After dark, he walked in the direction of the rear of the shack by fol-lowing a corridor that had been cleared through the forest. Leaving this path, he walked about fifty yards through the forest and circled a small pond behind the house. He planned to either pick a lock or break a window to gain entry, but neither option proved necessary. The front door was unlocked. He entered and turned on the lights. The one-room house was a shambles. It smelled of human sweat. Two unmade beds lined one side of the room, a dirty couch and chair the other side. In the middle of the room stood an oil burning stove. There was no cooking stove, only a hotplate. The dilapidated refrigerator con-tained little other than beer.

It didn't take Jack long to go over the room. He looked for a boat license, ignition key, boathouse rental agreement; anything that might indicate the existence of a boat or its location. But there was nothing; neither did he turn up any evidence of drugs. The cabin was a veritable treasure house of trash, however. It was littered with discarded beer cans, lunch meat wrappers, rolled up potato chip packages and moldy containers of dip.

Jack was preparing to rip up the couch and bedding when he heard a car approaching and saw the headlights rake the house. It was too late to turn out the lights or get out the front door. He went to the window opposite the door, opened it and dropped silently to the ground. He could just barely see above the window sill. One of the men who entered the house was Spider. Jack also recognized the other man, but couldn't place him.

"Wanna beer, Aldo?" Jack heard the Spider ask.

"I don't like this," the other man said. "Where's Gentry? He's supposed to be here."

"Be cool, man. I told you I didn't know whether he'd be here or not."

"He wasn't at the Stables, he's not here. Where's he at?"

"Someplace, man."

"Look, Spider, the deal is that I deliver today, here, to Gentry. He doesn't show, he doesn't get the stuff. It's that simple."

"Leave it with me. I'll give it to Alan."

"That ain't the deal."

"Alan trusts me."

"I don't."

"Ah, man," the Spider moaned.

There was silence for a few moments, and Jack sneaked a look. The muscular, bull-necked man was tapping his fingers on a box. Suddenly Jack realized where he had seen him before. He was the man standing with Banuchi when Jack took their picture.

"Tell Gentry I'll be back with the stuff again tomorrow night."

"I wouldn't do that if I were you."

"Why?" he asked, seemingly amused at the threat.

"Alan told me he wanted the stuff tonight. *Needs* it. You dig? It ain't here when he gets here, he's going to come knocking on the big man's door. Right in the middle of the night."

A long silence prevailed before the man spoke. "Okay, I'll leave it. I've stayed a lot longer than I like to. Especially with a big delivery like this. It's got to last a while until things cool down. Also, in a few days we're going to send someone over to help you guys expand your market. Listen to him. He knows his stuff." He started to leave, then turned to face Spider. "If I find out you didn't hand

140

all this junk over to your pal, I'm going to make you some custom-fitted concrete boots and drop you off the dam. I'll pass the word on that Gentry is threatening to see the man. He won't like that."

Jack moved to the corner of the house and made a mental note of the license number of the departing car. If crooks were smart, they'd unscrew the bulbs that illuminate the license tag, he thought. Then Jack went to the front door and kicked it open.

Spider reacted faster than Jack had expected. He came at Jack like an orangutan, but Jack sidestepped the flaying arms and stunned him with a punishing chop to the temple. While Spider was still sprawled on the floor, Jack kicked him hard in the rib cage. A sharp scream followed the sound of crunching bone.

While Spider lay writhing on the floor, Jack looked through the box. It was a deep box, rectangular, with several compartments. Beside the box sat a large plastic trash bag full of marijuana, which Jack had missed seeing from his vantage point outside the window. Jack tried to calculate the street value of the various drugs. There were at least one thousand of the five milligram Valium tablets at a buck apiece, and an equal number of 'Ludes and acid for about five dollars a hit. He hefted the bag of grass, figuring it must weigh about twenty-five pounds, at sixty dollars an ounce. But the big money was in the plastic bags of white powder. There were two bags, holding about a pound each. Jack tasted them in turn. One was coke, at a hundred dollars or more a gram. The other bag contained angel dust, at about half the price of coke. Still an expensive way to kill yourself. The grab-bag assortment of blues, yellow jackets, purple hearts, bennies, black beauties and meth probably wasn't worth five hundred dollars. They'd be used as free sample, promotion, he knew. All in all, it had to be a hundred thousand dollars worth of dope.

Jack turned his attention to Spider, who was rolled into a ball on the floor, moaning. "This is a real expensive assortment, Spider, but Valentine's Day is already over. What do you and Gentry plan to do with all these goodies, you hairy ape." When Spider didn't respond, Jack gave him a nudge in the ribs with his shoe.

"Sonofabitch," Spider spat at him.

"Look at it this way, Spider. I got the goods on you.

141

Right? All I have to do is call the cops and you'll get put away for possession. Maybe twenty years with this much shit. But you tell me what you do with all this dope and I'll split without saying boo. And you get to keep the box."

Spider moved into a sitting position for a more appraising look at Jack. "Honest?" he asked, grimacing with pain.

"I'm your friend, Spider. Be nice to me and I'll be nice to you. Lie to me once and I'll stomp on your sore ribs."

Fear in his eyes, Spider shrugged with resignation. "We sell the stuff."

"At the Stables?"

"Yeah, mainly."

"Make a nice profit, huh?"

"Yeah."

"Who's the big man?"

"I dunno. I just know Aldo Rinaldi, the delivery man."

"C'mon, Spider. I heard you tell him that Gentry would call the big man if he didn't leave the stuff. So that means you know, too."

"Honest, I don't know the big man."

Jack sent Spider sprawling with a swift kick to the chest. Spider choked off the cry of pain to cast a plaintive look at Jack. He knew he had him.

"Just a name, Spider."

"They'll kill me."

"I'll find out anyway. Tell me or go to jail, where they'll get you for sure."

"Banuchi," Spider mumbled.

"That's a good boy, Spider. Now, one more thing. Gentry, he killed his grandfather. Right?"

Spider shook his head vigorously in a negative response.

"Spider, it's gonna hurt like hell when I bust your ribs on the other side."

"Honest to God, Olsen, I don't know anything about that," Spider pleaded. "I was stoned that day. Passed out in bed."

Spider heard the car first, as Jack was preparing to deliver another well-placed kick. The ugly creature struck up an awful caterwauling that could be heard clearly through the open door. Jack hesitated only a moment before deciding to look out the front window instead of silencing Spider. The headlights were blinding, but Jack

142

saw the silhouette of a man standing beside an open door. Jack went out the back window in a headfirst dive, tucking his neck under and executing a perfect roll that brought him up running toward the trees. The slugs tore into the ground behind him and at his side. One plopped into the water as he raced around the pond, seeking the safety of the trees. From the sound of the gunfire, it was a .38, and whoever was shooting was taking deliberate aim. Luckily for Jack, the gunman was a poor shot.

Back at Kate's cabin, Jack went through duplicates of the pictures he had taken at Banuchi's. The drug salesman, Aldo Rinaldi, was the man standing beside Banuchi on the dock. Jack whistled, pleased. Then he spent the rest of the night sitting in the dark, near a window. In his lap lay the army-issue Colt .45 he had bought in Germany. He checked the magazine and pressed it back into the butt until he heard it click. He took some small comfort in the way the grip safety fitted snugly over the web between his thumb and forefinger.

SEVENTEEN

Cousins had been right about the drugs. The trail was clearer now, and it led directly to Banuchi. But Jack knew these new facts wouldn't be much consolation to Cousins; the old lawyer had died in the middle of the night. Whoever had killed Cousins had eliminated a determined foe of the Banuchi hotel, and a man who knew too much about Gentry's death. Also, Gentry's trust was one step closer to being dissolved, which would benefit the grandchildren, and perhaps others as well.

Jack felt low about Cousins's death. He had known the man only a month, yet he felt as if he'd lost his father. Cousins had been a man of grace, of wit, and of knowledge who was not overbearing. Jack was certain the old lawyer always had known the difference between right and wrong and had fought for his principles until the day he'd died. But most of all, Jack had liked the old man because Cousins had believed in him; he had seen hope for Jack at the very time Jack had needed an encouraging pat on the back.

Jack wasn't feeling totally good about himself. He explained to Kate, "I feel as if I were back in Chicago again. Every time I deal with scum, it brings out the meanness in me. Take Spider, for example. That was a nasty thing

I did to him, but I could just as easily have killed him, and it wouldn't have mattered to me then. That's what makes me feel bad when I think about it—that I can get so carried away by hate that even a human life doesn't mean anything to me."

"You're too sensitive, Jack," Kate said sympathetically. "Sometimes I can't understand how you could be a cop for ten years, and then I can understand why you had to quit. Just remember that Spider would have done the same or worse to you. It's natural to feel murderous toward his kind. Don't be so hard on yourself."

He knew her advice was reasonable, but he also knew he could be a chameleon. He reflected the environment in which he lived. He didn't have the strength of character to rise above it, to reform it, as did Kate and Cousins and Gentry. If he was going to be gentle, reasonable and understanding, he had to live that way. It was at that moment Jack knew finally, with certainty, that he could never go back to Chicago and his old way of life. He would have to start over and find something useful to do. Suddenly he wanted very much to be done with the Gentry case.

Jack received a response in the mail from Chicago regarding the pictures he had taken and his inquiry about Banuchi's companion in the St. Louis architect's office. On the latter score, he drew a complete blank. The man who called himself Jacoby had effectively masked his real identity.

But the pictures were a different story, according to Detective Lieutenant Grabowski. Banuchi's picture matched one on file in the police department's archives. The process of identifying Banuchi would have been very difficult, Grabowski said, if it had been necessary to sort through the mug shots by hand. But the name had rung a bell with the narcotics detective, and it turned out that there was a file on Banuchi, although it was not active.

Banuchi was a hometown Chicago boy, Grabowski wrote, who had graduated from the Loyola University School of Law in 1956. He had known connections with organized crime and for many years had been a fixture in court on behalf of mobsters charged with various crimes. He was known to be involved in the management of property owned by high-ranking Mafia chieftains, and several informants said Banuchi was being groomed for greater involvement in organized crime's nationwide investments, principally resort hotels. But then, inexplicably, Banuchi had dropped from sight about three years ago. Grabowski said there was no indication that anyone knew his whereabouts until Jack's inquiry. On the other hand, there was no reason for anyone to go looking for Banuchi. His record was totally clean, not even marred by a speeding ticket.

Grabowski said a blank was drawn on all the other pictures sent by Jack, except for one. He was Vincent Margossi—Mafia soldier, bodyguard, hit man. His rap sheet was as long as his arm. Margossi had served time twice, once for manslaughter and once when busted as a connection in the numbers racket. Currently, though, he was not on anyone's wanted list. Grabowski said Margossi had dropped from sight about a year ago and it had been expected that he would surface eventually in New York or LA—wherever they needed a fresh face for a dirty job. Jack knew Margossi as Aldo Rinaldi, the man who worked for Banuchi and delivered drugs to Gentry. He could nail that down for certain by tracing the license number of the car that had brought Spider home last night.

Grabowski concluded his letter by expressing interest in knowing more about the connection Jack had turned up, if only to update police files. He signed off after using both the carrot and stick approach, telling Jack that he would be doing a great service to the department by providing more information, and also reminding Jack that it would be a plus on his record when he sought reinstatement. Or a negative, Jack read between the lines. But he didn't have any qualms about filling in the Chicago police about Banuchi—whenever he knew the full story.

"Kate, help me sort this out, will you?"

"Sure, I'll play Dr. Watson."

"I see a man get killed in what looks like a boating accident."

"Except for the deliberate attempt to hit Gentry with the oar, which is probably what killed him."

Jack nodded vigorously in agreement. "Mrs. Lacy wants me to investigate Gentry's death. She thinks it was an accident, or at least acts as if that's what she believes. But then she throws in several qualifying factors. Gentry

146

had arguments on the telephone with unnamed persons, although she does identify Tom Wallace. She says she *thinks* Gentry changed his will. Then she turns up as trustee of the estate and soon after goes on a trip. Then there's the matter of the fifteen hundred dollar check. Was Gentry paying her such amounts regularly?"

"Jack, it's incredible that you could suspect Beth," Kate said in open-mouthed astonishment. "If she was involved in Gentry's death, all she had to do was keep quiet and everyone would have chalked it up as an accident. She didn't have to hire you."

Jack wagged his finger in a cautionary gesture. "But she knew that Cousins was suspicious, and that she would have to do something to show concern."

"Maybe she brought you in on the case because she thought you were too dumb to solve it." She laughed.

"The thought occurred to me," he answered wryly. "But what if she was blackmailing Gentry for fifteen hundred a month, or a week, and she forced him to change his will. Then had someone kill him."

"Blackmail him with what?"

"Gentry could have killed Eldon Lacy, or he and Beth Lacy could have done it together."

Kate bobbed her head in confusion. "But why would she then kill Gentry? Beth doesn't benefit from the will."

"Maybe Gentry was fed up with blackmail," Jack replied grimly. "Or maybe he was having attacks of conscience and was going to tell the real story of how Eldon Lacy died. Either way, she would have wanted to shut him up. Maybe she figured if she was in charge of a multimillion dollar trust, there would be some way to dip into the proceeds."

"Jack, that is an incredible hypothesis."

He shrugged. "Stranger things have happened. But let's go on. It turns out that Gentry did change his will and put his grandkids on a tight leash. That was motive enough for Barbara to kill him if she knew beforehand, and he may have told her when she sprang the abortion thing on him."

"But she seems to have an airtight alibi."

Jack frowned, begrudging the apparent fact. "Then there's Alan, and that's where things get complicated. Alan

147

admits he fought with his grandfather. The old man knew Alan was on drugs. Again, he might have told the kid he wasn't going to get all that money. Alan kills him, thinking that will take care of the problem. I'll bet we'll find out that Alan's alibi is full of holes." He paused, adding, "That's the money motive. Mrs. Lacy or the grandkids could have killed Gentry for his money. If that's the case, then only Mrs. Lacy benefited from his death."

"But all she gets is a fee as trustee," Kate protested.

Jack nodded knowingly. "I looked into that. Do you know what that fee could amount to? As much as thirty-five thousand dollars a year."

Kate was stunned momentarily. "Still, Alan and Barbara's motives seem stronger to me, whether or not they knew about the changes in the will. Besides, if Beth killed Gentry, who drove the boat?"

"How in the hell should I know," Jack answered and they both dissolved in laughter.

"Then there's the hotel motive," Kate said, picking up on Jack's line of thought.

"Right. We were lucky enough to figure that out, like Gentry. And our impressions are the same as his."

"Gentry was doing everything he could to prevent Banuchi from being able to build the hotel, not just on Gentry's land, but anywhere on the lake. So Banuchi gets rid of him."

"No, that would have been Margossi, Rinaldi, whatever his name," Jack said. "He's got the experience. And it is curious that Banuchi just happed to have such an iron-clad alibi that day, such as an afternoon meeting with the sheriff. Makes you wonder if he didn't plan it that way."

"If Banuchi did have Gentry killed, he isn't as cool as everyone thinks," Kate added. "He knew that a public shouting match with Gentry could make other people curious about the hotel. Besides, he might be under pressure from Chicago. Maybe the hotel's the real reason he was sent down here."

"That's a good point," Jack agreed.

"Maybe I should be Sherlock Holmes."

"Let's not forget Wallace," Jack continued. "He had a real strong motive for killing Gentry. Banuchi could build the hotel anywhere, despite his obvious preference

148

for Gentry's land. But for Wallace to profit, the hotel had to be built on his and Gentry's adjacent land. So Wallace kills Gentry, hoping the land will pass on to Alan and Barbara, who he figures he can deal with. In fact, the case becomes interesting here. Suppose Wallace and Alan Gentry plot the old man's death for their mutual gain."

"Have you checked with Bo Youngman yet to see if Tom's alibi holds up?" Kate asked.

"No, I didn't have time."

"Bo's a pretty straight guy. I'd say his word's good."

Jack was irritated at what seemed to be Kate's attempt to absolve Wallace. But he let it pass, asking her if she would check with Youngman.

"Then, there's the possibility of a Banuchi/Alan Gentry conspiracy to kill the old man," Jack continued. "There's the drug connection to further strengthen that bond. Or it could have been Banuchi and Wallace. All three of them, maybe."

"Old man Gentry didn't stand a chance," Kate said sarcastically.

"But I'm not sure I understand the drug thing," Jack said, frowning. "Banuchi's big angle is the hotel. Why risk that by dabbling in drugs, which could bring state or even federal cops down here? Especially when he's dealing with someone as flaky as Alan Gentry."

"What if the drugs are related to the hotel?" Kate asked.

"Sure they are. They'll sell them there, too."

"Maybe selling them now at the Stables is a test."

"A test. Of what?"

"A test to see what kind of opposition they were going to run into, so they could plan how to deal with it before the hotel was operating."

"Mel Davis!" Jack exclaimed. "He's the reason for the test. They had to see if they could buy him off on this issue. If they could, Davis would be a cinch to turn his head to the gambling. I remember what Cousins said about Davis having bigger political ambitions, and how Banuchi and his crowd would need to control some votes in Jeff City. Davis is a natural for that job, and he could handpick his successor as sheriff."

Kate came and sat on his lap, gently sticking her finger in his ear. "Now you got all the suspects weeded out, and

149

their motives. It's just you against the murderers, the mob, or both. What the hell are you going to do now, Jack?"

The burly sheriff rolled his head slowly in a circle as he stared past Jack at the activity in the hallway outside his office. Davis had made Jack wait at the front entrance for more than an hour before seeing him.

"I been getting a few complaints about you, Olsen," Davis said, chewing his gum slowly, like a cud. "You been around talking to a lot of people, making them uncomfortable."

"Who's complained?" Jack pressed.

"Oh, nothing official. Yet. But there was a man over around Hurricane Deck who turned you away from his house once and then had a prowler later."

"He say I was the prowler?"

"No, but he's suspicious, and so am I. You don't have any business on other people's private property. In fact, Olsen, you really don't have any business being an investigator."

"How's that?"

Davis, looking out the door, replied, "The first time you were here and told me Mrs. Lacy hired you, I didn't think much of it. But since that time, I been reading some in the state statutes. You hire out as a private investigator, you need to be licensed by the state. Being an ex-cop don't count, fellow. So, you see, you're breaking the law."

Jack matched stares with Davis for a few moments before replying. "Let's get back to that point later. First, can you tell me what progress you're making on the Gentry case?"

"We're still looking for the boat. I told you it might be hard to find."

"So you're making no progress at all."

Davis shrugged noncommittally.

"Sheriff, the last time I was here, I heard you say how crime was down in the county." Jack smiled. "Is that so?"

Davis concentrated, trying to fathom the change of direction, and then said, with no little pride, "Certainly it's so. Every category of crime is down since I took office, but especially burglary and assault."

"What's your secret?" Jack asked, playing to the sheriff's

150

ego, an approach that had proved successful during their first visit.

"I got the citizens helping me, reporting things. And I don't take no shit. I know all the bad boys around here and every now and then I pay them a visit. Let them know that if they start any fights in the local bars, or damage anybody's property while they're horsing around, I'll pull them in and crack their skulls."

"Do you read them their rights first?" Jack asked good-naturedly.

"Hell, yes. Right before I start doing a drum roll on their heads with my stick."

"What about the tourists that flood down here? It must be a real tough job policing them. I imagine they cause some trouble now and then."

"Yeah," Davis drawled, warming to the conversation. "Mostly, it's family squabbles, believe it or not. A man and his wife come down here to relax, go on a toot and get in a helluva fight. We don't drag them in or nothing. I just give them a little speech where I scare the hell out of them about what I'm going to do the next time. That usually takes care of it."

"I imagine some of the younger kids who come down here on vacation smoke a little grass, pop a few pills?" Jack watched Davis's reaction carefully, but the sheriff seemed wrapped up in a good yarn.

"We have some fun with those college boys who get stoned and then get too loud. We bend their fingers back a little bit and throw them in the cooler overnight. County attorney doesn't want to mess around with them if they only got a little stuff on them. But if we find a lot of grass, for example, or we think someone is selling the stuff, we prosecute the hell out of them."

"Sounds like a good record you're building up, sheriff. Seems like you ought to get re-elected pretty easy this fall."

"I think so," the sheriff replied, his attention again meandering to the activity outside his office.

"Ever think about running for state office?" Jack asked innocently.

"This'll be my third term coming up this fall," Davis replied confidently. "I got some good people working for me who can take over. There have been some folks urging me to think about being a state representative."

151

"But you don't have any local drug problem," Jack said, throwing the sheriff for a loop.

"No," Davis said, his eyes narrowing. He clearly didn't like Jack's interruption of his daydream about his political future.

"That's a lie," Jack said.

"Nobody calls me a liar," Davis snarled, standing.

"Sit down, you big prick," Jack said calmly, "and I'll tell you why I can call you a liar and get away with it. I'll also tell you why you're not going to arrest me because I don't have an investigator's license. Finally, I'm going to tell you why you're going to do exactly as I say in the future."

Davis sat down, his face black with rage. "Make it good, stumblebum. I need a laugh. When you're done, I'm going to pitch you out on your ass."

"First, sheriff, I'm the only one who's really investigating Gentry's murder."

"Ain't no murder," Davis said derisively.

"Actually, there are two murders now," Jack said evenly. "Gentry and Cousins. I'm going to prove it in both cases." Jack stood up and shut the door. "You won't take me off the case because I don't have a license. You do and I'll start talking to the state police. One thing I'll tell them is that drugs are being sold at the Stables and that you're turning your head to it."

"That's a lie," Davis said, clinching his fists.

"No, it's not. I figure you're being paid off and that the IRS boys can find the money someplace. A savings account. Safe-deposit box. Maybe you've been making some investments lately, sheriff? There's no way you can hide the money trail."

Davis turned pale, and Jack knew he had a captive audience.

"I know where the drugs come from and who owns you, Davis. Maybe even who owns the Stables. They're one and the same man. I have a feeling that I know something about the man that you don't. He's got mob connections in Chicago."

Davis's jaw fell. Cousins had been right again. The sheriff was on the take but he didn't know the full story.

"I could make one phone call and you'd have under-cover cops swarming all over this place," Jack continued.

"They'd love to know what Banuchi is up to. They'd probably have a few questions for you, too. By the way, what about Banuchi's alibi for the time Gentry was killed?"

"We were having a drink together," Davis protested. "Honest."

"How convenient," Jack said, as he lit a cigarette and blew smoke at Davis. "So far you're guilty of accepting a bribe, Davis. I'm going to give you a chance to do something to wipe out that debt. Okay?"

"Such as?" the sheriff asked, in a low but even voice.

"You find the boat that was used to kill Gentry, and the car that ran down Cousins. You've got the manpower to do it."

"We're doing those things already," Davis protested. "Both the boat and the car could be a thousand miles away by now."

"The boat's here," Jack replied. "I have a feeling. Second, you close down the Stables, cut off the drug traffic and pin the rap on Banuchi."

"That won't be possible," Davis replied, matter-of-factly.

"Try hard. Rinaldi is the name of a guy who works for Banuchi. I'm sure you know him. I want him in one of your cells right away. Any charge will do, but plant some drugs on him if you have to. Don't arrest Alan Gentry, but keep a close eye on him. Keep me filled in at all times. In fact, you have someone put a two-way radio in my pickup today. And don't bother telling me it's against the law."

"If I do all this?" Davis asked warily.

"Then, I'll let you resign," Jack answered, as he stood up and walked out the door. A chill ran down Jack's spine as he felt Davis watching him walk down the hallway. He realized that if he were dead, all of Davis's problems would be solved. He wondered how many other people had the same thoughts.

EIGHTEEN

After the funeral service for Roy Cousins, while everyone was waiting outside the church for the pallbearers, Mrs. Lacy approached Jack and asked if he would come to her home after lunch. Jack had been surprised to see Alan and Barbara Gentry at Cousins's funeral, and was even more so to find them seated on the sofa in Mrs. Lacy's living room. Alan alternated between blowing his nose and running a finger around the collar of an uncomfortable dress shirt. This time he wore a conventional tie. Jack wondered if it was Alan who had tried to shoot him, but the scrawny youth acted as if he'd never met Jack. Barbara, wearing a sexy black dress, was in a prim and proper mood.

Jack agreed to the offer of lemonade, but was disappointed to find that the glass curio stand was empty. The brightly painted figurines that he had come to associate with the house were gone.

Mrs. Lacy supplied the answer. "I spent all of yesterday packing them. It's part of the reason I asked you over."

"Looks like you're getting ready to move," Jack offered, standing in the middle of the room, facing the others.

"Yes. During my recent visit in New York State, I renewed a friendship with my cousin. We were very close when we were young and now we find that we still have much in common. We're both alone, for one thing. We like to do the same things. It makes a lot of sense for us to be with each other."

Jack wondered if the cousin was a man or a woman.

"We could live here, of course, but truthfully I'd like to leave the lake area. There are too many painful memories here. I'm not really interested in fishing or boating. And I miss some of the opportunities and conveniences of the city. We may locate so we're within driving distance of New York City." Mrs. Lacy smiled.

"That's not why you asked me to lemonade, Mrs. Lacy," Jack said. "What you want to talk about has something to do with these well-scrubbed children." Barbara was amused by Jack's remark, while Alan looked grim, slouching farther into the sofa.

"Yes, it does, Jack," she said, purposefully smoothing the pleats of her white dress. "I have decided to dissolve the trust as soon as the will is fully probated."

"What prompts this decision, if I may ask?"

"Much soul-searching, I assure you, Jack. In one sense, it's a selfish decision. The time I have left in life I would like to enjoy. The job of managing the trust, I'm certain, would be time-consuming and nerve-wracking. I'm not up to it either physically or mentally. With Roy dead, I find myself in the position of sole judge of Alan and Barbara. I don't like that, either. I could be strict and uncompromising and they would still inherit the estate someday. Or I can give them their just due now and ask them to accept the challenge of managing their grandfather's estate with maturity and judgment. After all, if they fail to act wisely, they hurt only themselves. After talking to both Alan and Barbara, I feel they will put forth their best efforts, and that is all I can ever really hope for, isn't it, Jack?"

Jack stood in the middle of the room, rocking on the balls of his feet. He couldn't help but smirk as he looked at Alan, sniffling into his handkerchief, a nervous tic rippling across his cheek. "Who initiated the discussions that led to this decision?" Jack asked.

"Barbara called," Mrs. Lacy said, "but I had been thinking of talking to both of them."

"What was said that convinced you, Mrs. Lacy?"

Before the widow could respond, Barbara interrupted,

155

"I'd like to speak for myself, Mr. Olsen. Grandfather and I had disagreements, as do all children and their parents. And, in fact, he acted as my father for most of my life. Many of my habits that he disliked I have also realized are not in my best interests. I have finished five semesters of college, studying to be a nurse. I believe that is a sign of responsibility. I believe I have changed and matured in recent years. I don't pretend to know enough to manage my grandfather's estate, but I can employ those who have the necessary knowledge and skills—the same people, in fact, who would advise Mrs. Lacy. That will give me a chance to learn and prepare for the day when I can wisely use this money for the benefit of myself and others."

Perfect, Jack thought. Barbie had snowed the socks off the old lady. But the performance didn't quite fit the image he had formed; nor did it match the sentiments she had expressed to him and others about her grandfather.

"Let's hear your speech now, Alan," Jack said.

The lanky youth seemed to struggle into an awareness of the conversation. "Like Barb said, man, we'll get good people to manage our . . . our money. And we'll work hard to learn."

It was short, but Jack didn't think that Alan could memorize too many words. Why couldn't the widow see it clearly? Or did she know the situation only too well? Something had happened to change her mind, he thought, recalling their first discussion about dissolving the trust. He couldn't believe it was anything so simple as a change of heart. Had they threatened her?

"Why tell me all this, Mrs. Lacy?" Jack asked. "There's nothing I can do to change your decision."

The widow smiled affectionately at him. "The last time I saw Roy Cousins, I told him what I planned to do."

"What did he say?"

"He was tired, as you know, and couldn't talk at length. He did give me a letter for you," she said, handing it over, "and asked that I trust your judgment. That's why I wanted you to know my plans. If you can give me any good reasons not to dissolve the trust, I'll listen."

Jack was never certain whether the widow was just a nice but naive old lady, or a very shrewd one. She might have surmised that he didn't have anything solid on the grandchildren, or he would have sprung it by now. Was she deliberately putting him on the spot? Then, if he couldn't produce, she could tell him there was no further need of his services. If he was about to be fired, Jack intended to make several people uncomfortable before he left.

"Tell me, Barbara, who would you consult about managing your inheritance?"

She pounced on the question with a ready answer. "As you know, Mr. Olsen, grandfather named several financial advisers in his will. Naturally, I'd follow their advice."

"Naturally," Jack parroted. "And what about Butch Banuchi. Would you seek his advice?"

Barbara's eyes darted to Mrs. Lacy, a cue Jack picked up quickly. "Yes, Mrs. Lacy, I know you talked to Banuchi. Did he give you the idea for dissolving the trust?"

"We didn't talk about the trust at all, Jack," Mrs. Lacy replied serenely. "Mr. Banuchi asked to see me for the purpose of explaining the details of the disagreement between him and Geoff over a new resort hotel on the lake. He said he knew I was concerned about Geoff's death because I had hired you. He said he wanted to be open about the hotel, and he was. Truthfully, I thought he made a good case. I can't say honestly that I would have taken Geoff's side on this issue."

Another snow job, Jack thought, remembering ruefully how convincing Banuchi could be. Either Gentry hadn't filled Mrs. Lacy in about Banuchi, or she was lying.

"According to the will, you share equally in the estate," Jack said to Alan and Barbara, "which I presume means fifty percent of all property. What do you intend to do with the land Banuchi wanted to buy from your grandfather?"

Barbara cleared her voice and said, "If Mr. Banuchi is still interested in the property, I would be willing to sell him the land provided Alan and I have veto power over any aspect of construction which is environmentally unsound."

She looked at Alan, who took several seconds to remember his part. "Yeah, I'd sell, too, under those conditions."

"You've both had health problems recently, haven't you?" Jack asked, startling them with the question.

"Yes, I was sick earlier in the spring," Barbara replied questioningly.

157

"Appendectomy, huh?" Jack sneered. "Amazing how good the doctors are these days. I didn't even notice the scar."

Barbara pursed her lips, looking like a cornered animal. Jack knew it was in her interest to preserve the fiction of the appendectomy, especially around Mrs. Lacy. But, again, the nagging question: was he to believe that Gentry had never told Mrs. Lacy about the abortion? What kind of relationship did they have?

"You've got a nasty cold there, Alan," Jack continued. "Seem to have it all the time, don't you?"

"Hay fever."

"Sure. Then you'll be happy to know that the source of your little sniffle is about to be shut off."

Jack watched as Alan's face successively reflected incomprehension, horrible realization and, then, fear.

It was Barbara who broke the trance. "We have to go," she said, literally dragging Alan after her.

"Lovely couple," Jack said, watching them through the triangle of glass that made up the lakeward side of the house.

"I know you have doubts about them, Jack, although I didn't understand the meaning of all your remarks," Mrs. Lacy said, taking his arm and leading him to the sofa. She motioned for him to sit beside her. "But give them the benefit of the doubt. It always pays off."

Doubts, he thought. He *knew* what they were.

"Jack, Roy Cousins said you have worked diligently to see that Geoff's killers are brought to justice. I appreciate that. Before you leave, I intend to pay you in full for all your time up to this minute."

"My final paycheck, huh?"

"Yes, Jack, and it may be for the best. I can't afford to continue to pay your fee. Also, I may have been unfair to Sheriff Davis. I don't have any real reason to believe that he won't do a good job. In my bitterness at losing Geoff, I became suspicious. Too suspicious, in fact. I still want the man responsible for his death to be found, but it really won't bring Geoff back, will it?"

She waited eagerly for his reply, and Jack didn't disappoint her. "Mrs. Lacy, in the course of this investigation, I've come to know and like Mr. Gentry."

158

"I knew you would, Jack," she said, laying a hand on his arm.

"I liked and respected Roy Cousins, too. We were in agreement about several things that will keep me on this case whether I'm paid or not."

"What things?"

"I had a feeling from the beginning that Mr. Gentry *might* have been killed on purpose. I told you that. As a result of my investigation, that suspicion has turned into conviction. As far as I'm concerned, Mr. Gentry was deliberately murdered."

She flinched at the word, but said nothing. He couldn't help but wonder if she was surprised that it was murder, or that he knew about it.

"Mrs. Lacy, have Alan and Barbara agreed to make a lump-sum payment to you for your services as trustee?"

He waited while she took a tissue from her purse and blew her nose. "I don't understand, Jack."

"Will you continue to receive money from Alan and Barbara after the trust is dissolved?"

"They suggested two thousand dollars a month and I told them that was really more than I needed." She said it matter-of-factly, Jack thought, as if it were her just reward. Two thousand a month wasn't as much as she could make as trustee. But it gets her off the hot seat, he thought. Whatever her role in Gentry's death, if any, Beth Lacy might wonder if she was next after Roy Cousins.

Jack continued to press the money issue. "Why did Mr. Gentry write you a check in May for fifteen hundred dollars? Did you regularly receive such amounts from him?"

"Oh, goodness no, not regularly. The fifteen hundred dollars was for the trip I just took. I had been planning it for some time and Geoff wanted me to stay someplace fancy, see the city with my cousin Martha, buy new clothes. Jack, who killed Geoff?"

The question came out of the blue. "I don't know," Jack answered. "Yet. But I'm not ruling out anyone." He remembered Cousins's admonition not to overlook anyone. "Mrs. Lacy, how many times have you met with Banuchi since I was hired?"

"Only the one time, Jack, when we talked about the hotel and development on the lake in general."

159

"You're certain? You haven't been consulting with him regularly?"

"Jack, I wouldn't lie," she replied, fixing him with an unflinching gaze.

"Tom Wallace. You mentioned his name to me once. Have you talked to him since Mr. Gentry died?"

She hesitated. "Tom brings me some wild berries occasionally, and other things from the garden. His mother gathers them. Yes, I think we've talked recently."

It had to concern the land, the hotel. Wallace wouldn't let that opportunity go by. "What did you talk about?" Jack asked. "The resort that Banuchi mentioned?"

"No," Mrs. Lacy said deliberately. "It was just small talk, Jack."

"He didn't urge you to dissolve the trust?"

"No."

"You're lying to me, Mrs. Lacy!" he thundered suddenly. "About this and God knows what else."

"No," she repeated calmly, a forced smile on her face.

"Mrs. Lacy, I can't have you dissolving the trust now," he pleaded. "It might prevent me from ever finding the people who killed Mr. Gentry and then ran down Roy Cousins."

"But you never told me about Roy," she protested. "Why would anyone kill him?"

"Because he knew too much. I might mention I've been shot at three different times so far."

The widow cradled her head in her hands, swaying slightly from side to side. "It's all so confusing. So unbelievable." She paused, then replied in a tremulous voice, "But this can't have anything to do with letting Alan and Barbara have their inheritance."

Jack was frustrated, angry. How could he stop her? It was critically important, after all, that she not hand over all the trump cards to everyone involved in the case. "Mrs. Lacy, if you dissolve the trust and try to leave the area, I'll somehow force a second autopsy on your husband's body—"

"Get out!" she interjected, before he could say ". . . to find out how he really died."

"You didn't," Kate asked, pleading for him to say it wasn't true.

160

"I had to stop her."

"Maybe you're right, Jack. You stoop too low, some-times." For the first time since he'd known her, Kate was disgusted with him. He felt a sense of panic clutch at his chest. Would it happen again, just as it had with his wife a thousand years ago?

"You have to admit that what she wants to do, dissolve the trust a month after Gentry died, is more than a little suspicious," he replied defensively. "If I let her do that, everyone who's involved in this case gets what he or she wants—Alan and Barbara, Banuchi, Wallace and Mrs. Lacy. Banuchi would get the sheriff back on his side, and they'd take care of me. Don't you see, Kate? What she was going to do was hand them the ballgame. Give the killers of Gentry and Cousins a clear road home."

Kate sat in a chair, her chin in her hands, shaking her head in bewilderment. "This started out like a game. We were snooping around asking questions, trying to catch a couple of scared kids or drunks. At least that's what I thought. Now the Mafia may be involved. Drugs. You fighting with Spider. Getting shot at. Blackmailing the sher-iff and Beth Lacy. It's just too much, Jack."

Jack sat down, too helpless to respond. That's when he felt the letter in his back pocket, the one from Cousins that Mrs. Lacy had given him.

It was a feeble scrawl, written the day Mrs. Lacy had visited the hospital before traveling to the East Coast. Cousins wrote that he anticipated Jack's response to her leaving, especially after hearing from Beth that she had talked to Banuchi and Barbara and was considering dis-solving the trust.

"But I doubt that Beth is our murderer or even co-conspirator," Cousins wrote. "Geoff was an astute judge of character and he entrusted his estate to Beth because of her honesty and decency, for he sensed, as you have come to learn, that he was surrounded by those who were neither honest nor respectful of human life and property. While it may seem incredible to you that Geoff never told Beth of his suspicions, he believed he was protecting her by *not* telling her these things.

"Jack, I want you to show this letter to Beth. Beth, please do what Jack asks. He is to be trusted totally. He knows more than both of us about the circumstances surrounding Geoff's murder, and he can bring the killers to bay somehow. Beth, beware of Banuchi, for he is a lion in sheep's clothing. Don't take advice from Tom Wallace. Finally, don't give Alan and Barbara the benefit of the doubt at this time.

"Jack, be careful, for your life is in danger, as I'm certain you know. When the money stakes are this big, men will kill without hesitation. I advise you strongly to see that the facts of this case are put into writing and committed to safekeeping. This can be an insurance policy on your life.

"Finally, Jack, steel yourself to see this case through to the end. Hold your breath against the stench that is involved. Rid our lake of this cancer before it grows beyond control. Do it not as a crusade against crime, but out of concern for this area and for the people you have come to love and who love you."

Kate broke the silence by asking, "What was in the letter?"

"It was from Cousins. Some last advice."

"What are you going to do now, Jack?"

"Keep stumbling forward," he said grimly. The letter, like a voice from the grave, had upset him. But it also gave him strength, confidence and an unyielding determination to get to the bottom of the case.

"Jack, I contacted Bo Youngman. He can verify Tom's alibi."

"Spider can verify Alan's alibi," Jack said sarcastically.

"Jack, Tom Wallace isn't the type," she pleaded. "He didn't do it."

"Like Cousins said, when the money is big enough, morality goes out the window. What about you, Kate? Would a quarter of a million dollars turn your head?"

That made it twice in one day he was kicked out of a house by a woman.

NINETEEN

Jack was consistent, if nothing else. The only person he had failed to confront was Banuchi. Therefore, the next morning he was in the mobile home-office. This time he accepted a cigar.

"I just checked the license numbers of the cars in your parking lot," Jack said, blowing two perfect smoke rings. "One of your employees, a Vincent Margossi, is a drug pusher. But then you already know that."

"What an outrageous accusation," Banuchi said, chuckling. His eyes bulged slightly, however, and Jack noted that as a signal of concerned awareness. "In fact, I don't even have anyone by that name working for me," Banuchi added.

"He calls himself Aldo Rinaldi down here, but he was Vincent Margossi in Chicago," Jack said, throwing the picture on Banuchi's desk.

Banuchi examined the picture carefully. "A friend told me you were taking pictures of me and my employees. You should have said something. I would have waved, or at least smiled. What do you think of that suit?"

"The Chicago police department not only identified Margossi, they have a fat file on you," Jack continued. "You didn't tell me you used to be a mouthpiece for the mob, Butch."

"The import-export business, Mr. Olsen. Remember? Your friends in Chicago have made a grievous error."

Jack laughed at Banuchi's ability to slip every punch. He was the perfect lawyer for the syndicate. His coming to the Lake of the Ozarks was obviously a promotion. They wanted someone very capable to be in charge of a project with the potential of making them millions.

"Not only do I know about your mob connections, Banuchi, and that you're a drug supplier, I also know that you bribed the sheriff. That's a crime, too. Naughty, naughty."

Banuchi leaned back in his chair, smoothing out the wrinkles in his vest.

Seeing that Banuchi was prepared to listen to all of his story, Jack continued, "I'm sure you paid Davis with cash, so the payoffs can't be traced to you. But I can find the cash and raise a lot of embarrassing questions. Davis knows that. So you see, I've neutralized him. Now he has more fear of me than love of your money. Who else have you bribed, Butch? Surely the sheriff wasn't the only one."

"It seems as if you have a habit of spreading malicious gossip about people, Mr. Olsen," Banuchi said, as pleasantly as if he were commenting on the weather.

"And I know why you bribed the sheriff," Jack said rhetorically. "You wanted him in your hip pocket when you got around to your grand project—the resort hotel." Jack pitched the architect's card on the desk.

As with the picture, Banuchi examined the card at length. "You certainly are a thorough investigator, Mr. Olsen, even though there doesn't seem to be any purpose to all this busy-work."

Ignoring the verbal jabs, Jack continued, "The plans are real nice, Butch. I was especially taken with the computer setup. How clever of you to know that people will absolutely flock to your hotel to play electronic hockey—and other games."

Banuchi leaned forward, resting his chin on his hands, which were clasped together in prayerful fashion. "Mr. Olsen, it's apparent I have misjudged you. I took you to be a plodding, not-too-bright person. Now I learn that you have a wonderfully vivid imagination. It's a mistake I don't make usually—underestimating people."

"But there was a fly in the soup. Right, Butch? Mr. Gentry wouldn't sell you the land you wanted, *and* he checked out your hotel. Funny, isn't it? How many people looked at your plans."

"Yes, I'm afraid I'm rather disappointed in MacMillan and Company. I doubt seriously if I shall do business with them again."

"Gentry was going to try to queer the whole project by fighting a rear-guard battle against you with zoning restrictions, building permits, public debates and God knows what else. Suddenly, Mr. Gentry gets iced. Makes you wonder, doesn't it?"

Banuchi seemed genuinely amused. "Mr. Olsen, you wanted to justify your fee so much that you concocted a murder."

"Finally we're in agreement, Butch," Jack replied. "Mr. Gentry was murdered. And Roy Cousins died of complications resulting from an attempted murder. It's just a matter of time before I can prove who was responsible for these two deaths. You may not have covered your ass well enough, Butch."

"Please elaborate, Mr. Olsen."

"Of course, it's unthinkable that you would have run down Mr. Gentry or Cousins personally. After all, we can't expect you to take chances that might soil some of your expensive suits, can we?"

"Of course not," Banuchi agreed.

"Let's suppose—just for speculation, mind you—that you had other people do Gentry in. And I find out who they are. And they squeal on you. What then, Butch?"

"As you say, Mr. Olsen, pure speculation. But it has been nice chatting with you. Have you ever considered writing fiction?"

Jack snubbed out the cigar, smiling at Banuchi. "You probably didn't know Roy Cousins well."

"Not well."

"But you know he was a smart man."

"Yes, I'd agree with that assessment."

"Cousins is the man responsible for your downfall in many ways, Butch. Maybe that's why he was hit by a car. He told me it would be difficult, perhaps impossible, to stop you by trying to reveal that the hotel was intended as a gambling casino. He suggested I follow the drug trail.

He was right: it led here. When we round up the guys with the boat, and the drug addicts, and squeeze them all a bit, I'd guess we'll wring your name out of them. That'll stop your hotel, don't you think, Butch?"

Jack met Sheriff Davis on the way up the steps to the parking lot.

"I was looking for you, Olsen," Davis said, blocking the way. Jack didn't like looking at the silver-plated sunglasses; it made the sheriff look foreign and deadly.

"I didn't get my car radio." Jack scowled. "And you haven't done the other things I asked, either."

"No, and I'm not going to, stumblebum."

Jack wondered about the change in the sheriff's attitude from the day before.

"I been thinking about your visit to my office, Olsen. Accusing a publicly elected official of accepting a bribe is slanderous. Then there's still the business of you acting as a private investigator without a license. And you're still bugging people, Olsen. I may be able to get a complaint against you. All in all, I got enough reason to run you in."

"I see your boss had a talk with you, fat boy," Jack said. "He had somebody call and tell you I was here?"

Davis reached for the back of his belt and produced a pair of handcuffs. "Please put up a battle, Olsen."

"I get it," Jack said. "You and your boss decided you'd get me in jail and then maybe I'd try to escape and get myself killed. Then you could all get on with the good things you're involved in, like murder, drugs, bribery, gambling."

Davis swung the handcuffs, but Jack was expecting it and ducked. At the same time he swung at the paunchy stomach. The sheriff went down like a ruptured balloon, a surprised look on his face. He sat on the steps, his mouth opened in a gasp for air, but no sound came out. He reached for his gun, but Jack stepped on his hand and ground it like a cigarette butt.

Jack spoke rapidly to Davis. "Before you start screaming for help, you'd better read this letter." Jack took the envelope from his back pocket and handed it to Davis, while moving aside for some people, who looked questioningly at the sheriff.

The letter was to Detective Lieutenant Grabowski. It read:

Dear Ed,

In the unfortunate event you're reading this letter, I'm either dead or in immediate need of your help. In the latter case, check the Camdenton, Missouri, county jail.

You asked that I tell you more about Banuchi, the Chicago hood who's set up operation here in the lake area. First off, he and Margossi, whose alias down here is Aldo Rinaldi, are dealing drugs in the area. A bar called the Stables is where the sales are going down. A guy named Alan Gentry and his pal, Spider, are doing the actual selling.

The local sheriff, Melvin Davis, is on the take from Banuchi. You can get a line on that by looking for an account, or safe-deposit box, in Jefferson City, St. Louis, Kansas City or possibly Springfield.

Check with a St. Louis architectural firm by the name of MacMillan and Company. Get hold of the plans Banuchi had drawn up for a new resort hotel to be built on the lake. Show it around the department and I'll bet you'll come to the same conclusions I did—that the hotel is to be used for gambling and prostitution.

I'm certain two men—Geoffrey Gentry and Roy Cousins—were killed because of their knowledge about the hotel's real purposes.

Cheers.

Jack plucked the sunglasses off Davis's face. "You didn't think I was so dumb as to leave my backside uncovered, did you? This is a copy of a letter someone has and will mail if anything happens to me. Just in case you think it's Kate, it isn't. It's a friend who lives in Chicago." Jack admitted to himself that without Cousins's advice, he'd be in Davis's jail, waiting for an accident to happen.

"What's this about the hotel?" Davis asked. Jack laughed, amazed at the old lawyer's savvy guesses. All Davis knew about was the drugs.

167

"Never mind," Jack said. "You get your ass up to your car and get someone out here to put a radio in my pickup. I'm staying up the road at the Shoreline Inn. You have my truck up there in two hours. Tell your dispatcher to give me any information I request, anytime. Hear?"

Davis plodded obediently up the steps ahead of Jack, who occasionally prodded him in the back with a finger.

"You call me on the radio or the phone," Jack continued, "and tell me when you're going to raid the Stables. Make it no later than tomorrow noon. Arrest everyone that's high, but especially Gentry and his pal, Spider. Get a warrant for Alan Gentry's cabin and go through it for dope."

Leaning against his squad car, Davis looked like a beaten puppy. He was sweating profusely, and large perspiration stains darkened the tan uniform.

"Make your choice now, Davis. You either side with Banuchi or with me. But let me give you a piece of advice. His number is up. It's all in the letter you read. One way or another, he's going down the tubes. Are you with me?"

The sheriff bobbed his head affirmatively, in several quick jerks.

Jack wagged a threatening finger in Davis's face. "The last time I told you to arrest Rinaldi, you ignored me. I want this guy in jail today. Search his place, too. I have a feeling that he's about to come looking for me. And that would get the letter sent. So you can see why you need to get him off the streets. Do it now while you're here."

When Jack got to the motel, he found an envelope taped to his door. Inside was a note: "Dear Jack, I forgive you for being an asshole. Please come home. I love you. How about a thick steak tonight for dinner and a piece of me for dessert? Love, Kate."

An inquisitive deputy delivered the pickup within the two-hour limit, but Jack ignored his subtle attempts to start a conversation and find out about the two-way radio. About six, he packed his clothes, paid his bill and went to dinner. It was everything Kate had promised, and by ten o'clock they were dozing in bed, totally satiated.

The sound of the horn seemed to come from far away until it pierced his shield of sleep and made Jack realize it was the pickup. Then it stopped. He got out of bed and pulled on his jeans. Kate rolled over and moaned, but otherwise was not disturbed from her sleep. Jack looked out one of the living room windows at the spot where he had parked the truck. The lights were on, shining into the forest.

He walked around the inside of the cabin, looking out every window. Nothing was moving, although he knew someone was out there. It's probably some kids out bushwhacking who decided to have a little fun at my expense, Jack thought. Just in case, he stuck the .45 in his waistband before opening the door and stepping outside. Again, he looked around carefully, but it was a sultry, overcast night and his range of vision was limited. He moved cautiously to the end of the cabin away from the bedroom. He sneaked a look behind him before peeking around the corner at the pickup. He walked gingerly, pulling out the gun. He listened for something, anything, but could only hear the sounds of the night—the cacophony of frogs calling to each other and the creaking sound of a boat dock as it was slapped by the waves.

The window on the driver's side was rolled down, although he distinctly remembered rolling it up against the possibility of rain. He gave the inside a perfunctory glance, since there was nothing to steal, then reached through the window and shut off the lights. He looked around for a few minutes, slowly relaxing. He put the gun back in his waistband and headed for the front door. It had to be kids, and he figured they were long gone by now.

What he saw at the entrance to the house made his blood run cold. It was the dog, Mudball, with its stomach slit open, intestines spilling onto the ground. Someone *had* been behind him. He injected a shell into the barrel of the automatic and pushed off the safety. He thought of going to the pickup and using the radio to call for help, but he decided to do that from the phone inside. Besides, he was suddenly sickened by the thought that he hadn't locked the door behind him. Kate was inside, unprotected.

As he was preparing to step over the dog, while checking left and right, Jack was knocked to the ground. Someone had jumped on him from the roof. The shock sent him crashing to the ground; suddenly the gun was no longer in his hand. A strong arm grabbed Jack and pulled him to his knees. Jack went for the knife hand as soon as he saw the flash of the blade. Even though he was holding off the knife with both hands, he could feel its steady progress toward his face. Desperately, Jack fought to get away from the powerful force behind him, but he only succeeded in allowing his opponent to immobilize him further with a scissors hold. The arm around his neck prevented him from screaming for help and also shut off his air. What saved him was that his grip loosened suddenly as waves of unconsciousness washed over him and the knife found its flesh in the arm of the intruder.

There was a snarl, a curse and a brief opening of the viselike hold, which Jack took advantage of to struggle free. The knife was on the ground. He kicked it away, frantically looking for the gun. But his attacker recovered quickly and Jack came under siege from a flurry of fists. He saw only a blur of a man wearing a black hood and a long-sleeved shirt. One punch caught Jack flush in the eye, and he hit the ground hard, but had the presence of mind to roll quickly and get to his feet to avoid being pinned again. He found his voice and yelled hoarsely for help. A crunching blow to the face shut off Jack's lights.

He came to with his head cradled in Kate's lap, as she passed a bottle of ammonia under his nose. His face felt numb and he couldn't see out of his left eye.

"What happened to him?" Jack asked, feeling a sharp pain in his nose as he spoke.

"I yelled at him and then shot," she said, holding the Ithaca twelve-gauge shotgun in her right hand. With its bottom ejection port, it was a good gun for a leftie. "I missed," she added.

Fear brought Jack quickly, if unsteadily, to his feet. "My God, he could still be out there somewhere."

"I know," she said, shivering.

Jack had Kate stand in the doorway and cover him with the shotgun while he searched for and found the .45 and a switchblade knife.

"Look at what he did to Mudball," Kate cried, as he closed and locked the door.

"I know," he said, putting an arm around her and steering them toward the bathroom, with its one high window. They stayed there awhile to collect their thoughts, he on the stool with his head in his hands, while Kate stood beside him.

"Did you get a look at him?" Jack asked.

"It all happened too fast," she said. "He was large."

Kate looked at him, and he saw the horror spread over her face. "Oh, Jack, your nose is broken. It's all crooked. And you have a deep cut in your eyebrow." Then she began to sob uncontrollably.

Jack looked in the mirror and nearly cried himself. He ran the sink full of steaming hot water and soaked a towel in it.

"Kate, get hold of yourself," he said, taking her in his arms. "I need your help. Take another towel and tear off a long strip that will go around my head. And keep the shotgun near."

The towel was nearly too hot to handle. He quickly applied it to his face, molding his nose until he could at least breathe. Then he took the strip of towel from Kate, soaked it in cold water and tied it tightly around his head so that it went across the cut and acted as a compress. He knew he'd need stitches, but that would have to wait until morning. They weren't going to leave the cabin at night.

Later, Jack did venture into the living room to call Sheriff Davis. He told the sheriff what had happened and asked if Rinaldi had been jailed. Davis said the man apparently had left town. With that, Jack launched into a tirade against the sheriff and threatened to send the letter in the morning. Within a half hour, Davis and a deputy were at the cabin to stand guard for the remainder of the night.

While Kate sat in a rocking chair in the bedroom, cradling the shotgun, Jack succumbed to exhaustion. Before he drifted off to sleep, he thought again of the steel grip that nearly choked off his life. Besides Rinaldi, two others filled the bill: Barbara's boyfriend, Hank, and Tom Wallace.

TWENTY

The doctor thought Jack had done a tolerable job on the nose and decided not to try to straighten it further. The gash over his eye took six stitches.

Surveying his taped nose and eye, Jack said, "It looks like I fought for the heavyweight championship."

"And lost," Kate quipped.

Over Jack's protest that he didn't need a chauffeur, Kate insisted upon driving him over to see Mrs. Lacy. She said he still looked a little wobbly and that he might need her intervention to gain an audience with the widow.

But Mrs. Lacy was very gracious, and she read Roy Cousins's letter attentively.

"Roy also believed Geoff was murdered," she said in a still-disbelieving voice.

"Yes."

"And he was right in warning you to be careful," she said, reaching toward his battered face although failing to consummate the touch.

"Cousins also was right about Banuchi and Alan and Barbara," Jack added. "You shouldn't have anything to do with them."

"You suspected me," she said, dejected and defensive.

172

"I did think dissolving the trust was the best answer, Jack. I wasn't conspiring with anyone. When you were here the day before yesterday, you only confused me. I didn't know what to do."

Jack looked away, and Kate spoke for him. "Jack had to be suspicious of everyone, Beth. Otherwise he wouldn't have come this far. We just had to prove ourselves to him."

Jack was stunned. He was so stupid. He had even suspected Kate. Why? Out of jealousy? She had saved his life. He put his arms around her and squeezed tightly.

"What can I do to help you, Jack?" Beth Lacy asked, with a broad smile.

"Don't dissolve the trust," Jack said, putting an arm around each of the women.

"All right. For as long as I'm alive or until you tell me differently, I'll stay on as trustee of Geoff's estate."

With his binoculars, Jack surveyed the Stables until he found the telephone line. Trying to be as inconspicuous as possible, he walked behind the building and snipped the wire. Back in his pickup, he monitored the progress of the task force assembled by the sheriff to raid the Stables. Jack was afraid someone would see the raid developing and telephone the tip to the Stables. For that reason, two of the four carloads of deputies were in unmarked vehicles. They would be the first to arrive from a staging area about three miles south of the bar. As soon as he was informed that the lead cars were within a mile of the Stables, Jack got out of the pickup and went through the front door. He slouched against a wall, a hat shielding his face from view. When he saw the two cars arrive, Jack pulled out the .45 and stepped into the main bar area.

"Everyone stay right where you are," Jack commanded, moving behind the bar. To the beefy bartender, he said, "You get out in front, flat on the floor on your face." Jack figured that if anyone in the place was armed, it was likely to be the bartender. By this time, Davis and his deputies had burst into the bar, brandishing pistols and shotguns.

"Two of you, upstairs," Jack barked, and the deputies responded immediately without questioning his authority. "Get everyone up against the wall," he told the other deputies. "Shake them down." Jack had taken the precaution of being officially deputized by Davis, to eliminate any subsequent legal problems that might arise because a civilian was in on the raid.

"There's a kitchen," Davis said, propelling his bulk with surprising agility in that direction. Jack followed through the swinging doors and was greeted by the sound of a garbage disposal at work.

"Hi, Mel," a man with curly gray hair said. "Just doing a few dishes here." On his arm was the tattoo: "Born to sin."

"This is Clyde Lewis, the manager," Davis said sheepishly.

"Getting rid of the garbage, Lewis?" Jack said, surprised only that they had waited until the last minute. Jack regretted being so candid with Banuchi.

But they didn't come up empty-handed. Several of the patrons, making the trip from the bar stools to the wall, emptied their pockets on the way. Cleaning up the floor yielded several ounces of grass and a few hundred pills.

"Well, well, if it isn't the Bobbsey twins," Jack said, walking down the line of patrons and stopping in back of Gentry and Spider.

"I see someone finally shoved in your face, prick," Spider said, obviously in pain from trying to keep both hands on the wall.

"These two got anything on them?" Jack asked the deputies performing the searches.

"No, they're clean," a hatchet-faced deputy answered. "Unless they're the ones with the holes in their pockets."

The two prostitutes joined the gathering, and Margo was solicitous about Jack's face. "You're still the sexiest thing to come in here lately," she said, as she sidled up to Jack and slipped her arm through his.

"She had some grass in her purse," a deputy said sourly.

"Margo, I can't believe it," Jack said with feigned indignation.

"Honest, honey, I thought it was tobacco. I was going to roll my own. You know, I like to lick 'em shut."

Jack turned to Davis. "Well, sheriff, it looks to me like you've got cause to shut this place down."

"I'd say so," Davis agreed gruffly.

"Just a minute," Lewis said. "I ain't responsible for what customers bring in the bar. I can't search everyone who comes through the door."

"The girls?" Jack questioned, jerking a thumb at the two hookers.

"We rent rooms," Lewis protested. "Sometimes it's guys and sometimes gals. Nothing illegal about that."

Davis looked to Jack for guidance.

"Haul them all in, sheriff. There's enough evidence here to give us cause to ask a few questions."

When they raided Alan Gentry's place and the hotel room vacated by Margossi, alias Rinaldi, other sheriff's deputies could not find the slightest trace of drugs. Jack was grim at the news. The fact that Davis had delayed several days in carrying out Jack's orders might have cost him the evidence linking the drug traffic to Banuchi.

The sheriff could hold everyone caught in the raid for several hours without filing charges. Jack told Davis to concentrate on interrogating the locals he thought might break and admit to buying drugs at the Stables, or those who could provide evidence of prostitution. Jack knew it was useless to try to pry that information from Lewis, the tough bartender, or the two streetwise hookers.

Jack asked for a closed room for himself and Spider. "How're the ribs?" Jack asked, as Spider circled to keep the conference table between them.

"Broken, you sonofabitch. Just like your face. If you think you're going to beat on me again, I'll guarantee one good punch will land on your nose."

"Oh, God, I couldn't stand that, Spider." Jack laughed. "Of course, if you're thinking of that, this nose doesn't slow me down in moving like those ribs do for you. So why don't you just sit down and we'll have a civilized talk."

Spider did as he was ordered, keeping a wary eye on Jack, who remained standing.

"Naw, Spider, I don't feel like fighting today. I just want to finish that conversation you and I were having a few nights ago before we were interrupted. By the way, who was doing the shooting that night?"

Spider smirked. "Alan took a couple of shots at a prowler."

Jack made a mental note: Gentry carried a gun. "Before Gentry showed up, you had fingered Banuchi as the source of the drugs."

"I didn't say that," Spider replied sullenly. "You got it all wrong, man."

175

"They talked to you, huh," Jack smiled. "Rinaldi do that before he left town? Threaten to come back and fit you for those concrete boots?"

"Don't know what you're talking about."

"You got reason to be scared, Spider. Rinaldi is Banuchi's man, and Banuchi works for the mob. Surprised? Why? Who else has the connections to come up with drugs like you've been getting, Spider?"

Spider turned his head slightly to the side, indicating an interest in Jack's information.

"Banuchi already knows I'm the guy who turned the sheriff on him," Jack continued. "But they don't know exactly how I got onto the drug trail in the first place. You and I know I just happened to be window-peeking at Alan's place at the right time. But I'm going to tell them that you're an ear, Spider."

"What?" Spider asked, incredulously.

"An ear. You know, man, a guy who listens and tells. I'll have Sheriff Davis let you go in a few minutes and tell all the other people who got arrested that you're the guy who squealed. Then I'll let the word out that you fingered Banuchi."

Spider's mouth formed in an O-shape, but nothing came out.

"The mob's got a long arm, Spider," Jack prompted, sympathetically. "I'm afraid you're going to have an accident, Spider."

"All right, all right," Spider conceded. "I figured it would end soon anyway. I may be ugly, but I'm not dumb. I knew they were using us to get the drugs going. Until they could see if the sheriff could be bought. Once the trial period was over, I figured they'd bring in their own guys. That's what Rinaldi said that night at the cabin. You heard him."

Jack nodded his agreement.

"When that happened, I knew they'd want to get rid of us. In fact, you really screwed up my plans that night," Spider added ruefully.

"What do you mean?"

"I'd gotten Alan off on a wild-goose chase so he wouldn't be around when Rinaldi made his delivery. I planned to take the box and skip."

Jack whistled. "Why?"

176

"Because there's murder involved, man, and I don't want any part of that."

"You told me you didn't know anything about that."

Spider shrugged.

"Was it you and Alan in the boat?"

Spider raised his hands in supplication. "Honest to God, man, it wasn't me."

"Who then?"

"I don't know. Really. Alan's a bigmouth. He told me he offed his grandpa to get all that money, but he was mum about the other guy. I think even he was afraid."

Jack paced the floor, thinking. "That big box of goodies, Spider. The bag of grass. Where are they? It didn't show up in the raid. Surely they didn't flush a hundred grand of shit down the drain?"

Spider replied meekly, "No, Alan moved it after you got away that night."

"Where's it at?"

"There's a barn west of Gravois Mills," Spider replied. "Inside is an old beat-up forty-nine Chevy without a motor. The drugs are inside the gasoline tank."

Jack smiled, feeling triumphant. "Thanks, Spider. I'll tell Davis to let you go with the rest of the pack, and we won't say a word."

"There's more," Spider said begrudgingly. "You're gonna find the boat." He laid his head on the table, moaning. He knew his chances of not becoming a witness in court had evaporated.

"Hey, man, you're gonna protect me. Right?"

Jack found the drugs and the gleaming new boat with its gray lightning stripes. How could a thing so sleek and beautiful be an instrument of death, he wondered. Then he remembered the steely coolness of a new revolver. Jack didn't tell Davis about Spider's revelations, knowing the sheriff was a reluctant partner.

He waited at the barn for some time, hoping Alan, whom he had ordered released with the rest, would show up. By the time he gave up and returned to his pickup, it was nearly eleven. He started to call the sheriff's dispatcher to have someone come get the boat. But as soon as he identified himself, the dispatcher interrupted to say that there was an urgent call from the sheriff.

After making certain that deputies would impound the boat, Jack called Davis on the radio. The sheriff's news was startling. Having the goods on Alan Gentry was academic; he had been killed by his sister.

Jack arrived about midnight to find the sheriff and Barbara sitting in her living room. She was sipping bourbon on the rocks, to steady her nerves. The coroner and several deputies were in the woods east of the house, still examining the body.

"What time did you say he came?" Jack asked, noting Alan's car in the driveway.

"It was just after nine," she replied, cupping the glass with both hands. I was watching this show on TV and it had just ended. I was in the kitchen fixing a sandwich when he arrived."

"What did he want?" Jack asked.

"Money," Barbara replied. It was the first time Jack had seen her in jeans. While he found the night oppressively hot, she had on a man's long-sleeved dress shirt, which was torn in several places.

"He said he had to get out of town, tonight," she continued.

Jack had considered that Alan would run when he told Davis to release him about eight o'clock. But he had banked on Alan coming after the drugs. He wanted to confront Alan, threaten him with a long jail sentence and get him to implicate Banuchi. But it had never happened. What had Gentry done for an hour before showing up at his sister's house? Jack wondered.

"Did you offer him money?" Jack asked.

"Not at first," she said defiantly. "He gets the same allowance I do. Why should I give him part of mine, too?"

"But you did finally offer him money?" Jack guessed.

"Yes, after I saw how upset he was. I mean delirious, almost. He was ranting and raving. He wanted me to go with him to Mrs. Lacy's house and make her give us Grandfather's money." She paused and shook her head in a gesture of hopelessness. "Why he thought she'd have cash is beyond me. And he wanted to break into Grandfather's house to see if there was any money there. Really, he was impossible."

178

"Go on," the sheriff prompted, having heard the story before Jack arrived.

"I refused to do either of those things, of course," she said, pouting. "Then he started hitting me."

Jack looked closely at Barbara's face through his one good eye. There wasn't a mark on it; in fact, her make-up appeared flawless, as usual.

Looking at Jack, she said, "Mainly, he hit me in the arms and back."

"Where's your boyfriend, Hank?" Jack asked, curious as to why he wasn't there to protect his girlfriend. Also, he wanted a close look at Hank's left forearm, to see if there was a knife wound.

"He was only here *temporarily*, Mr. Olsen," she chided. "By now, I suspect he's in California."

Jack asked, "Did you run outside after he started hitting you?"

"No. He made me write him a check for five thousand dollars on my checking account, which is ridiculous, since I only have a balance of two hundred dollars. He seemed satisfied for a while and he sat in there at the dining room table drinking beer. He took some pills he had with him." She pointed at a vial sitting on the table.

"After a few drinks, he started in again, cursing everyone and everything. Demanding his money from Grandfather's estate. I tried to calm him, but then he got mad at me and pulled a knife."

"We're looking for it in the woods now," Davis explained to Jack, who was examining the bottle. There were four pills left. All Quaaludes.

"He try to cut you?" Jack asked.

"I took one look at his eyes and didn't wait to see," she replied. "I ran upstairs to my bedroom, where I keep a gun, and locked the door. But he kicked it in."

"Sure did," Davis confirmed.

"I scared him with the gun and he backed away," she said, "and I was able to get out the door and down the stairs. That's when I ran out of the house."

"Where were you going?"

"Anywhere. Down the road to the neighbors."

"From the lights and men outside, I gather the shooting took place over there," Jack said, pointing to the east. "Most of your neighbors are the other way."

"I'm sorry, Mr. Olsen, if I wasn't thinking clearly," she replied icily.

"So he followed and caught up with you," the sheriff repeated.

"Yes. I had to shoot him," she said, burying her head in her hands and sobbing fitfully.

Jack looked at the body as they prepared to take Alan Gentry away in an ambulance. There was an angry black hole in the left side of his chest.

"Three-fifty-seven magnum," the coroner said in a monotone.

"Big gun for a little girl," Jack mumbled, looking at the frontier-style Ruger Blackhawk, its long barrel swallowed up in the meaty grasp of the coroner. He formed a mental picture of the revolver bucking in Barbara's grasp. Had she fired one-handed or two-handed?

"What time did she say she shot him?" Jack asked Davis.

"She said it must have been about ten," he replied. "She called about five after ten, according to the dispatcher's log. It all seems on the up and up to me."

"The body was there in the woods?" Jack asked, pointing toward an area still illuminated with floodlights.

"Yes," the fat coroner confirmed. "Found the gun and the knife there, too." Why a knife? Jack wondered, remembering that Gentry favored guns.

"She said she dropped the gun after firing," Davis said, shrugging his shoulders in response to Jack's questioning glance.

"You sure he was killed on that spot, not somewhere else?" Jack demanded of the coroner.

"Positive. He lost a lot of blood right there."

"What about bruises on the body, like around the head?"

"Nothing apparent now, but we can check closer," the coroner replied, looking questioningly at Davis.

"Do that," Jack said. "And check around here, especially the house, for bloodstains."

"Why?" Davis asked, and Jack was tempted to snap at the sheriff, telling him to do as he was told.

"Please?" he asked, instead.

180

TWENTY-ONE

Jack and Sheriff Davis met with the county prosecuting attorney, a human dynamo named Ron Thomas. As a result of their conversation, the young attorney persuaded the circuit court judge to convene a grand jury. On the one hand, the jury would investigate the death of Geoffrey Gentry II. There was evidence linking Alan Gentry to the killing of his grandfather. The boat was traced to a dealer in St. Louis, who identified Alan Gentry as the man who had purchased it. A farmer volunteered that he had rented the barn to Gentry.

Spider accepted an offer of protective custody. He also hired a lawyer, who gave him good advice about not making public his private confession to Jack. In return for immunity from drug-related charges, Spider said he would testify that Alan had admitted killing his grandfather. Spider's testimony, therefore, would establish premeditation and a motive—money. Jack didn't doubt that Alan had killed his grandfather for the money, but he doubted that that was the full story. Spider continued steadfastly to deny any knowledge of Alan's partner in the crime, and Jack tended to believe him.

The grand jury also was asked to hear testimony regarding Alan Gentry's role in the drug traffic at the Stables. The bar, which turned out to be owned by Banuchi Enterprises, was closed temporarily. In this area, Jack realized that Spider was walking on eggshells. He would finger Alan as a pusher and even identify Rinaldi as the deliveryman. Jack knew that Spider didn't want to go that far, but Spider feared Jack's testimony and didn't want to perjure himself. Jack appreciated the fact that a warrant undoubtedly would be issued for the arrest of the absent Rinaldi but was skeptical that he would ever be found. The mob, like the government, had its relocation service. On the other hand, Rinaldi was a link between the drugs and Banuchi, his employer, and that would lend some credence to Jack's allegations, whenever he decided to make them.

On the advice of his lawyer, Spider would refuse to testify about Banuchi. Spider only had hearsay knowledge in this area, according to his lawyer, and Jack conceded the point. What *evidence* did he have that Banuchi was involved? Besides, it was entirely possible that Banuchi had contacted Spider and given him a choice of words. The words, Jack was certain, were "silence" and "death."

Jack wasn't at all certain what he would tell the grand jury. Should he introduce the hotel plans, voice his suspicions and try to link the deaths of Gentry and Cousins to their opposition to the hotel? Was it the time to produce proof that the sheriff had been bribed? Jack feared that he couldn't substantiate all of those charges, at least not at the time.

As a result, everything was placid on the surface. Banuchi did business as usual. Barbara remained at home, grieving for her brother. Sheriff Davis was proud as a peacock, accepting the accolades of his fellow officers and the county attorney for busting up a local drug ring *and* solving a murder. Only around Jack was Davis reticent, uncertain what Jack would do eventually with the knowledge that Davis had accepted a bribe.

For the moment, Jack planned to do nothing, thinking he could still use the sheriff. Kate was happier, too. She had met Tom Wallace on the street and he didn't have a knife wound in his arm. Jack admitted that was a definite mark in his favor.

The dog days of summer were upon them. By midday, the blazing July sun would turn the asphalt roads into a gooey mess. The grasses were burned brown except for those lawns and golf courses that were watered daily. There was an ever-present danger of forest fires and an increase in the public announcements urging people not to be careless with fires and cigarettes. Jack started doing more fishing again, early in the morning or in the evening, since nothing, including the fish, seemed to move during the day. He began making plans for the upcoming vacation with his children, and started thinking about what he would do in the future. But something kept gnawing at him, and one evening after dinner he asked Kate if they could talk it out.

"I'm uneasy about the way Alan Gentry died, for one thing," he said.

"What Barbara told you seems natural enough to me," Kate said. "Alan got out of jail. He knew the game was over. He wanted to get out of town. Who else could he go to for money?"

"Banuchi," Jack said firmly. "But even then, Alan had to know that Butch would want that large cache of drugs."

"Why wasn't Alan followed?" Kate asked.

"I didn't want him followed for several reasons. I didn't want him or Banuchi or Banuchi's people to spot a tail. I didn't trust Davis enough to want him involved. And I was certain Alan would come after the drugs."

"But he didn't."

"No, and that puzzles me," Jack replied. "He was let out of jail shortly before eight. I checked that. Yet Barbara says he didn't show up at her house until shortly after nine. What did he do for that hour or more?"

Kate bobbed her head from side to side in contemplation. "He drove around and thought about his options?" she offered.

"He didn't have a car at the jail. Yet he shows up at Barbara's with his car. Somehow he got to the Stables to pick it up."

"Did a deputy possibly drive him there?"

"No, I checked that, too."

"It had to be a friend, then. He called someone."

"Right," Jack agreed.

"So that's how the hour evaporates," Kate said, puzzled at Jack's reluctance to accept an obvious possibility.

"I guess so," he said, fidgeting nervously. "I just keep

remembering how I told Banuchi that his ass was in the wringer whenever I was able to put the pressure on the guys who ran down old man Gentry, as well as the people involved in the drug scene. I didn't realize at the time that one man—Alan Gentry—was the key person in both areas. With Alan dead, the trail to Banuchi dries up, and all that's left is a bunch of local hopheads from the Stables. You see how convenient Alan's death was?"

"Yes," she admitted. "But if he was killed on purpose, then Barbara is one of Banuchi's people."

"Why not?" he asked.

"But her story is good, you have to admit," Kate countered.

"Too good. First, there's the thing about the booze and the pills. I can buy the fact that Alan is naturally agitated when he arrives. He's been busted. The drugs will be cut off. I can even see him slapping her around. But then he starts in on beer and 'ludes, according to her. First, I know he doesn't have any drugs on him when he gets to her place."

"That's not necessarily true," Kate interrupted. "He didn't have any when he left the sheriff's office. Whoever gave him a ride to his car could have given him some pills, or he could have had a bottle in his car."

"Okay. But is he going to get into another rage after drinking booze and taking a drug that's a sedative? The opposite should have happened. He should have gone to sleep. I wonder how well Barbara knows her drugs?"

"You can't know for sure how he would have reacted," Kate said. "His mental state at the time could have had a lot to do with his reaction."

Jack shook his head. "I doubt it. It's more likely he was in a stupor. That would have made it so easy for her to lead him into the woods and blow him away."

"They checked to make sure he wasn't killed someplace else, like you asked?"

"Right," Jack replied. "He was killed there on that spot. No doubt about it, according to the coroner."

"What would Barbara gain by killing her brother?" Kate asked.

"Half of a multi-million dollar estate."

"But Mrs. Lacy isn't going to let that happen now. I'm sure Barbara knows that."

"So the only one who benefits from Alan's death right now is Butch Banuchi. Alan's death ends the drug trail, and it prevents us from ever knowing why Alan killed his grandfather, or who helped him do it. Did he do it because he feared being disinherited? Or did he do it because Banuchi made that the price of a free supply of drugs?"

"Maybe it was a little bit of both," Kate said.

Jack was sorely tempted to plant Alan Gentry's cache of drugs in Banuchi's office. Then he could badger the county attorney into securing a search warrant. Jack's ploy would be that Spider would finger Banuchi as the ultimate drug source. It would be enough to persuade the eager county attorney.

Then, when the drugs were found, Banuchi would post bail and leave town. There was no way he'd come to trial to face the real possibility of evidence, albeit circumstantial, being introduced that related to his character, speculation about the purpose of the hotel and its relationship to Gentry's death. Banuchi also would fear that Spider or Sheriff Davis could be induced to talk.

But Jack didn't want to stoop that low, not to mention that it would be against the law. Besides, while that scenario would get Banuchi out of town and stop the hotel, at least temporarily, it would also let Banuchi off scot-free. That Jack didn't want. He decided to have a face-to-face encounter with the mobster, however. He told the sheriff where he was going, and said it loudly enough for several deputies to hear, just in case Banuchi had ideas about detaining him.

Taking Jack aside, Davis was curious and scared. "What do you hope to accomplish?"

Jack shrugged. "I don't know exactly. Somehow I want to smoke him out. Make him afraid. Give him time to think. Maybe he'll do something stupid. Then I can nail him."

"Then it'll come out about me," Davis whined.

Jack felt sorry for him; the sheriff thought it a real possibility that Jack would let him off the hook. "Just for the record, Davis, how much did you get from Banuchi?"

Davis mumbled, and Jack made him repeat the figure. "Five thousand a month," the sheriff said.

Jack whistled. "Wow. They *really* bought you. For how long?"

"About a year. Look, Olsen," Davis pleaded, "we've got to talk about this. Sure I did wrong. Everyone makes mistakes. But I've been doing a good job lately, haven't I? Whadaya say we just forget about the money? I'll donate it to a charity. Wherever you say. How about it?"

Jack grinned, taking a perverse delight in watching the cocky sheriff sweat.

Banuchi, resplendent in a yellow leisure suit, greeted Jack as if he were a long-lost brother. Jack endured the usual ritual involving the offering of cigars and drinks.

"You're getting to be a regular visitor," Banuchi said, as if they were friendly rivals about to enjoy a good-natured tête-à-tête.

"Yes, I like to come by once a week and threaten you, Butch," Jack said, and they laughed together.

"What is it this time, then?"

Jack took a deep breath. "I won't cover old ground, about your mob connections, your proposed gambling casino, or the fact that you're a drug pusher."

Banuchi nodded agreement. "It would only cause hard feelings."

"I'm not even going to spend a lot of time talking about how you're probably behind the deaths of Geoffrey and Alan Gentry and Roy Cousins, although I'm certain that you are."

Banuchi shook his head, clucking disapproval.

"Truthfully, I don't know that you can ever be nailed for those murders," Jack said grimly. "At this point in the game, you're winning big."

Banuchi smiled, accepted Jack's remarks as a compliment.

"You've got real problems ahead, though, Butch. I've busted up your drug operation, and run your hit man out of town, and the sheriff is dangling on the end of my string. A grand jury has been convened. Mrs. Lacy won't dissolve the trust unless I say so."

Banuchi spoke quietly, dangerously. "You're a resourceful man, Mr. Olsen. I said that before."

"Yes, and I'm going to be harder than hell to kill, as you know," Jack warned. The two men stared at each other.

186

Jack spoke first. "I've decided it's time for me to go on the offensive. I have a lot of information. I can raise a lot of questions. I'm going to grant several newspaper interviews. Perhaps even television."

The perpetual pleasant smile faded from Banuchi's face.

"You can appreciate the appeal of this story to the national press, Butch. Scenic lake area plagued by mysterious killings, a drug ring, prostitution. One of the successful businessmen in the area was previously the mob's lawyer in Chicago. There are plans afoot for a new hotel, which has several intriguing features. Maybe I'll add a few surprises. Like revealing that the sheriff has socked away sixty thousand dollars in the last year. What do you think, Butch? Will they eat it up or will they eat it up?"

Banuchi smiled. "It doesn't sound real. They may not believe you."

"We'll see," Jack replied.

The conversation obviously over, Banuchi asked solicitously, "Your face, Mr. Olsen—does it hurt much?"

"Only when I laugh, and I'm in real pain right now."

Banuchi looked directly at Jack. "That was a nasty fall you took, Mr. Olsen. Accidents are the number-one cause of death for people in your age bracket. You'll have to be very careful in the future."

Her name was Mauvis Mabley, and she knew that Kate's young man worked for Beth Lacy. So she thought that Jack would want to know that Beth had been taken to the hospital shortly after noon.

Jack feared the worst as he and Kate arrived at the hospital and found Mrs. Mabley in a dither. She was a short lady, with a purplish tint to her hair, and she wore the high-heeled laced shoes favored by so many elderly women.

"I came by her place about eleven-thirty," she told Kate, "like I always do on Thursdays. Beth and I like the salad bar down at the Tripoli. Maybe a carafe of nice white wine, too. Anyway, I couldn't raise her, no matter how hard I pounded on the door. Now, that's not like Beth. She's so punctual. And polite. If she wasn't able to go for one reason or another, she would have called, or left a note. I sat on the patio for a spell and waited. Her car was there, and I thought maybe she was at a negihbor's house. But

187

when noon came, I started to worry. After all, when you get to our age . . ." Her voice trailed off while she continued to twist her handkerchief.

"What did you do then?" Jack asked.

"I went up to Mr. Gentry's place. Walked. I could hear the mower going. I figured maybe Lloyd McGinnis was up there working. He didn't want to, but I made him come down to Beth's house. The doors were locked, though, and Lloyd didn't want to break a window or anything. But he brought down a ladder and climbed up to the balcony off Beth's bedroom. Yelled down to me that he could see her in bed. Then I knew something was wrong. Beth never takes a nap during the day. Lloyd knocked on the glass door, but he couldn't raise her. He was getting scared then, too, so he ran back to his pickup and got a crowbar and pried open the sliding doors. Beth was unconscious. Lloyd let me in the house and I called the ambulance."

"Have you talked to a doctor?" Kate asked. "Did they tell you what the matter was?"

"No," she said. "They just told me not to worry." She looked to Kate and Jack for confirmation of that statement, her face a picture of pure innocence.

"Doctors can do miracles these days," Jack assured her, then went in search of a nurse, who said that the doctor would be out shortly to speak to them. Jack looked at his watch. It was nearly two o'clock.

When the doctor came to the waiting room half an hour later, he looked tired. He was dressed in surgical green, a tall man with a pointed nose and ropelike veins in his arms.

"Hi, I'm Dr. McEvoy. I understand you want to know about Mrs. Lacy's condition." He took off his glasses and began to polish them with a handkerchief. "Mrs. Lacy is a diabetic, as we learned from Mrs. Mabley. I had my nurse call her doctor. A mild case, he said. She's supposed to take one hundred units of insulin per day. NPH, or isophane insulin, a long-lasting preparation. This morning Mrs. Lacy took a massive overdose. How much I don't know. She's suffering from insulin shock."

"Is it serious?" Mrs. Mabley asked, in her precise and slow manner of speaking.

"We're taking measures to counteract the insulin, of course. We were lucky to find her within a few hours of the overdose. That's a plus. But her age is a negative factor. The next twenty-four hours will be critical."

Jack drew the doctor aside. "Could I talk to her for a moment?" he asked.

"She's unconscious," the doctor replied. "Are you a relative?"

"No, just a friend," Jack said. "Tell me, how could this happen? Didn't she give herself shots each day?"

"Yes, and it's just that routine that is often dangerous. In the treatment of diabetes with insulin, diet and exercise are very important. Insulin shock can occur when a diabetic forgets to eat or has a delayed meal. That's one possibility. Frankly, there's another. It's not unusual for a person Mrs. Lacy's age to take an overdose on purpose. Was she despondent lately? In ill health?"

"No, not that I know of," Jack replied, preoccupied with a third possibility. "Doctor, is there any evidence of violence? Any indication that Mrs. Lacy might have been forcibly injected?"

Dr. McEvoy was aghast. "My God, son, are you serious?"

"Deadly serious, doctor."

TWENTY-TWO

By noon the next day, Mrs. Lacy was conscious. The doctor said she was lucky, but Jack was appalled at the extent to which she seemed to have aged. Her eyes were ringed with black circles and seemed to have sunk into her head. Her mouth hung open when she spoke and her lower jaw bobbed feebly, causing her speech to be slurred.

Still, she was able to tell them what had happened. She had been sitting on her patio about nine-thirty, taking some sun, when someone grabbed her from behind.

"Did you see who it was?" Jack asked anxiously.

"No," she gasped. "Strong arms held me like a vise. Someone else slipped something over my head. A bag. Couldn't see." Silently, the doctor lifted one of her arms to display bruises in the outline of fingers.

"They carried you upstairs," Jack guessed, wanting to help save her breath.

"Yes."

"They injected you there?"

"Yes."

Sheriff Davis intervened. "Did they say anything to each other?"

"Nothing," she said, her head rolling to one side.

"That's really enough, gentlemen," Dr. McEvoy said.

Jack raised his arm. "Wait a minute, doctor. Three people are dead and there have been attempts on other people's lives. Only a few more questions. It's important." Taking Mrs. Lacy's hand, Jack looked into her eyes and smiled. "Beth, one was very strong, you say. Was he also tall? Remember when he lifted you?"

"Yes, he was tall," she said, responding to his comforting touch.

"Did you smell anything unusual?" he asked. "Cologne, perfume, anything?"

She shut her eyes, straining to remember. "I don't know, Jack. I'm so sorry. I was too scared."

He sympathized, remembering his panic when the same strong arms were choking the life out of him.

"I didn't even feel the shot," she said, eyes opened wide in wonderment.

"Were you expecting anyone?" Jack asked.

"Only Mauvis about noon," she replied, then adding as an afterthought, "Mrs. Wallace had called the day before and said Tom might stop by with berries and things from her garden—squash, cabbage, onions, corn." She drifted off into a troubled sleep.

The sheriff put out an arrest order for Tom Wallace. Jack and Kate sat in the pickup at an outdoor drive-in in Camdenton, drinking Cokes and listening to the radio traffic. It was about four o'clock in the afternoon when Wallace was spotted driving south on Highway 54. Jack and Kate arrived just as a deputy finished frisking Wallace for weapons.

"I'm not supposed to move him until the sheriff gets here," the deputy explained, according Jack the deference that had now become usual.

Wallace's hands were handcuffed behind him, and he leaned against the squad car. There was no knife wound in his arm, as Kate had already determined. Looking at the tall man, Jack mentally gauged his strength. Wallace was lithe, agile; in his younger days, he might have been poetry in motion. He was obviously strong, but Jack didn't think he possessed that brute, overwhelming strength that he had endured. Suddenly he felt sorry for Wallace.

"Jack," Kate pleaded, taking both his hands and looking

191

directly into his eyes. "He didn't do it." Tears trickled down her cheeks. When she cried, he ached. "You've been jealous, Jack, for no reason. Once Tom and I were romantically involved. But that's over. What isn't over is a lifetime of friendship. He and I started grade school together. He was Bert's best friend. I know him. He doesn't kill people. You can help him, Jack. Please."

Jack walked over to Wallace, who smiled—not a cocky smile, or a smirk, but one that was resigned.

"Cigarette?" Jack offered.

"I don't smoke," Wallace said.

"You've got a few minutes," Jack said. "Tell me everything."

"You know everything, Olsen. I leveled with you all along. I wasn't the other guy in the boat the day Gentry was killed."

"Go on," Jack said, conceding the point.

"Sure, I talked a lot to Banuchi. He approached me first about selling my land for a new resort hotel. Gentry wouldn't go along, and we argued. After Gentry died, I tried to get Alan to talk to Mrs. Lacy. I told you that at the Stables. You said I wanted that quarter of a million dollars awful bad. Maybe you were right. I did want it. Wanted to get off the farm. Stop being called a pig farmer. Maybe open a marina or buy a small resort. Get my mom into a nicer place. Settle down with a girl like Kate. But want it bad enough to kill? Never."

Jack believed him, but there was one question left to be asked. "Were you at Beth Lacy's house the day someone tried to kill her?"

"Sure," Wallace replied. "I got there about one-thirty. No one was home. I left the vegetables in a box on her doorstep. Surely someone found them?"

They were still there when Jack and Kate stopped by Mrs. Lacy's house. Only the wild berries had dried out in the sun. Jack talked to the sheriff, who admitted he didn't have any witnesses to place Wallace at Mrs. Lacy's house. But Tom admitted he was there, the sheriff argued. It was only a question of getting him to admit he was there in the morning and not the afternoon. Jack noticed the sheriff had regained his swaggering confidence and was acting as if he were the driving force of the investigation and Jack didn't matter anymore.

192

"Don't worry," Jack told Kate. "Tom didn't do it, and he won't be in jail long. Find him a good lawyer."

"How can you be sure they won't pin it on him?" she asked.

"Because I checked, and Banuchi has left town, just as I thought he would after our recent conversation. If he and Tom were in this together, Banuchi would have told him he was leaving and Tom would have known that the hotel was on the back burner now. He wouldn't have had any reason to kill Mrs. Lacy."

"Who did that to her, then?"

"There's only one logical choice—Barbara!"

"Right. With Beth gone, she inherits the estate."

Jack felt serene, ambling along in the pickup, savoring the last light of day. As he turned down the road to Barbara Gentry's house, he caught glimpses of the lake through the forest. Every evening when the winds died down at sunset and the boats were all tied up, the water became like glass. He thought that a flat stone, thrown just right, could skip all the way to the opposite shore. It was nearly over. Tomorrow he and Kate could sleep late. They'd pack a picnic lunch, nap in the early afternoon and then fish for their supper. Things would get back to the way they had been.

Barbara seemed pleased to see him. She was wearing short shorts and a tight T-shirt that accentuated her perfectly formed breasts. On the shirt was the legend: "WHAT YOU SEE IS WHAT YOU GET."

"Mr. Olsen, it's so good of you to come," she purred, leaning against the edge of the open door. "I have wanted so much to talk to you."

After she ushered him inside, he did a brief scan of the room to make certain they were alone. He didn't want to precipitate any premature violence, or tip his hand, by openly wearing a gun. But taped to his ankle was the compact Smith & Wesson .38 he had liberated from the sheriff's collection. Less than seven inches long, weighing only about fifteen ounces, it was a perfect weapon to conceal. Its frame sidewalls surrounded the hammer, which wasn't likely to get fouled in the tape if he was in a hurry to remove the gun.

"You alone?" he asked.

"Not anymore," she replied coyly. "Would you like a drink?"

"No, this really isn't a social call, Barbara. I'm here to accuse you of the attempted murder of Mrs. Lacy, the murder of your brother and perhaps even conspiracy in the death of your grandfather."

She clasped her hands together in schoolgirl anticipation. "Oh, how exciting!"

"You tried your whole bag of tricks on Beth Lacy, didn't you," he said, selecting a chair which commanded a view of the dining room and hallway. "First you played the mature young lady for her. A very convincing performance, actually. An errant child who has finally seen the light and realized that Grandpa was really your best friend." Barbara seated herself on the floor, in cross-legged Indian fashion, directly in front of Jack. "But you and I knew all along that you thought he was a bastard. And you enjoyed humiliating him in public with your unwanted pregnancy and abortion."

"Ah, ah," she said, wagging a cautioning finger. "Someone has been telling stories out of school."

"What did your grandfather say when you told him about the abortion?"

Barbara cocked her head and twisted her mouth in comic recollection. "Well, sir, he was pretty damn mad. He said he was going to disinherit me."

"He said essentially the same thing to Alan when he found out about the drugs, I'd guess," Jack continued. "Is that when the two of you decided to kill him?"

"Oh, Mr. Olsen." She laughed, a beautiful princess sitting at his feet. "You're such a good investigator." Her voice lowered to a level of confidentiality. "It wasn't exactly like that. I didn't hobnob with Alan, you see. He wasn't my type. He was dirty, nearly illiterate. A common criminal."

"Criminals come only in the common variety," Jack stated. "Who was in the boat with Alan?"

"Well, it wasn't me," she replied indignantly.

"Rinaldi?" Jack asked, naming his prime suspect.

"Nope," she laughed.

"Who, then?"

"I can't tell you just yet," she replied enigmatically.

Jack tried, but couldn't fathom the remark. "So you

conspired to kill your grandfather, hoping to inherit all his money?"

"I sure did," she said gleefully.

"Then you were surprised at the reading of the will."

"Terribly disappointed," she said, pouting. "I didn't think he'd had time to change the will. On the other hand, it wasn't as bad as Grandpa threatened."

"Was Banuchi involved in planning your grandfather's murder?"

"Actually, he first suggested it to Alan, not me," she replied, matter-of-factly. "Butch needed to get rid of Grandpa because he knew too much about Butch's hotel. You know all that. So Butch told Alan that Grandpa's death was the price of an endless supply of drugs."

It was just as Jack had thought. Alan had served two purposes for Banuchi: murder and drugs. "How'd you get involved?" he asked.

"Alan let it slip to me that he was going to kill Grandpa as a favor to Butch. He could never keep his mouth shut, especially when he was high. That's when I took over planning Grandpa's death. I figured that if it was going to be done, it might as well be done right."

"You contacted Banuchi?" Jack asked, astounded.

"Sure," she said proudly. "He appreciated my organizational talents, as well as other things I did for him."

"I bet," Jack replied drily.

"We cut a deal," she continued. "I was to get rid of Grandpa and then sell Butch the land. He'd build a hotel and I'd get ten percent of the gross profits for the first five years. That, and all of Grandpa's money. I was going to be rich. From the beginning, I knew I'd have to get rid of Alan eventually."

"There's one thing you didn't count on," Jack interjected. "Your grandfather's estate was tied up in a trust fund."

She pouted again. "Nothing works perfectly, does it?"

"You nearly talked Beth Lacy into dissolving the trust, when she was emotionally exhausted after Cousins's death."

"But you queered that deal, too, Jackie," she cooed.

"So you gave her an overdose of insulin."

She shrugged resignedly. "That didn't work, either."

"Who ran down Cousins?" Jack asked, barely able to control his temper.

"That was Rinaldi. See, you get to pin something on him after all. 'Course, he's skipped town now."

"Did Banuchi tell you everything about the hotel?"

"Only that it would be the finest and fanciest on the lake," she said rhythmically. "And Butch never lied about things like that."

Jack snorted. "The hotel was to be used as a sophisticated, computerized gambling casino. And sex for hire."

"Oh, goodie, goodie." She clapped her hands. "I was going to be the madam of a den of iniquity."

Jack had never met a woman exactly like her. She appeared to be totally amoral. "Did Banuchi tell you to get rid of Alan?"

"He *asked* me," she said, blinking her eyelids seductively. "You see, Alan had served his purpose. Basically, he was a careless boy with a big mouth. You were putting a lot of pressure on him. He was ready to crack and tell everything he knew."

"How'd you kill him?"

"Oh, that was fun," she said, rising to her feet and moving out of the room.

Jack followed her into the dining room. There he stopped, where he could see her in the kitchen.

"I'm just mixing a drink, honey," she said over her shoulder. "Sit down there at the table and I'll be right with you."

He waited until she returned, and when she sat down, he pulled out a chair that gave him a view of all entrances to the room. The dining room had windows on all the exterior walls. Jack shuddered, feeling enveloped by the darkness.

"When they let Alan out of jail, he called Butch," she continued, sipping the drink. "He'd gotten into that habit, instead of working through Rinaldi. Butch called me and asked me to take care of it. I liked that. It showed confidence in my ability." She beamed in remembrance of the compliment. A Barbie doll wired with dynamite. "So I picked Alan up and brought him back here. Served him beer spiked with 'ludes. Told him Butch would be by at ten with twenty-five thousand dollars and an airline ticket. Alan was real pleased at the idea of taking a vacation."

"But you had other plans for him."

"Shortly before ten he was a lamb," she replied. "I took him out into the woods. You know why he went?" She was bouncing on her chair with glee. "I told him we'd caught you and had you tied up out there. He wanted to kick your teeth out. He stood out there in the woods whispering, 'Where is the bastard, I'll kill him.' Instead, I killed him." The smile faded from her face. "It was a real funny feeling. Good. You know. He just looked at me. Stupidly. It was so silent in the woods. Just the sound of the insects. Then I pulled the trigger. Man, now I know what they mean by 'blowing people away.' Alan, he was just gone. Poof. Nothing left but the carton."

He'd talked to them before. It was an understatement to say that they were interesting. Cold-blooded killers. Psychopaths. They were fascinating, in fact; totally devoid of human compassion. And this one had planned her grandfather's death, wasted her brother and attempted to kill Beth Lacy, he thought.

"Except for you, it would have worked beautifully," she continued, seemingly sad. "You just wouldn't let go. You're like a bulldog. Are you ferocious in bed, too?" She lit a cigarette and regarded him coolly.

"Your nursing background came in handy when you did the needlework on Mrs. Lacy," Jack said. "Who's the strong guy, Barbie?"

"Oh, you mean who carried Mrs. Lacy upstairs?" she asked rhetorically. "You mean the guy who helped Alan run down Grandpa? Actually hit him with the oar. The guy you wrestled with? The same fellow who drove Alan's car out here?"

Jack tensed, thinking he heard a noise outside. "Yeah," he said.

"Hank," she said, motioning to the kitchen. Suddenly, he was at the end of the table. He moved like a cat, and, like a cat, he stopped there to stare at his prey. There was one strip of tape around the gun. Jack calculated quickly that he didn't have a chance. He'd have to choose a better time.

"If Hank had done you in that night like he was supposed to, everything would have been all right," she said nonchalantly. "We'd have gotten Mrs. Lacy to dissolve the trust and the sheriff would have come back to the fold."

197

"I had *him*, Barbie." Hank pouted. "It was her with the shotgun who fouled things up." Jack stared at the bandage around Hank's left forearm.

Jack was perplexed and angry at himself. "I talked to a witness who placed both of you at the party, at least fifteen minutes before your grandfather was killed."

Barbara walked to Jack's side and tweaked his cheek. "How careless of you. You're not such a good private eye, after all. *I* arrived at three-fifty-nine by boat with another guy. One of Hank's bodybuilding friends. Hank came later, after Alan dropped him about half a mile down the shoreline from the party. In the confusion—everyone was drunk, dearie—people just didn't notice."

Then Alan got the boat out of the water, put a tarpaulin cover on it and took it to the barn, Jack guessed. He stalled for time, crossing his leg so the gun was nearer his hand. "What good will it do to kill me now? Mrs. Lacy's alive. The doctor knows someone tried to kill her. Kate knows I'm here."

Banuchi appeared in the kitchen doorway, behind Hank. "I think we can surmount all those little difficulties, Mr. Olsen," he said. "It is insightful of you to know that your death is imminent."

Jack felt the beginning of cramps in the pit of his stomach. He had made several miscalculations, the chief being that he hadn't expected Barbara to have so much company. He should have suspected something was amiss when she so readily confessed her involvement in murder and attempted murder.

"You didn't think you could really scare me into leaving town, did you, Mr. Olsen?" Banuchi continued, taking a chair at the table. He had on black gloves and was holding a pistol equipped with a silencer. Hank moved in one fluid motion to Jack's side of the table. He stood with his hands on his hips, about six feet from Jack. A perfectly co-ordinated muscle machine.

"It would have been foolish for me to run," Banuchi continued, "when I can solve all my problems by getting rid of you."

"That will look suspicious," Jack countered.

"To whom?" Banuchi asked. "It will look like an accident. Besides, everyone's attention will be focused on the trial of Tom Wallace for attempted murder of Mrs. Lacy.

Sheriff Davis is going to build an airtight case against him. I'll guarantee it."

Jack tried not to panic. "And Mrs. Lacy?"

"We'll get another shot at her," Barbara said, studying her fingernails.

"Satisfy my curiosity about one thing," Jack said, trying desperately to think of a way out of his predicament.

"Certainly, Mr. Olsen," Banuchi replied.

"Who shot at me up the road from here?"

Banuchi lit a cigar. "Mr. Rinaldi did that. He had orders not to kill you. I didn't want you talking to Alan again, or the sheriff. At the time, I thought we could scare you off the case. A terrible miscalculation, I admit. I decided to have you killed after Mr. Wright told me you'd visited his office and viewed the plans for our hotel."

"Let's get going," Barbara said impatiently.

"You gonna come nice like," Hank asked, "or shall I break your face again?"

Jack asked pleasantly, "Where are we going?"

"A boat ride, I think," Banuchi answered. "You're known to fish in the evenings, Mr. Olsen. Tonight you are going to have an unfortunate accident and drown. You remember, I warned you, once."

Hank snapped open a switchblade knife and motioned for Jack to follow Barbara and Banuchi through the house, out into the yard. Jack calculated that his best bet was to feign a twisted ankle, fall to the ground and come up with the gun. He figured his chances were nil against the catlike Hank.

Before Jack could play out that scenario, Mel Davis stepped from the shadows.

"It's getting crowded here," Jack said.

Davis smirked. "I wouldn't miss this party for the world, stumblebum. It's your turn to squirm."

Jack appealed to Davis. "Since you've been listening to all the confessions, you know how much trouble you're in."

"Don't matter," the sheriff replied, chewing his gum slowly. "Looks like I'm on the winning side."

Banuchi, poised as always, interrupted. "Just for the record, Mr. Olsen, I've confessed to nothing. I learned a long time ago that you can't be held accountable for what you don't say."

The moon was bright and cast eerie shadows, giving

199

Jack the chilling feeling that he was walking through a graveyard.

"There's a letter," Jack said, desperate for a way to divert them from their intended purpose.

"What kind of a letter?" Barbara demanded.

"Sheriff Davis and I had a heart-to-heart talk this afternoon," Banuchi answered. "It seems the sheriff has been held at bay with the threat of a letter that sets forth Mr. Olsen's various suspicions."

Jack felt a renewed hope. "The letter is in Chicago, with a friend. If I die, it will be sent to another friend on the Chicago police force."

"What do we do, Butch?" Barbara asked, less certain of herself than at any other time during the evening.

Banuchi, hand on his chin, thought for a moment, then smiled. "The solution is simple. We find out who has the letter and have my friends in Chicago take it away from him."

"How do we do that?" Hank asked, bewildered.

Banuchi smiled. "Oh, I think you can get Mr. Olsen to tell us, Hank. Use your imagination."

A look of growing comprehension and then pure rapture spread across Hank's face. "Sure he will," he purred.

Barbara's face was twisted in a snarl. Her eyes bored into Jack. "After we're done with him, we'll go over and lean on Kate Carter awhile, just to make sure he was telling the truth. In fact, it would be a good idea to get rid of her, too."

Something moved along the trail leading to the boat dock. "Why don't you lean on me now," a voice growled from the dark.

It was Kate! Jack hit the ground, rolling, pawing for the gun. He heard the splat of the silencer, then the roar of a shotgun. On his knees, gun in hand, Jack faced an enraged and charging Hank. Jack pulled the trigger reflexively as the blond-haired beach boy bowled him over. The shot caught Hank squarely in the throat, and he lay on the ground, fearful as a wounded animal. Blood squirted from the hole with every beat of his heart. Banuchi also was lying on the ground, dead from the shotgun blast. Kate was covering Sheriff Davis, who was pale and trembling.

"How'd you get here?" Jack asked, rushing to Kate's

200

side. Barbara was devoted to a clinical appraisal of Hank, as he lay dying.

"By boat."

"Why?"

"I had to protect my investment," she answered. "I'm getting too old to attract another good man."

TWENTY-THREE

It was early September. The summer Jack had wished for so desperately in February oozed on pitifully slowly. He went to Wisconsin for a week's vacation with the kids. Then he and Joyce spent several pleasant days with the kids in Chicago, although Jack became increasingly restless to return to the lake and Kate.

He testified before the grand jury about the incredible story that had begun with Geoffry Gentry's death. He realized that several of his suspicions, such as the real purpose of the Banuchi hotel, could never be proved. Still, there was an official record; public officials throughout the state would be on the alert should the mob try to revive the hotel scheme in some other form.

Davis was indicted for accepting a bribe and conspiring to kill Jack. The gullible sheriff indicated he would be a prosecution witness in the case of the People versus Barbara Gentry. At her arraignment, she pleaded innocent to the charges that she had conspired to kill her grandfather, murdered her brother, attempted to murder Beth Lacy and conspired to murder Jack. Despite the fact that he and Davis would testify that Barbara had confessed to these crimes, Jack was not overly optimistic about the prospects for conviction. The evidence was largely circumstantial. Jack knew what a smart lawyer could do with the case.

But he was even more dissatisfied that Vincent Margossi, alias Aldo Rinaldi, remained at large and beyond the remedies of the law for his role in the death of Roy Cousins.

Beth Lacy was home recuperating. When Kate and Jack went to visit, he was pleasantly surprised to find the glass curio stand once again filled with the fascinating and lifelike figurines.

"Will you still go east?" he asked, taking her hand.

"Maybe, but not this year," she said, touching the scar over his eye. She looked more like her old self again. "The lake seems cleaner now, almost new," she said. "I find myself anxious for the autumn and the blaze of colors that will ripple through the forest."

"They don't have that in the city," Jack agreed. He remembered Roy Cousins, leaning against a building in June, able to see the winter's snow in the summer sun. All things change and the circle becomes a whole, he thought. It's a matter of faith; a hope for the best in tomorrow.

"What will you do, Jack?" Beth asked.

He drew Kate close to them, and the three held hands. "I'm going to build a home on the west shore for Kate and me. And I'm going to help organize that area development council Mr. Gentry provided for in his will. That's something I think I'll enjoy. I believe in it, and it will help everyone who lives on the lake, or wants to enjoy it."

"Good for you, Jack," Beth said, squeezing both their hands.

On the way to the pickup, Kate stunned him with the question: "Since you're going to build a home for us, will you marry me?"

He was humbled that she wanted him; embarrassed that she'd asked first. "Goddammit, Kate, why couldn't you wait awhile?" he said. "I was going to get around to asking you in my good time."

"Well?" she demanded.

"Sure I will," he answered.

"Good. Now the only remaining mystery of this case can be revealed."

"What's that?" he asked, mystified.

203

"The real reason I came over to Barbara's that night to save your ass."

"What was the reason?" he asked, not certain if she was serious.

"So my first child wouldn't grow up without a father, silly."

He gawked after her as she strutted up the hill toward the pickup. Then she stopped, beckoning for him to follow along.

VINTAGE FICTION BY A MASTER
A HARD-FAST THRILLER WITH
A PURE-SHOCK ENDING

CHINAMAN'S CHANCE
by ROSS THOMAS

The search for Silk Armitage, a beautiful blonde rock star with some secrets to spill about the CIA and the Mafia, embroils two colorful rogues in a worldwide intrigue from Saigon to Scotland to a sunbleached crime haven near Venice Beach, California, where a deluxe cast of henchmen, musclemen, and maniacs—both nympho and psycho—struggle to find her . . . and kill her . . . and love her.

"A SPICY, FAST-PACED THRILLER . . . interlaced with serious, brilliant writing . . . a classic of the genre."
The Washington Post

"I READ IT IN ONE COMPULSIVE GULP, AS I USED TO DEVOUR HAMMETT AND CHANDLER."

Frank DeFelitta

MAIN SELECTION OF THE MYSTERY GUILD

Avon 41517 $2.25

CHINA 3-79

AVON ⬡ THE BEST IN
BESTSELLING ENTERTAINMENT

- [ ] **Chance the Winds of Fortune..**
  Laurie McBain   75796 $2.95
- [ ] **The Heirs of Love**   Barbara Ferry Johnson   75739 $2.95
- [ ] **Golden Opportunity**   Edith Begner   75085 $2.50
- [ ] **Sally Hemings**   Barbara Chase-Riboud   48686 $2.75
- [ ] **A Woman of Substance**
  Barbara Taylor Bradford   49163 $2.95
- [ ] **Sacajawea**   Anna Lee Waldo   75606 $3.95
- [ ] **Passage West**   Henry Dallas Miller   50278 $2.75
- [ ] **The Firecloud**   Kenneth McKennay   50054 $2.50
- [ ] **Pulling Your Own Strings**
  Dr. Wayne W. Dyer   44388 $2.75
- [ ] **The Helper**   Catherine Marshall   45583 $2.25
- [ ] **Bethany's Sin**   Robert R. McCammon   47712 $2.50
- [ ] **Summer Lightning**   Judith Richards   42960 $2.50
- [ ] **Cold Moon Over Babylon**
  Michael McDowell   48660 $2.50
- [ ] **Keeper of the Children**
  William H. Hallahan   45203 $2.50
- [ ] **The Moonchild**   Kenneth McKennay   41483 $2.50
- [ ] **Homeward Winds the River**
  Barbara Ferry Johnson   42952 $2.50
- [ ] **Tears of Gold**   Laurie McBain   41475 $2.50
- [ ] **Monty: A Biography of Montgomery Clift**
  Robert LaGuardia   49528 $2.50
- [ ] **Sweet Savage Love**   Rosemary Rogers   47324 $2.50
- [ ] **ALIVE: The Story of the Andes Survivors**
  Piers Paul Read   39164 $2.25
- [ ] **The Flame and the Flower**
  Kathleen E. Woodiwiss   46276 $2.50
- [ ] **I'm OK—You're OK**
  Thomas A. Harris, M.D.   46268 $2.50

Available at better bookstores everywhere, or order direct from the publisher.

"C.I.A., Mister Fletcher."

"Um. Would you mind spelling that?"

"Enough of your bull, Fletcher."

"Okay, guys. What's the big deal?"

"You are going to tape the most private bedroom conversations of the most important people in American journalism."

"You're crazy. What have you got on me?"

"Taxes, Mister Fletcher."

"What about 'em?"

"You haven't paid any."

Fletch's Fortune

BY THE
BACK-TO-BACK
EDGAR AWARD
WINNING AUTHOR OF
FLETCH AND
CONFESS FLETCH

Snatched from bliss on the Riviera, Fletch was flown to the journalism convention with a suitcase full of bugging devices and a bizarre assignment: dig up some juicy scandals on Walter March, the ruthless newspaper tycoon... Then Walter March was found lying face up with a long pair of scissors stuck in his back. It was the crime of the century. And a hell of a story.

A blockbuster of suspense by
GREGORY McDONALD

"... the toughest, leanest horse to hit the literary racetrack since James M. Cain." —PETE HAMILL

 Avon/76323/$2.25

FF 7-8